GREY RANDALL: PRIVATE DICK
CASEFILE #1

Lily White
Rose Red

CATT FORD

Dreamspinner Press

Published by
Dreamspinner Press
4760 Preston Road
Suite 244-149
Frisco, TX 75034
http://www.dreamspinnerpress.com/

This is a work of fiction. Names, characters, places and incidents either are the product of the author's imagination or are used fictitiously, and any resemblance to actual persons, living or dead, business establishments, events or locales is entirely coincidental.

Grey Randall, Private Dick

Cover Design by Catt Ford

ISBN: 978-1-61581-471-8

Printed in the United States of America
First Edition
June, 2010

eBook edition available
eBook ISBN: 978-1-61581-472-5

Dedicated to Kennedy and Liriel,
for their unfailing support and belief in me.
And to E.N.

Author's Note

This story is set in 1948 in the United States, a time when people of color, homosexuals, and women were overtly considered second-class citizens and it was accepted that they had fewer rights. In an attempt to be historically accurate, I have used language that some may find offensive, such as the N word, "colored," and "queer." The reality of the time shapes the story and the characters.

In 1948, homosexuality was illegal in Nevada, and if caught, men could be and were sent to jail. African Americans were forced to live separately and were not permitted inside casinos and hotels, except as menial employees.

Catt Ford
June 2010

Prologue: Welcome to Vegas

THEY even have a song about it: "How Ya Gonna Keep 'Em Down on the Farm, Once They Seen Paree?" Well, I wasn't going back to some farm; I was born and bred in New York, the city. You can't get much bigger than that, even if I hadn't seen Paris at all. I spent most of my time on exotic tropical islands that didn't seem quite so exotic after you feel one of your friends bleed down your neck. Even so, after the war, you could find whatever you wanted on liberty in Hawaii. I don't remember everything about that visit—I was too drunk most of the time, too sexed up some of the time—but judging by how bad I felt when I boarded the ship for America, I must have had a damn fine time.

When we landed in California, I took a day to look around and then I hopped the train home. Got off when we hit Las Vegas to stretch my legs. That's where I met the dame; she wasn't wearing diamonds and mink, she was just a pretty girl with a little oval face and a nicely pointed chin. Nothing else stood out about her unless you counted the fear in her eyes. Once I got her problem straightened out, my train was long gone and my bags with it. By then I had a new friend and a new life, one that I hadn't been banking on.

Las Vegas didn't seem much like a city to me in those days. First it was a desert, surrounded by mountains. The footsteps of the Indian peoples who scraped a barren living there were swept away by the merciless wind, leaving no trace behind. Flat, brown, dry, with just a few buildings sprouting out of nowhere and Route 91 running right down the middle.

The color that matters most in Vegas is green, so whatever patina of morality city leaders like to hang onto, you gotta look underneath for the real deal. And that's the bills. The railroad came through in 1905, scoring trails of iron across the valley as people passed through on their way from somewhere to somewhere else. The railroad took their share, selling land around the tracks for jacked-up prices in a fixed auction. They parceled out the city by block, providing for man's creature comforts in Block 16, the area set aside for drinking, gambling, and whores. The year 1931 saw the legalization of gambling, even though the fact that it was against the law hadn't made a noticeable dent in the action before that.

Prohibition ended in 1933, leaving the city not quite so dry. But Las Vegas wasn't dead yet; it became a vacation destination for movie stars and mobsters like Bugsy Siegel, Max Hamilton, and Davie Berman. There were stars like Ava Gardner, Frank Sinatra, Sammy Davis Jr., and Lily McIntyre. The Rising Star and the Flamingo opened in 1946 on what would become the Las Vegas Strip, and overnight Sin City was born.

Now in 1948, drinking and gambling might have been legal, but many other things were not. And that's where I come in. I do things that the cops can't. In the city of neon, I shine a light on things that some people would rather remain in the dark.

My name is Grey Randall, and I'm a private dick.

Chapter 1: Miss Lily Comes to Call

YOU'VE heard of the big fish in the small pond. That was Vegas in 1948 for casino owners, mobsters, and movie stars—but not for me. I'd had a few jobs since I landed in town and even did some very clever work, but it was all small potatoes: the cashier with sticky fingers operating the till at Woolworth's on Fremont, the dame who slipped the leash her bookie boyfriend had her on and was seeing a blackjack dealer on the sly. And then there was my favorite case, the newsboy who cut in on the other kids' territory. I never thought I'd be catching a twelve-year-old criminal mastermind, but he had the goods all right. Went around on the other boys' routes, collecting a day early. He was counting on the fact that most people just don't look that close at the kid who rides by and tosses the paper on their front step. And he was scoring big-time, at least till I got on his trail. Probably had a blooming career ahead of him when he got a little older.

No, I was the little fish in the big pond. None of the bigs came around calling on me to get their problems solved, at least not until that one day when *she* walked into my office.

Femmes fatales had been noticeably absent since I hung out my shingle, but the day she opened the door without knocking, I knew I'd hit the jackpot.

She was a doll all right, a little out of my age range, maybe in her early forties although she didn't look it, but everything was positioned right where it should be. She was tall and slim, dressed all in black: the fashionable suit with the big shoulders, expensive furs, the jaunty hat with a little veil and a sweeping feather, but the somber color just set off her shiny red hair and that famous peaches and cream complexion. They said it extended way down past what I could see with all her clothes on.

"Mr. Dick," she announced in a velvety tone that spoke of seduction and made you want to get dirty.

"Call me Mr. Randall, that's my name, Miss—?" I stood up politely. My mother was a stickler for proper manners.

"You may call me Lily."

I admired her strategy. By putting us on a first name basis right off the bat, she managed to stay incognito and get us on a cozy footing. A lot of people don't like admitting that they need a dick's help. But I recognized her, all right. Miss Lily McIntyre had been a dancer, not just *a* dancer, only the most famous dame to have ever strutted her stuff on a Vegas stage. She wasn't hoofing for dough any more, but retirement seemed to agree with her.

There was something about her that suggested that if she were yours, each day would be filled with fascinating and exciting surprises. Her laugh made the little lines around her eyes stand out a bit more, despite the expert make-up. She might be getting on in years, but she was still an astoundingly beautiful woman. And she had something that transcended beauty, that elusive quality called charm that would make her the center of attention when she was eighty. She flashed me the kind of smile that had probably gotten her that fur stole around her shoulders and the sparkly bracelet on her wrist. She really piled on the rocks, but she could carry the weight.

Miss McIntyre came a little closer, and I got a whiff of her perfume. Expensive, just like everything else about her, from the diamonds sparkling in her ears to her exquisite coiffure. She had on a four-string pearl choker with a diamond and emerald catch; probably she thought that was toned down for days, but under it I caught the glint of a fine platinum chain studded at intervals with diamonds that disappeared down into the deep V of her silk blouse. I'm no expert in women's fashion, but hers was top-drawer. First class all the way for a dame like her. I wondered who was keeping her now that dancing wasn't paying the bills.

"All the girls must love you. Such beautiful eyes and those long, thick lashes, simply wasted on a man. You've got something, haven't you, Mr. Randall?"

I couldn't help smirking. "I don't know about that."

"You're skinnier than I thought a private dick would be."

She had a way of saying "dick" that made it sound very dirty, and I could tell she liked doing it.

"Wiry. I'm wiry, not skinny."

"Of course. Wiry, but tough." She ran a gloved fingertip over my cheekbone, the one that had healed a little funny. "Where did you get that?"

"You didn't come here to get my life story, did you, Miss Lily?" I caught her hand and held it away from my face.

She just smiled and strolled to the window, looking down at the street through the blinds. I wondered if I'd remembered to dust them lately.

"Would you like to sit down?" I went around my desk to hold a chair for her.

Of course she homed in on the good one, the green leather chair. She sank down onto the seat, light as a feather, and crossed her legs. Stems a million miles long, and they looked good, damned good. She made sure I got a good gander by surreptitiously hiking her skirt up above her knees, which were worth the attention. Knees in general can be problematic, but if shorter skirts came in, Lily wouldn't have to be ashamed of her knees at all. I wondered how her toes were.

I retreated behind my desk, glad to have that shield between us, sat down, and waited.

She said, "Nice office, Mr. Randall."

I had to laugh. It was pretty basic and located on the side of town that dames like her just don't get to very often. "You didn't come to admire the décor, either."

"What are your rates?"

She had me hoping she wasn't shopping for a kept boy. Maybe she hadn't read the sign on my door. "Depends on what you want me to do."

"I want you to find and catch a killer for me, Mr. Randall."

I sat up straight. Murder? Now we were talking! Miss Lily McIntyre *and* a murder case. I rubbed my hands together, and she seemed amused by my eagerness. "Why me? Why not the police?"

Her peachy, luscious lips thinned for a moment, and that was a pity. She had nice lips, meant for smiling in that come-hither way she tried on me earlier. She couldn't know she was wasting her ammo. "The police have had forty-eight hours to catch him, and they're no nearer to finding out the truth than they were when they first found her body."

Her?

"Sometimes it can take a while, Miss Lily, even for the cops. Believe me, they like stamping 'case closed'. Makes them look good to the public."

"A while will be too long. Time is of the essence, Mr. Randall. And I have it on good authority that you're the man for the job. Perhaps the *only* man who can solve this case."

Of course a guy likes to hear that, but I also wanted to know who gave her the word. "And who told you that?"

She smiled. "Does it really matter?"

"Maybe. We can come back to that." I pulled out a pen and a pad of lined paper. "Who got murdered and when?"

"You're very businesslike. I like that." She let the fur thing slip off her shoulders, and somehow she managed to make it look as hot as if she'd just taken it all off. It had to be a practiced technique from her dancing days, when word was if the stakes were high enough, she did more than just shake her stuff. "It was a woman, only a girl, really. Miss Marguerite Saint-Ville. Very talented, and only at the beginning of her career."

"And who was this girl to you?"

"A protégé," Miss McIntyre said. "And a charming young friend."

I was beginning to have an inkling that she was lying to me. They all do, the people who bring me their troubles. They want me to dig them out of a hole, but they never want to tell me the whole story. They seem to like making you work for the money. "You taught her to dance?"

"You can tell I'm a dancer, then? You're very observant, Mr. Dick. May I ask how you knew?"

"You have a certain… grace. And it's my job to be observant."

"I see," she said. "Every year I take on a student or two. However, Miss Saint-Ville was different. Special."

"In what way?"

"She was a lovely girl, and she should have been a star. She could dance, sing, entertain. She had a bright future ahead of her."

Suddenly I understood the all-black get-up. I would eat my hat if I didn't find out there was a closer acquaintance between the two than just teacher and student. But Miss McIntyre didn't betray any sign of grief. Not that she would show any emotion she chose not to. Those soft furs and silky glad rags covered a lady made of steel.

"When was she killed?"

"Two nights ago." Miss McIntyre leaned forward and gazed at me intently. "She was found in an alley, in the warehouse section behind Union Station."

I got the sense of some powerful emotion being held firmly in check. "What was she doing there?"

"I was hoping you'd find that out, Mr. Randall," she said somewhat tartly. "So far no one has been able to tell me a thing."

"How was she killed?"

"Strangled."

I looked up from my notes. "Personal."

Miss McIntyre shrugged, but her gaze was intent upon me. "I'm not sure what other motive there could be. She wasn't rich."

"When was she found?"

"After two a.m."

"Were any of her belongings stolen?"

"Her purse was there, although the money was gone. Can't you find all this out from the newspapers?"

"I will, Miss Lily. I just want to get your take."

"I wasn't there. I know nothing about what she was doing or why." Miss McIntyre uncrossed her legs, giving me a little flash of the top of her stocking. She was still watching me carefully, although I had no idea what she was hoping to see. "You're going to find all that out for me."

"What if I find out something you don't want to know?"

She gave me a determined smile. All steel, that lady, although she wanted you to think otherwise. "Truth can be a harsh mistress."

"All right. Why was she killed?"

"Isn't that supposed to be *your* job?"

"Never overlook the basics. I'd feel like a damned fool if I didn't ask and I found out later you knew all along. And I'll need a photograph," I said.

She opened her handbag and flashed me a photo. "Autographed?"

I coughed. "Er, not of you, ma'am, of Miss Saint-Ville. Although…." I caught sight of the picture she was offering. "If you don't mind, make it out to Grey Randall." Hell, I'm not gonna pass up a photograph of a beautiful woman wearing only pearls and a G-string, although most of the good stuff was left to the imagination between the lighting and the pose. My mother didn't raise any stupid children. I was smart enough to play along when a dame showed a yen to flirt. No sense raising questions I didn't want to answer. Besides, having her autographed photo on my desk could only help when future clients came to call.

She smirked as she signed it, obviously thinking she had me back on a leash. But nobody puts Grey Randall, private dick, on a leash. I may let them think so, but only till I get what I'm after.

She slid it across the desk with a smug look as I took a glance before putting it in the top drawer to file later. "I was a dish, wasn't I?"

"Was? You still are. And now the photograph of Miss Saint-Ville, please."

After fixing me with a gaze that bored right through me, Miss McIntyre seemed to make up her mind about me. She opened her bag again and took out another photograph.

It was a black-and-white publicity still, the kind used by actresses, singers, and dancers, shot with professional lighting. Still, the girl had been lovely, beautiful, even. Which in itself could constitute a motive.

"Boyfriend?"

"Yes. More than one, I suspect."

"Don't you know?"

"She spoke of seeing more than one man. She never mentioned any names." Miss McIntyre made a graceful gesture with her hand. "You understand, in the entertainment business, one meets a number of... admirers, shall we say?"

"And maybe one of them got a little out of hand?"

"Perhaps." Miss McIntyre didn't seem too shocked by the idea.

"Was she a hooker?"

"No, Mr. Randall, she was not!" she snapped.

"Not even amateur? Look, Miss Lily, entertainment is a tough business to break into. Sometimes girls have to do things to make ends meet—"

"She was a lovely girl. Not in my league as a dancer, of course," she added modestly, "but these days what passes for talent would barely have landed you onto a casting couch back then. Not that I'm past it. I can still do a high kick over your head."

She peered at me deviously, just hoping I would ask. Well, I'm a gentleman, and I can never refuse a beautiful dame.

"I may need to see that, just as part of the case, ma'am," I murmured.

"Call me Lily," she said. She rose languidly to her feet, letting the stole slip behind her to the floor, and came around my desk like a panther on the prowl, sleek and dangerous.

She approached my chair, and my nostrils were filled with the feminine scent of her. I sniffed, trying to identify it. Lily of the valley. I can always tell.

She swung her leg up and over my head with no apparent effort, remaining perfectly balanced. Obviously she had a cleverly concealed slit in her skirt that I'd missed, cut up to the thigh. I applauded. Hey, even a hard-nosed, booze-swilling, seen-it-all dick like me can appreciate talent when I see it. That and she had on some really glam lace-topped stockings.

"Very nice," I said, keeping my breathing steady. After all, I was a dick, a private dick, and I know complications when I see them. "What does that have to do with your case, Miss Lily?"

She remained standing in front of me, crowding me. Not that I minded. But it was odd how she didn't back away from me. Almost as if....

I gasped when she suddenly planted her right foot on my chest, my hands gripping the arms of my chair, ready to take her down if she proved dangerous. She leaned forward slightly, increasing the pressure on my chest, applying enough pressure that I knew I would see the mark that the heel of her expensive shoe left there tomorrow.

She leaned closer, saying, "Mr. Randall, dancers are very flexible."

"So am I, ma'am, and if you don't take your foot off my chest, I may have to show you, and I don't think you'll like it very much."

She smiled and increased the pressure of her heel. "If I really put my weight into it, this heel would cut right through you like butter."

I grabbed her ankle, the hose silky to the touch, and pushed her slowly away from me. "I think I get the picture. You could have just told me."

She shifted her balance instantly, swinging her leg up and out of my grasp with a little flash of smooth white skin above the black garter, spinning away from me before walking back to her chair with a provocative roll of her hips. Even at her age, she was… flexible. She bent to retrieve her stole and pick up her bag.

"Miss Saint-Ville knew how to take care of herself." She wasn't even breathless when she sat down. "Sometimes a girl has to know how to get out of a sticky situation."

I brushed off my tie, trying to pretend that it hadn't hurt. "Nice move."

"I was holding back. If I really put my weight into it, this heel would have made you think twice."

"I believe you." I did. She had dancer's legs, slim but strong. I wouldn't want to meet her in a dark alley at night if she were mad at me. "So she could have taken a man by surprise with that move."

"I know a lot of other moves as well."

"And you taught her everything you know."

For the first time, I saw a flicker of emotion cross her face. "Not enough, apparently. I taught her all I knew, except how to stay alive." She looked sad for a moment, but then it was back to business. "You never gave me your rates."

"A hundred a day, plus expenses."

"You can open your mouth all right." Miss McIntyre smiled at me as she looked over the office. I knew that she knew I was lying, but she must have wanted someone on the case right away and was willing to pay for it. "I can do better than that." She opened up her bag and pulled out a five-G stack.

"Look, you want someone killed, get yourself another dick," I said.

"I'll take care of that part after you find the man," she said. "I know a lawyer or two."

"I don't carry out revenge," I told her. "I'll find him for you, but I'm not going to kill him. I may not even be able to produce enough evidence to bring him to trial, but I'll find him."

"You're very sure of yourself," she purred flirtatiously as she settled back in her chair.

"I should be. I've never failed to get my man yet," I said casually, although I didn't let on exactly what I meant by that. It was the keeping them that was the tricky part.

"Oh, I have complete faith in you, Mr. Randall," she assured me. She crossed her legs and leaned forward, one silk-clad leg against the other making a hushing noise like rain, and said, "All you have to do is find him. I have ways to take care of him later. If you catch him before the week is out, there could be a bonus in it for you as well."

"What kind of bonus?"

"That's up for negotiation." Something in her smile made me feel like we were talking a whole different currency here.

"You're a fascinating lady, Miss Lily."

She threw back her head and laughed. "I'm no lady, darling. I'm a woman, full-grown."

"Yeah," I agreed. "Armed and dangerous."

"Who knows, maybe I could teach you something."

"Oh, I have no doubt of that." Even though she wasn't packing the right equipment, I'm sure I could have learned a lot from her. "Where do I call you when I catch him?"

"I like your style, Mr. Randall. You're confident. That's good in a man."

"Thank you, Miss McIntyre. And your number?"

"So you knew all along? I see I've found the right man for the job." She recited her number. I didn't make a move to write it down, and she seemed to approve. "This job is likely to be difficult."

"Trouble is my business, Miss McIntyre, and I'm open twenty-four hours. Why the time limit?"

"We don't want to give him time to—dispose of the evidence, shall we say?" She stood up, and I circled my desk to pick up her fur thing and set it on her shoulders. She put her hand over one of mine with a grip of iron. "I suspect that you won't let me down, Mr. Randall.

But before you let anyone know that you're working for me, get yourself a new tie."

"What's wrong with my tie, other than your footprint on it?" I looked down at it. Dark blue with red and yellow stripes. It was just a regular tie.

"It's hideous. A handsome man like you can do so much better." Then she turned and walked out.

"Hideous?" I muttered, staring at my tie.

"*Hideous*, darling!" Her voice floated back from the hallway, followed by a throaty laugh.

I went to the window and waited for her to emerge from the building. A middle-aged colored man was standing by a big shiny limousine, and he held the door open for her when she came out. A Lincoln two-tone, midnight blue, 1948. I would have loved to drive that car. He handed her into the back seat and circled the car to get in the driver's side. I watched it start to roll and turn at the corner.

She was lying. Miss Lily McIntyre was lying to me, from start to finish, but somehow I could tell this was the start of something big for me.

All I had to do now was find out what the fuck it was I was really supposed to be finding out.

I sat down and entertained myself by trying to read my name backwards on the frosted glass in the door: evitceteD etavirP lladnaR yerG. Yerg! What was I thinking? I had to get to work. I had a case to solve.

COPS don't exactly love private dicks. If a dick cracks a case that they couldn't solve, it makes them look bad. Dicks can do things the cops can't, at least not that the fuzz can be caught doing. For instance, we can lean on a suspect a little harder or bribe them to go canary. If I'm on a case, I can work it full time without having to stop and hand out a ticket for jaywalking.

On the other hand, cops swing a lot of weight that I don't have. I can't *force* a witness to see me if they refuse. A cop can get a warrant to get face to face, even if they can't make a witness sing.

So it's pretty safe to say that the cops weren't going to be overjoyed to give me the bird's-eye lowdown on this caper. Still, I was on good terms with a few city employees. Everyone in Vegas had known of Captain Billy Woods of the downtown precinct since he'd come to Vegas two years ago, but I didn't know him personally. I had a guarded relationship with his second in command, Lt. Tom Steele, and a not-quite-so-guarded friendship with my old pal Reggie Harding.

It always helps to have an inside man, and it helps to know where he goes to tie the feedbag on. Reggie liked this little diner over on 3rd, Nancy's Diner. I'd never set foot in there before, but that was where I headed now to get the scoop on the case.

Even if Reggie wasn't working on it, cops are terrible gossips, and he'd know all about it. Besides, neither of the other two would have given me the time of day. Woods would probably have said something about ongoing investigations, and Steele liked to pretend that private dicks didn't exist. Which was fine by me; I just wished I could pretend *he* didn't.

I parked my heap across the way from the diner and waited till I saw Reggie go in and take a booth. I had a sneaking suspicion that he might make a bolt for it when he saw me, especially if word got around that Miss McIntyre had hired herself a dick.

I waited till he was shoveling it in before I opened the door to the joint slow and careful, so as not to jostle the bell. I slid into the seat opposite him before he even knew I was there. He started to stand up, but I hooked his feet out from under him, and he dropped back onto the vinyl-covered bench with a thud.

"Anyone would think you weren't happy to see me, Reg."

"Fuck off, Randall!"

"Can I help you?"

I looked up to see a fortyish waitress standing by our table, chewing gum and holding her order pad. She was dark-haired, a little plump for her uniform, and had a shrewd pair of eyes that chased back and forth between me and Reggie.

"A cup of joe," I said.

"It's okay, Nancy. This is Grey Randall. Friend of mine."

I stood up and held out my hand. "Pleased to meet you, Miss Nancy."

She looked surprised but stuck her pencil into her hair-bun and took my hand in a firm grip. "I don't like trouble in my place, Mr. Randall."

"I won't cause any, Miss Nancy. You can count on me."

"You break any china, you pay for it."

"It's a deal." I smiled at her, and after a moment, she smiled back. It's wholesome living and my irresistible charm, gets them every time. Obviously, as Lily had pointed out, it wasn't the tie.

"I'll get your coffee."

Reggie snorted in disgust and glared at me some more as she walked away.

I sat down. "Calm down, Reg. If you play your cards right, I might buy you a bowl of chili."

"I already paid for it."

"Next time, then." I smirked at him, and he glowered back. "I need a favor."

"Go find someone who owes you one."

"I already did."

Reggie picked up his spoon and dug around in his bowl of chili with it. He wouldn't look at me, and I didn't blame him. He didn't like being reminded. Neither did I. It was a two-way street.

"Whaddya need?"

"Miss Marguerite Saint-Ville."

He shot me a cagey glance. "That's a big favor."

"I said I'd owe you."

"I didn't hear you, but you will. Who brought you in on it?"

I thought about not telling him, but it always pays to show a little good faith. Besides, I knew he could keep his yap shut if there was something in it for him. "Miss Lily McIntyre."

He didn't seem surprised to hear that. In fact, he snickered and took another bite of chili.

"Good to see your appetite's coming back. Share the joke."

Nancy came back and plunked a cup of coffee in front of me.

"Thanks."

"You're welcome. Don't mess up my boy here." She ruffled Reggie's hair before leaving.

"You're such a ladies' man," I teased.

He gave me a sour smile and smoothed his hair back down. "Yeah, that must be it. Anyway, Miss McIntyre about chewed the lieutenant's ear off over the case," Reggie said. "Didn't think we were trying hard enough."

"And are you?"

Again, he gave me a hard look, as if trying to see if I was kidding him. "Some of us are. Lieutenant Steele is. He doesn't like murder."

"I don't blame him. Especially on his watch."

Reggie went back to grooming his chili instead of eating it. He was beginning to give me the impression that there was more to the case than met the eye, not that much actual information had met my eye so far. "What did she tell you?"

"Not a lot. Just that this Saint-Ville frail was a protégé of hers, that means student to you—"

"Thanks, maybe you can explain what pain in the ass means next," Reggie said sarcastically.

"If you ever looked in a dictionary—"

"I'd find *your* picture under it. What else did she tell you?"

"Miss Saint-Ville was found in the train yard, in an alley, around two a.m. Monday morning, strangled to death. Her purse was next to her, but the money was stolen. Miss McIntyre has no ideas about anything, like what the girl was doing there, who she was meeting, or if she even had a boyfriend, except that she had a few that nobody knows the name of. The end."

Reggie snickered. "She didn't tell you much."

"Suppose you do. Did you work on it?"

"Took the crime scene pictures." He was a good photographer, and once the lieutenant found out that tidbit of information, Reggie was often rousted to do it even when he was off duty. For overtime pay, of course.

"And? Can I see them?"

"The lieutenant wouldn't like that." He shook his head doubtfully.

I sighed. "Paint a picture for me. What was in that alley when you got there?"

He gave me a sharp glance to see if I was pulling his leg. "The girl's body. Her purse was next to her, as if someone went through it and then tossed it down near her."

"Signs of a struggle?"

"That whole area looks like a permanent struggle. Broken bottles, rubbish, discarded furniture...." He shrugged, but he was still tense, still holding something back.

"Describe the body."

"It was a dead body. Not pretty. Strangling isn't a nice way to go."

"Start at the top and tell me about her clothes. Any sign of sexual assault?"

Reggie shook his head. "None of that. She might have put up a fight, but she was fully clothed. No sign that someone took 'em off and dressed her afterwards. She had on kind of a sequined number like a dame might wear onstage. Brassiere, panties, garter belt, stockings, shoes, earrings—"

"What kind of earrings?"

"Diamond. Nice ones."

That little tingle had a hold of me now, that feeling I get when I'm finally on the trail of some facts. "So this thief who went through her purse after her money didn't like these diamond earrings and left them for the next taker?"

Reggie gave me a smug grin, and I knew he'd led me up the path on purpose to see if I was following along. "Maybe they didn't look good on him. He left a diamond bracelet too. Or possibly he thought they were rhinestones."

I nodded. I knew that someone on the force must have had them vetted, or he would have left out the bit about the jewels. "What about her hat?"

He looked startled. "She wasn't wearing one."

"So maybe she wasn't expecting to go outside."

"Maybe she was meeting someone she knew and just slipped out…."

"Slipped out of where? Was she shacked up in an empty warehouse?"

"Maybe someone brought her there by car."

I considered that. "Could be. Any tire tracks?"

"Yeah, go figure. On asphalt where a hundred trucks drive through everyday."

"What about a coat? It's winter. It gets cold at night, even in the desert."

"She had one of those flimsy evening wrap things women tote around, but she'd dropped it before she was killed." Reggie was looking at me like I was missing something that he'd expected me to hone in on.

"Why don't you just spill it?" I said.

"You didn't get this from me, right?" He peered around anxiously, but the snitches were off duty for the night. Nancy had been reading a newspaper and eating a piece of pie behind the counter when she saw I wasn't planning to wreck her joint.

"Come on, Reggie!"

"Keep your shirt on." He glanced around again and leaned forward to whisper, "There's a clue in that alley, something our boys didn't pick up. You go back there after dark when the newshawks have gone to roost and you'll find it."

I sank my voice low as well. His paranoia was catching. "What the fuck? Why didn't you scoop it when you had the chance? You could have made sergeant."

"Shut up!" he hissed. "Look, it won't mean anything to anyone but you. Everyone saw it, they just didn't get the significance of it, get my drift?"

"No," I said. "Seems like you got it, so why didn't you just—"

"Let me explain it to you in words of one syllable. Go down there and take a look, snoop." He stood up and wiped his mouth with his napkin, even though he hadn't made much of a dent in his bowl of chili.

"Why after dark?"

"That's all you're getting from me. Do your own legwork."

He left without a backward glance, and I didn't try to stop him. I knew from the tone of his voice that he meant it. Also that he was going out on a limb for me. If the lieutenant found out that Reggie spotted a clue and hadn't blown the whistle, well, he could be off the force or scrubbing the johns for the rest of his career.

While I sat there puzzling over what kind of clue it could be that would only mean something to me, I pulled his bowl of chili closer and sampled it. It was excellent, much better than I would have expected given the kind of dive this place was. The coffee was good too, and that surprised me. Maybe Nancy had more on the ball than I thought.

While I ate, I came to the conclusion that this clue, whatever it was, had to have a meaning that other people would get too. After all, if it meant something to me, it had to mean something to Reggie too, or he wouldn't just—

Aha. Something we had in common, then. Perhaps some potentially career-ending fact about us that we wouldn't care to have become public knowledge. While that told me why he was being so cagey, it still didn't tell me exactly what to look for, but at least I knew there was something the cops had missed, maybe something that could break the case wide open.

I finished the chili before I left. Who says there's no such thing as a free lunch?

Chapter 2: The Meaning of a Clue

IT COULD have been a setup. I didn't want to believe that of a friend, but a man has to be careful in my line of work.

After leaving the diner, I went straight to the train yard, ignoring what Reggie said about waiting till after dark. But when I got there, I realized the wisdom of his advice. However the place looked at night, by day it was full of trucks and men on forklifts bustling around moving freight.

Not much chance I could slip down the alley unnoticed in that hubbub, but I took note of the location. A few amateur criminologists standing behind the rope, including some newshounds with flashbulbs, helped mark the spot.

I parked my jalopy a couple of blocks away and took a walk, glancing into the alley as I passed by. This wasn't the glossy face of Vegas. Here on the wrong side of the tracks it was mostly warehouses, some shacks left over from when the tracks were first laid, and tumbleweeds, blowing through the alleys in front of the constant wind that came in from the desert.

The cops were long gone, having collected their evidence and left the scene of the crime. I took it easy, casing the dirty windows for a glint of sunlight off a pair of binoculars. Or a rifle. I saw nothing to get my motor running. I returned to my car and sat there reading the paper, wondering if anyone was going to ask questions about just why I was sitting there.

But the stray cat and lone drunk I spotted weren't interested. They just went about their business and ignored me.

Along about dusk, everybody had gone home or onto more exciting pursuits. I got out of the car and stretched, in case anyone was watching. They weren't. I could see the glow of the neon lighting up the dark blue sky past the station over on Fremont. Everyone on the other side of the tracks was having a good time, with the lights and the booze and the gambling.

It was quiet here, quiet as the grave. The alley was so dark I couldn't see a thing. Luckily, private dicks carry a lot of the tools of the trade, which in this case was a flashlight. I was going to need it; none of the bright lights penetrated into the alley. I flicked it on and proceeded, taking each foot of the alley slowly, hoping to see this item that the coppers had missed.

Next time I saw Reggie, I was going to thump him. The police were careful; they didn't tend to leave anything behind, even if it didn't look like clue. I mean, if the dame dropped her bag, it's not like they'd leave it there all handy for me, maybe with a note tucked inside it, saying who had it in for her. Or a message in invisible ink.

Yeah, right, it should be so easy. In my dreams.

I peered down the alley. It was empty, as far as I could tell. No way to tell from this end if there was some way out down there, but if there were, a smart broad would have taken the emergency exit instead of riding the dead-end train to nowhere.

I decided to play it cagey. If anyone saw me, I might look like a fool, but better a live fool than a dead one. I drew my gun, keeping the flashlight in my left hand. I hoped it wasn't going to come to squirting lead, not yet. It would be murder to get killed when I didn't even know anything about the case yet. Yeah, I gave myself a laugh with that one.

I swung the flashlight around, and the place lit up like a jewelry store, glints of light dancing everywhere off pieces of broken glass and bottle caps. Evidently it was a dump for winos after they had their way with their bottles. If Miss Saint-Ville had scattered a cache of stolen jewels here, it might have escaped anyone's notice, except she'd left a dead body with it. That tended to draw a bit of attention from the cops.

I edged down the alley, peering into the niches that had been bricked up along the sides of the buildings. Probably windows in the old days, judging by the brick arches over them. Reggie had said she was found all the way at the end, propped up against the brick wall that backed the alley. I could see the reflection of chalk lines, drawn around where they'd found her.

Bad way to see your last sunset, trapped like a rat in a maze with only a man who hated you enough to off you for company.

Zip. I saw nothing that conveyed any secret knowledge to me. And what did I really know about her? Miss McIntyre hadn't exactly been forthcoming. Maybe I was better off in the archives of the newspapers. But Reggie hadn't sent me on this wild goose chase without a reason. We were friends, but he knew I wouldn't let him get away with sending me here to look for nothing.

I tracked my light across the pavement, trying to overlap each pass. When I finally found it, it looked like a bottle cap unless you knew what you were looking for. The kind of thing I would expect to see in a dirty alley. I could see how the cops missed it.

But when I moved the light back to take a second look, there was something about the shape inscribed on the bottle cap that caught my eye....

Standing there looking down at it, suddenly I was three thousand miles away, in a war zone on a stinking hot island in the Pacific. Looking down at two twigs, one short, one long, laid out to form the same symbol on that disc.

The sign that only a select few of the soldiers recognized, a sign that said there was action behind the bushes or in the back of a nearby Jeep.

The sign of the Lambda.

A Greek symbol belonging to an exclusive fraternity of men. The story went that the Lambda was placed on the shields of gay men and their lovers, men who were part of the fighting elite of the Greek army. Men who were honored for their bond.

Maybe the first queer who thought to use the sign had a good education along with a perverted sense of humor, because the U.S. Army didn't think of us as part of any elite fraternity. They tended to take a dimmer view of queers, even ones who enlisted to fight for their country. But station a couple of platoons of men on an island without any women, and even the straightest amongst them might get a little bent with frustration.

Some men hooked up for the duration, and the officers tended to turn a blind eye unless they made it obvious. But if you wanted some hot man-on-man action with no strings, this was the symbol you looked for: scratched into the dirt beside a path, or maybe two spoons placed at right angles tipped you off. If the bushes were shaking, you just waited your turn.

I recognized it, and when Reggie found that sign down this alley, he must have too. But being a cop, there was no way he could draw attention to it, because then he'd have to explain how he knew what it meant. It must have really gone against the grain with him to have to leave a potential clue to a murder in place because he couldn't risk explaining how he knew what it meant. And now I had a pretty good idea as to who had sent Lily McIntyre my way.

I put the gun away and crouched there, fingering the disc. I chuckled softly to myself.

"What's so funny, peeper?"

Oh fuck! It *was* a set-up! I was terrified that Reggie had sold me so he could make sure the clue was found, and I was going to turn around to find a hundred cops standing behind me, guns drawn.

My heart was racing as I drew my own gun again and rolled on my shoulder, aiming it upward at the shadow looming over me, before I recognized his ugly shoes and relaxed.

"Artie, fuck off! You know better than to creep up on a man holding a gun!"

He sniggered. "You weren't holding it, *Greyson*. You put it away."

"Don't call me that, it's Grey," I said automatically, stowing the piece in my holster and retrieving the disc. My hands were shaking but I didn't let him see.

"I hear you landed yourself a keeper." He used both hands to trace the curves of an exaggerated female figure.

"What don't you hear?" I got to my feet and slapped the dust off my pants with my hat.

Artie shrugged. "Thought you might need more man muscle, my son."

I glared at him. "Not yet. I'll call you if I need you."

"No phone."

"I'll send up a smoke signal." It didn't matter. If I needed help, Artie would show up. He had a nose for trouble.

"What did you find? Is it worth anything?"

"Who says I found anything?"

He laughed. "Yeah, it's not everyday I can walk up behind you, Grey. Ears like a bat."

"A bat?"

"You know, sonar, or radar maybe. Whatever they have."

Sometimes Artie surprised me with the weird stuff he knew, what with being a boxer. You wouldn't think that would leave him much time for reading, especially if another fighter had rung his chimes in a bout. The rest of the time he did odd jobs for the criminal element to get enough money for gym fees.

I held out the disc so he could see it.

"A bottle cap," he said in a disgusted voice.

"Turn it over."

He did, and I held the light so he could see it. He poked it with a finger and then looked up at me with a little grin. "Feeling horny?"

"Brings back old times, doesn't it?"

He nodded, but his expression was quizzical. "You mean, you're not a member?"

He knew I was queer, like I knew he was, but it wasn't something we ever chatted about. In fact, I suspected that he swung both ways, but he was a meat-eater if there was any to be had. He liked beefier guys than me, and I didn't much want him, but we'd drunk out of the same bottle once or twice, and he'd told me some stories.

"A member of what?"

Artie nodded at the cap. "This place. It's the ritziest queer club in Vegas."

"Not like the dives you hang out at?"

He shrugged. "The club is more high class. They call it Lambda, but there's no name on the door. Doctors, lawyers, fancy nances getting their rocks off before going home to the missus."

Just goes to show how out of touch I was. I'd heard there were clubs, but experience had taught me to stay out of them. I had two hands, and I was equally good with both. One of the benefits of being ambidextrous in certain areas; if I got tired of my pal Lefty, there was always Righty.

"Where is this place? And what makes it so tony?"

Artie pointed at the cap. "That's your ticket in. Members only. It's over that way. I gotta show you. No street names in the train yard."

"In the train yard?"

"Keeps the passing foot traffic down. You gotta know about it to find it."

"Okay, show me the way."

"I could show you something all right, soldier." He chuckled and turned to lead the way, his hulking shadow ominous against the brick walls.

"So how do you know about this joint if you don't go there?"

"Word gets around. I know a few guys." He smacked his lips, and I got the drift. Artie liked a good mouthful.

"What's the drill?"

"Same as a speak. You knock three times, some goon slides back a spyhole in the door. Show him the sign, he opens up."

"And what the hell was a skirt doing carrying this around?" I muttered out loud without really meaning to.

"Could have been the fella," Artie pointed out.

I looked at him. That was way too smart for him to come up with on his own, and anyway, he was smirking again. "Spill it."

"She was a torcher, or so I heard. Heard she worked at that club."

"A queer joint? Employing a dame?"

He shrugged and pointed. "See that door?"

I looked. I still had the flashlight in my pocket, but I had the feeling the management wouldn't take too kindly to lights being flashed around. I mean, they'd gone to a lot of trouble to keep it discreet, locating in a spot that was virtually deserted at night. No lights showed anywhere, but I could hear the faint sound of music.

"Want I should stick around?"

"Nah, they see your ugly mug, they'll probably shoot me before they'd let me in. Encouraging a bad element to hang around. Take a powder."

"Have fun." His dirty leer along with his flattened nose made him look more menacing than he really was. Artie wasn't a very successful boxer.

I waited till he eeled out of sight before I snapped the brim of my fedora to the correct angle and went up to the door. It was a good strong one, with iron hinges and a big handle. There was a square of metal fastened to the brick wall, but instead of a name, it just had the same symbol engraved on it: Lambda.

I could see why Reggie said wait until dark; he knew me. He knew once I was on the scent I'd want to case the joint out right away, and they probably didn't have daylight hours. I took the disc out of my pocket and knocked on the door. The lookout slid open, and with it came music, louder now, and the acrid scent of cigarette smoke.

I held the disc up to where a pair of eyes glinted in the dim light. Without a word, the owner of the eyes slid the lookout shut, and the door opened for me.

He was big, about as big as Artie, although his nose was still the original shape he'd been born with. Good-looking too, but I wasn't here to tomcat around. His face relaxed when he gave me a glom, and he nodded, gesturing for me to go on inside. What can I say? It's a secret fraternity with a select membership. Sometimes you just know, and he could tell I was one of them.

I walked down the short hallway to the room that opened up into a nightclub scene that could have given the Morocco Room at the Rising Star a run for its money. The bar was located in the center of the room, which was an unusual spot for it, but it made room for the tables and dance floor. It was glossy black and bathed in blue light that shone upward on the faces of the two bartenders. There were booths lining the walls and small tables in the space to my right. The atmosphere was smoky and hot. Booze, drugs, illegal gambling, and a hint of more deviant sins swirled just under the surface of what you saw. You could get whatever you wanted there, legal or not. You just had to know who to ask. Some of the booths had the curtains drawn, and I could guess what was going on behind them.

To my left was a small stage, two steps up from the dance floor. When I first walked in, the sight of men dancing together in a clinch hit me. It was something you don't see everyday, so it seemed strange. It gave the place a forbidden, secret kind of allure, but I liked it. I acclimated real quick, and I realized I was in danger of feeling a little *too* comfortable there. After all, I wasn't there to socialize.

A band was playing, and I did a double take when I saw the piano player. He was very good-looking, tall, broad-shouldered. Dark hair that was curly rather than frizzy. His eyes were half shut, hidden behind dark lashes as he poured himself into his music, but I got the impression that they were lighter colored. However, what really caught my attention was that he was black. Well, a handsome shade of brown, actually, kind of medium-toned.

You just didn't see many colored men in a white club in those days, but nobody seemed to be too hysterical over it.

Straight ahead of me, the wall behind the bar was lined with dark blue damask curtains, stretching from one side of the room to the other. As I watched, the curtain twitched and a dame came out. Or was she? She was tall, taller than I was. She was also colored and her face was severely beautiful, her shoulders broad and her hips narrow. The busy dress she wore exaggerated what she had, the sequins shining under the lights as they glided over her body, drawing the eye to follow the curves, although she seemed more flat than round. Her hair was skinned back, and there was a flower behind her ear. When she bent to speak to the piano player, her voice was low and sultry. I relaxed as soon as I twigged that she was a transvestite, a T-girl. It was hard to pick that out unless you knew what you were looking for, but hey, I'm a private dick. I'm observant, what can I say?

I suddenly realized I was making like a totem pole and attracting a little attention as I stood there gaping. I headed for the bar and slid onto an empty stool.

The colored girl started to sing, and the piano player closed his eyes almost like he was in pain.

"What can I get you?"

I turned to face the bartender. He wasn't queer, I knew it right off, but he seemed right at home there. He was an older man, with gray showing at his temples. He waited patiently for my order.

"Scotch. Rocks."

He nodded and went to get a glass.

I don't like to drink on the job, but what're you gonna do. If I'd asked for a Shirley Temple I'd have had to turn in my tough guy credentials forever. And tonic by itself—just inflict me with malaria or I don't want to know about it. At least the ice would dilute the giggle juice a bit.

He came back with my drink and took my money. I spun on the stool and rested my elbows on the bar to look over the crowd. Now that I was here, I could feel that familiar let-down of the daily guard, the comfort of being among my own kind. There was something about being in a room filled with only men, other queers on the hunt. In a joint like this, we were all after the same thing, and we didn't have to front.

Except that's not what *I* was there for. I saw one or two guys I wouldn't have minded slipping into the bushes with, but then I noticed a familiar face. He was seated in a booth as far from the stage as he could get.

I edged through the crowd, staying close to the wall until I reached his table. I slid onto the seat opposite and grabbed his wrist so he couldn't take off on me.

"Well, hello, Reggie. Fancy meeting you here."

He jerked and turned his face to stare at me. I could feel his muscles jumping under my hand, but he didn't try to give me the slip.

"Grey. I've been waiting for you."

"Yeah, sure you have." I let go.

"Honest. I knew you'd find it. Then it was just a matter of time."

"Why didn't you just tell me?"

Reggie shivered. "I don't like saying the words, even in private."

"To a friend."

"Even to you."

"So, which one of them was it? The skirt or the killer?"

"Don't know, could have been both. She worked here." Reggie nodded toward the black girl onstage, singing her heart out to the oblivious piano player. "She was a singer like Miss Tina."

"Canary, huh? So they were sisters under the skin?"

"No, she was for real. No gaff. No hiding a roll of quarters under a garter belt or girdle."

I nodded at the slim colored girl. "That one's only packing dimes."

Reggie laughed for the first time, and that made me realize that he was looking pretty sad. "Yeah, so I've heard. No, the Saint-Ville broad was a real live girl, but what better place to hide out if you're on the lam?"

I considered that. "What kind of broad ducks for cover with a bunch of queers?"

"That I don't know. I don't know why the owner took her on, either. I'm pretty sure he knew she was legit."

"And who *is* the owner?"

"Name's Phil Martin."

I nodded. I'd heard of him. He ran a string of nightclubs, and you needed backing to make a success of that. "And *he's* tied in with the mob."

"No direct evidence of that. And this wasn't a mob hit."

I rolled my eyes. "Yeah, I know. Usually they don't take the time to strangle you. A clean bullet to the head is more their style."

Reggie's eyes were mournful again, and I followed his gaze. He was watching the black dude play.

"He's your type," I commented.

"What do you know about it?"

"I've noticed," I said smugly.

"Yeah, well I know your type too, peeper, I wouldn't get too mouthy!" Reggie snarled at me.

"Okay, what's my type?"

"The kind where you never see his face, because where *you* meet them, it's too dark to see."

That stung. Reggie knew why I was the way I was, what happened to make me run when it was over, but I guess he couldn't help lashing out. He was hurting, I could tell, but I still would have pasted him one, except it wouldn't get me any further on the job, not to mention this wasn't the place to get into a dustup. "So what's with the piano player? You think he did it?"

"No!"

I jumped at the vehemence of his tone. "All right, settle down. I was just asking. How can you be sure of that?"

"He was dizzy for her. He wouldn't have hurt her." Now that his anger fizzled out, Reggie sounded defeated.

"And you're dizzy for *him*. Is he even queer?"

Reggie laughed bitterly. "As a three dollar bill, but when she walked into the place, it was like he was bewitched or something."

"And did she go for him?"

"She sure gave that impression. I don't know for sure." Reggie knocked back his drink and set the glass sharply on the table.

"Sounds like motive to me. If she told him to take a walk, he might have lost his temper—"

"Or maybe Miss Tina stuck a shiv in her when she horned in on her territory," Reggie interrupted.

"Except she was strangled."

"Details. Maybe you can make it stick."

"So you got competition for the player?"

Reggie nodded but wouldn't answer.

A dark-haired waiter with a big nose slid up to the table. "Can I get you a refill?" he sneered.

"Yeah. Same again," Reggie said through clenched teeth.

The nasty number didn't even glance my way, just picked up Reggie's empty.

"Excuse me," I said, loud so the waiter couldn't pretend he didn't hear me.

"I suppose *you* want a drink too," he said with an exasperated sigh. I wasn't quite sure he could even see me around the schnozz.

"Like you care. What's the name of the broad singing?"

"Miss Tina? Don't even start, you wouldn't stand a chance with her," the waiter said with a contemptuous smile.

"Her?" Maybe he'd be more forthcoming if he knew she wasn't pulling the wool over my eyes.

He grimaced, which was maybe his idea of a smile to acknowledge my keen sense of observation. "She doesn't go for pipsqueaks like you. She likes 'em big."

"I heard there was another singer. White dame—"

Grudgingly, the waiter conceded that he was going to have to talk to me. "You're too late. She was good and the boss was gonna make her a headliner, but she never came back."

"Do you know why?"

"Do I look like the town crier?"

"No, you look like an anteater." I had the satisfaction of seeing the sneer on his face give way to confusion, if only for a moment, before the condescending expression came back. He hurried off to get Reggie's refill.

"I would have said possum," Reggie commented.

"What did I ever do to him?"

"He's always like that. Ignore him."

It was telling that Reggie didn't laugh at my joke. He leaned forward, his eyes as cold as black ice. "Jazz didn't do it. He's not a killer. He wouldn't do something like that."

"Jazz?"

"My—the guy on piano."

"Proof?"

"No proof. I just know him."

"You're a cop, you know better. I can see the D.A. now, taking your feelings as evidence. Does he have an alibi?"

Reggie shrugged helplessly. "I can't check it out. Maybe you can."

"His name is Jazz what?"

"Jazz Morgan."

"And he works here—"

"Shut up!"

A hand fell on my shoulder, and I looked up into the bluest eyes I'd ever seen.

"Good evening, gentlemen. Everything all right here?"

Reggie was nodding, and I wondered how he could stay so calm. The man whose hand rested on my shoulder was more than good-looking. Slim and smart in his suit, but built. I could see the muscles move under the fabric. And his face was gorgeous. He could have given any movie star a run for his money, and he was staring right at me with a quizzical look on his face.

I kept it suave. "Yeah—things are—just great! Fine! A—a nice place—you have here—"

The man took pity on me. Dimples dug deep into his cheeks as he flashed a grin, showing off his pearly whites. "Is this your first time here, Mr.—er—"

Put on the spot like that, I didn't have time to make up an alias. I admit it, I was flustered, and being caught by surprise like that, my mouth may have been hanging open until I remembered to shut it. It wasn't good business to get known as a private dick with an interest in dick. Besides, he seemed straight as a board.

While I was deciding, Reggie helpfully piped up. "His name's Randall, a friend of mine from the service," he announced with a malicious smile.

The beautiful man stifled a snicker, still holding out his hand to me. We shook.

Sparks. It was electric, just feeling his hand in mine. Or maybe I should say, mine in his. His hand was big, strong and warm as it closed around mine. I struggled to meet his grip without letting out a sound. Like a needy gasp. He was so hot I almost melted out of my seat.

"Randall. That suits you," he smirked at me.

If I weren't used to the undercover gig, I might have given away the show, but as it is, I think I carried it off with a lot of cool. "Um—yes—it's my first time—no, that isn't what I—I meant, I've been around—no, I haven't been around—it's just—"

He cut me off, to my relief. "I hope to see you here again, Mr. Randall. I enjoy meeting new people in my clubs." He released my hand and got up to go. "Gotta make the rounds. I'll see you a little later."

My head was spinning. What did he mean? Was I supposed to wait around? Did he really want to see me, or did he say that to all the guys? Or just the new guys?

He moved on to the next table, and I watched him bend over to exchange some words. His shoulders were broad, tapering to narrow hips, and his legs were long. His hair was so dark it could have been black for all I could tell in the dim light. He worked the room, going from one table to another, with a word and a smile for everyone. I could see how this place was such a success. If he smiled at me like that, I would have laid down right on the floor for him. In fact, I don't know what kept me in my seat.

"Suck your tongue back in, Grey." Reggie was shaking with silent laughter, sure he had one on me now.

I was a little too stunned to pull the wool over his eyes. "Who the fuck was that?"

"That was the owner."

"Yeah, no shit. His name, Reggie."

"Trouble with your memory? I told you before, Phillip Martin. AKA Mr. Big, to us on the force."

Of course. We had already covered this, hadn't we? "AKA Mr. Beautiful," I muttered to myself.

"To those suffering from chronic blue balls, maybe."

Fuck, he heard me. Reggie was smirking at me now. He was so fucking pleased with himself.

"Just to make sure I'm following along, bear with me here." I had to get his mind back on the case before he laughed himself silly at my expense. "The dame, Miss Saint-Ville, was hired by Mr. Big to sing at night here at Lambda, a queer club, even though he knew what she was. Jazz Morgan falls for the frail, leaving you sighing and horny in the shadows. So maybe you did it."

That snapped him to. "Fuck you, Grey! I wouldn't kill a woman for that!"

"No? What would you kill her for? How much?" Maybe I just had to let off steam after my scare in the alley earlier, even though Reggie hadn't shopped me.

"You know me better than that!" He was glaring at me like he wanted to burn me right there.

"You have a motive."

"There were other men in her life with better reasons. You think they liked it that she was making eyes at a Negro?"

"What other men?"

He closed his lips firmly and shook his head.

"You know who did it, don't you?"

"I don't know for sure. All I know is she had other men in her life."

"You could just tell me. Once I know where to look, I'll find the evidence, and then we can all go home." I nodded toward Jazz. "Maybe when he knows for sure, it'll let up for him."

Reggie looked tempted, but he shook his head again. "I don't know who they were. I just know it wasn't Jazz."

"You're being a big fucking help."

"Yeah, that's what I live for. To help a private dick make the cops look bad. Look, I did what I could, steering the flash broad your way. You stand to make a bundle, while I—"

The sarcastic number came back and put the drink down in front of Reggie, who shut his trap smartly. The waiter glared at me, daring me to order another drink, but I shook my head, so he gave a sniff and left.

I watched Jazz Morgan as he let his heart pour out his fingertips. I couldn't tell if he was sad about the girl or mad at himself for wandering across the line. Two lines, really. I'd seen him glance over here a couple times, always when Reggie wasn't looking, but I didn't mention it. Didn't want to give Reggie a bum steer. "You got it bad."

"Just because you have ice water in your veins doesn't mean the rest of us just want to fuck and run like hell."

"Better than getting hurt," I shot back.

"You can't hurt a man with no feelings."

Two for two! He was on fire tonight, and that was below the belt. Now I didn't feel so bad about that crack earlier. Reggie knew, better than anyone else, that I had feelings. I knew he was just angry, but still—

"Sorry."

"It's okay."

Reggie stood up. "Listen, you know I like to mess around with photography."

I nodded.

"I took some publicity stills for the owner. In color. I'll get you a set of prints."

"Thanks." I wasn't sure how that was going to help. I already knew what she looked like, and she was dead. Where she was, I wasn't going to be following her. But I took the olive branch for what it was.

The curtain moved again, and the owner, Phil Martin, reappeared. I thought he was looking right at me, but his movement was so smooth, he could have been looking anywhere.

Reggie sniggered. "Your type?"

"Aim for the moon," I joked, to put him off the scent.

"You're not kidding; he's straight as an arrow. Just in it for the dough. Always has a stable of beautiful dames on a string. Runs a bunch of clubs, remember?"

"Yeah, I remember." I got up and walked out with Reggie. I'd had enough smoke and mirrors for one night. I was *not* running away. "When can I have them?" I asked once we were outside. The clear, cool air and silence were refreshing after the atmosphere in the club.

"Stop by the precinct in the morning. Around ten o'clock, my coffee break. If you lay off Jazz, I might let you see the photos from the crime scene."

"I'll be there."

Reggie turned and walked off to where his car was parked. I heard the slam of the door and the motor turning over. The sound of his engine faded into the night, and I walked over to a building across the way, leaning against the wall. I could have told myself this was research.

I could stand here and wait till Jazz Morgan came out and tail him home. Or I could just look him up in the phone book later, assuming he had a phone. I could wait until the owner, Phil Martin, came out, but he probably had a limo pick him up after hours around back. Or I could wait for that sarcastic number and show him the back of my hand.

Reggie might be right about his friend Jazz, but he had no proof. And I had to wonder how come he, a cop, felt comfortable enough to sit around in a queer bar at night. And even more, how he got so hand in glove with the straight club owner that he was taking photographs for him. Maybe Reggie had concocted some story about being a photographer by day, which wasn't such a bad cover story at that. Everyone knew that fellas in the artistic pursuits were a little limp in the wrist, and he got to earn some extra dough on the side.

I'd have to ask him. Having decided that, my thoughts were free to roam back to Mr. Martin, AKA Mr. Beautiful. I had a feeling he was trouble with a capital T. Trouble for me. A club for queers run by straights, first the bartender and now the owner. Of course, it didn't make good business sense to squeal on your clientele, and I imagine that Mr. Martin, AKA Mr. Big, had plenty of practice keeping mum if he had connections.

I hadn't had such a yen for a fella since the service, and I thought I'd put all that behind me. First finding the disc with the symbol, then the club where I felt right at home, and then seeing Mr. Big, a guy who was way out of my league—it got me off balance. And that's part of why he'd made me so nervous.

I still had a job to do. I pushed myself off the wall, realizing I was sporting some wood. Seeing a guy that tasty will do that to you. I was tempted to whip it out and jack off right there, in a back alley in the train yard. I could nip behind a building, and no one would be the wiser.

But I wasn't twenty anymore. I could control myself. Time enough for that when I got back to my place. I looked down to see that I had traced the sign of the Lambda in the dirt by the wall with my shoe. Hastily, I stamped on it to erase the drawing. Talk about the subconscious.

The moon was only a crescent in the sky, and it was on the move, the roaming hunter of the night, sending long shadows over the deserted streets. It was dark as I walked back to my car, and the darkness had a gnawing hunger. You could hide from it in the light, but at night it calls to you like a siren on some desolate rocky shore, luring you to your doom.

I had a feeling it would be better if Mr. Big and I didn't meet again, no matter how much he knew.

I stuffed the hunger back into the box and locked it. Then I started my car, driving for home.

It felt like the shine was gone from this job, but I was no quitter. I would solve it somehow.

Chapter 3: You Have to Know Charlie

IT SEEMED to me that a little research was in order, which meant a visit to my friend Charlie Taylor at the library. I wasn't too popular down at the office of the *Las Vegas Review-Journal* ever since they caught me trying to boost a section from the archives.

That meant a stint in the basement of the library, going blind scanning through loops of microfilm on the viewer, but at least Charlie would leave me to it.

I headed over to the library on 4th and Mesquite and parked around back. I stopped at the front desk to say hello to the head librarian, Mrs. Fielding, and ask where I might find Charlie.

Mrs. Fielding primmed up her mouth and nodded toward the fiction section. "Shelving books. Hopefully."

I grinned and thanked her. I knew what the disapproving expression was about; Mrs. Fielding thought Charlie could be spending her time better, but even the boss didn't like to cross Charlie. She was smart, and her tongue had a sharp point to it.

I plunged into the nonfiction section, peering through the shelves to see a ladder with someone sitting on the platform at the top, and went around to that aisle. Mrs. Fielding's suspicions proved correct. As usual, Charlie had gotten interested in some book and calmly sat down to read it instead of doing her job.

I put my hands on the ladder and leaned in closer so I could see her little oval face and nicely pointed chin over the pages. "Hi, Charlie. Read any good books lately?"

She didn't even glance at me. "Keep your day job, Grey. You'll never make it as a comedian."

"Good looks will get you anywhere."

"Too bad you don't have any then."

Now that the social niceties were over, I got down to business. "I need to get into the basement. Gimme the key."

"Please, Charlie, I'm here to beg you for a favor. Would you very kindly interrupt your important work and allow me to do some free research in the archives, which are off-limits to the general public?" she retorted.

"Please, Charlie. I only asked for the key so you wouldn't have to interrupt your important work and climb down from there. I know the way."

She shut her book with a snap and shoved it onto the shelf between two other books without looking, but I knew it was in its proper place. Charlie didn't tolerate books wandering away from their appointed Dewey decimal slot. "That's so kind of you, Grey. I know you wouldn't want to cause me any inconvenience." She kicked my hand away and came down the ladder two steps at a time, disdaining my assistance.

Not that I was stupid enough to offer. Charlie had a temper, and I didn't want her to rip my head off my shoulders. At least not at the start of a case. "I'll pay you back."

"You don't have anything I want," she said with a glance from behind her glasses.

Those sidelong glances always got to me, but no point dwelling on it. We weren't an item and we never would be, and she was one of the few who knew why. But we were friends at least.

She took her glasses off and shoved one temple-piece down the neck of her blouse to hold them in place. Charlie only needed them for reading, and she looked prettier without them, if only because she unerringly chose the ugliest frames in existence. Not that vanity was a driving force in her life. That much was made clear by the brown cardigan she was wearing.

"I'll buy you a party dress," I said by way of witticism. I didn't think she even owned a dress; I'd never seen her in one, at any rate.

"For the next time I'm invited to the ball, is that it?"

"Right."

She turned and led the way to the back stairs, her wide-legged trousers flaring around her slender legs as she strode purposefully in front of me. She had a big bunch of keys on a ring that she had snapped to her belt, and she used one of them to unlock the door that said "Staff Only."

The door led into the staff room, where they took their breaks, and then we went out the other side into a small hallway, where the stairs were located.

The cellar was cold, perfect for archives. It was always cold down there, even when it was hot as blazes upstairs in summer, with all the windows open and the fans blowing.

"What are you after?" she asked, frowning at me.

Her fierce expression didn't fool me. I knew she was just as happy to be down here, away from the patrons of the library. She might have had to be polite to them up there.

"*Journal-Review*, Monday morning edition, police blotter," I said. I planted the back of my lap on the table and swung my legs as she went to the shelf and extracted a reel of film.

"I'll thread it for you."

"I can do it," I offered.

"It'll be quicker if I do it." She peered into the viewer, pulling the film along until she reached the right section. She stepped away and let me sit down to look at it. "What're you working on?"

"Murder. Some girl named Saint-Ville was offed Sunday night behind the train station," I said.

"Woman," Charlie corrected me automatically.

I ignored her. "And here it is."

"I said I'd cue it up for you," Charlie snapped. "She was young, beautiful, and someone strangled her. Her valuables were stolen. She was found in an unusual place where she had no business to be that late at night—"

"Blaming the victim, Charlie?"

"It was probably something to do with a *man*," she spat in disgust. "She probably thought she was *in love!*"

"Just because you were disappointed in love—"

"Have you *ever* heard me say so?" she exclaimed. "Just because I'm *sensible* and don't go around falling for men's lines—"

"Can it, Charlotte!"

"You call me that again and the cops will be investigating *your* murder," she said grimly.

"You're too smart for them, they'd never put the finger on you, *Charlie.*" I went back to reading my article. I peered at the accompanying picture, but it was just the empty alley. The *Journal-Review* didn't print photographs of murder victims, deeming the citizens to be too delicate for images of that nature, despite the fact that Vegas was a tough town and half the population had flocked to the site for a glimpse. But they did print a photo of the victim while still alive, the same publicity still that Miss McIntyre had given me. It didn't tell me any more about Miss Saint-Ville this time around.

Neither did the article. Either the cops were sitting on the facts, or the paper preferred lurid speculation to reporting. Captain Woods had been interviewed and had a few words to say about the horrible nature of the crime and how his department would never rest until they found the killer, the usual stuff about their high percentage rates in solving crimes and getting a conviction. The Las Vegas Police always gets their man—or *a* man, at any rate.

"What else have you got on this case?"

Her voice dripping poisoned honey, Charlie said, "If only you'd called ahead, I would have spent *all* my spare time researching it for you, but since you didn't—"

"Would you mind? So far I know nothing about the victim. I don't know who she knew, or where she worked or lived. I don't know if she preferred coffee or tea. I don't know who to ask about her."

"Who's your client? Can't you ask him?"

I knew this would impress her. "Her. Miss Lily McIntyre."

"Hot stuff." She *was* impressed. And why shouldn't she be? Lily McIntyre was a legend in this town. "What'd she say?"

"Not a lot. She gave me the impression she didn't know her very well, but someone had to."

"And if they do, why would anyone print it up?"

"Because she was a dancer, an entertainer. Surely her name must appear on some list of wherever she worked," I explained. "Public relations."

Charlie heaved a deep sigh, but I could see from the gleam in her eyes that I had her hooked. There was nothing she liked better than the challenge of a difficult research job. "Only a thousand places she might have danced in Vegas, but I'll see what I can find. There are a couple of magazines that might have something. The street guide will give me her address, and that will tell you something about how she lived."

"You're wasted in your job, you know."

Charlie could look really pretty when she smiled, and she smiled at that. "Sometimes you know how to pay a pretty compliment. But I don't come cheap."

The five large Lily McIntyre had given me was burning a hole in my pocket, so I said rather grandly, "You never do, but I'm flush this time. Name your price."

"There's a new Jane Austen collection coming out next year," Charlie said hopefully.

"Knew you were a closet romantic," I teased, and I ducked when she reached for the empty film canister, pretending she was going to throw it at me. I knew I was safe though. As if she'd damage library property.

"Jane Austen writes about *sensible* women with superior brains and morals—and they aren't always *pretty!*"

"But you are. See you, Charlie. Gotta see a man about a girl." I went closer and dropped a kiss on her cheek.

"Since when are you interested in girls?"

"I like you, don't I?"

"You like getting me to do your research for you." But she was pleased, I could tell by the glow.

IT WAS a short drive up Mesquite to the police station. I parked on the street and went up the front steps into the lobby, where a middle-aged desk sergeant labeled Thomas sat behind the cage.

"I'm here to see Officer Reggie Harding," I announced airily, galloping by him to the door that led to the offices behind.

"Hey, hang on! Who the hell are you?"

"Grey Randall. It's okay, I know the way." I waved my hand at the desk sergeant and breezed through the door before he could get up. I saw him reaching for the phone, but I figured once I got to the photo lab, I'd be home free. It was dark in there, and they'd never spot me.

It was just my bad luck that when I turned the corner I ran right into a big man who practically filled the hallway. He was handsome and genial, brave and stalwart. Captain Woods liked himself so much that other folks thought there had to be something in it and liked him too.

Big Billy Woods came by his name honestly. He was at least six foot five, towering over me. His wavy, black hair was on the longish side for a cop, but he didn't bother with the uniform except at press conferences. Today he had on a stylish navy blue suit that had obviously been tailored to fit. His face was open and friendly, his lips were curled into a smile, and I suppose some might have called him handsome.

In stark contrast was a wizened gnome in uniform, Sgt. Bert Guthrie, who was almost always to be found a few paces behind the captain. He sneered at me under Captain Woods's arm. He was a few inches shorter than me, which put him under periscope depth for the captain.

Sergeant Thomas plunged through the door after me and skidded to halt when he saw the Captain, saluting instinctively. "Sir, I just—"

"I'll take care of it, Sergeant, back to your post."

Sergeant Thomas nodded and backed away.

Captain Woods gave me the once-over. "Reporter?"

"Nope." I grinned up at him. "I'm a big fan of Lieutenant Steele's. I just came to visit, maybe share a gab over old times." I tried to edge around the captain. If he was busy, maybe he wouldn't have time to deal with me, but Guthrie seemed like he was going to give it the old college try, shifting to block my way. "I know the way," I assured them.

"I'm sure Lieutenant Steele will be happy to see you. I'll show you to his office," Woods said. He waved his hand, indicating that I should take the lead. Maybe it was a test to see if I knew where Lieutenant Steele's office was. Well, I'd been hauled in there before, so I flew there straight as a homing pigeon.

I raised my hand to knock, but Captain Woods reached past me and opened the door.

My nemesis, Lt. Tom Steele, stood up at attention, all natural irritation at seeing me wiped from his face in an instant. "Captain Woods, sir! What's the problem?"

I could just tell Steele was dying to glare at me, but he wouldn't in front of the captain. I sauntered in like I owned the place, hoping it would annoy him. "Hi, Lieutenant Steele."

"No trouble, Lieutenant. Just an unescorted visitor who says he's looking for you."

"I know him, sir," Steele said grudgingly, answering the unspoken question. His face was wooden, and he stood there stiff as a board.

Captain Woods smiled over my head in my general direction and then ignored me. I was beginning to feel like a forgotten chip on a poker table. Whatever was going on between them had nothing to do with me, and the tug of war was just beginning, with me in the middle.

Captain Woods was much better at this game. But maybe he'd had more practice. He kept the smile glued in place, at any rate. "Let's see now, who is this young man?"

"He's a private investigator, sir."

I noticed that Steele didn't mention my name.

Captain Woods couldn't hide the little grimace that crossed his face, but maybe he enjoyed that Lieutenant Steele obviously didn't like me, either.

I stood there looking between them, wondering at the contrast. Lieutenant Steele was older, in his forties, with a seamed, ugly face that looked like a bulldog. Short and stocky, wearing a tweed sport coat and dark gray trousers, he stood ramrod straight, like an ex-Marine, which is what he was. He was your basic dedicated, honest cop. You can find them by the score all across the country, trying to make a dent in crime.

"I'll get rid of him, sir," Steele grunted.

"The public is always welcome here," Captain Woods rebuked him in a deep voice. I was starting to wonder if he was thinking of running for something. He flashed me a vote-winning grin without meeting my eyes. "As long as they follow *my* rules. We have nothing to hide."

Maybe it's just me, but as soon as I hear someone say that, I want to throw them up against the wall and frisk them. Especially when they say it in such a friendly tone. I could see the face of his sidekick, Sgt. Bert Guthrie, peering around Woods's shoulder, nodding and agreeing. On the other hand, maybe it's just my knee-jerk reaction to higher authority, left over from being in the service.

Captain Woods had to duck a little to make it out of the doorway without bashing his head, but he did it automatically, like it was habit. Guthrie gave me a sharp glance out of his weasel eyes before bringing up the rear, trotting after the captain to keep up.

The lieutenant came to parade rest before he remembered I was there to enjoy it. He slammed the door shut as soon as soon as Captain Woods was out of sight and circled his desk, leaning both hands on it to snarl at me. "What the fuck are you doing here, shamus?"

I could tell he didn't like being put on the spot like that with me there to witness it, and I didn't blame him. To put him at ease, I decided to irritate him.

"I'm a member of the great public you serve, Lieutenant," I said in a wounded tone. "I just came down to drink in the atmosphere of the corridors of power and admire the efforts of you brave men in blue."

"Whatever damn reason you had for coming here, it wasn't that. If I find you're here to hijack one of our cases, you might just find yourself spending a night in the gray-bar motel, courtesy of the city of Las Vegas."

"Me?" I put my hand on my chest. "I would never—"

"Yeah? Like you didn't on the Fitch case?"

"You got me all wrong, Lieutenant. I just came down to pick up some of your crimestopper tips. So I can be as good as you one day. You're my hero."

"Nuts!" He sat down and glared at me. "I suppose you came to see your pal Harding." He picked up the phone and barked into it. "Thomas, send Harding to my office on the double. I don't care if it's his mother's birthday, get him down here." He slammed the phone down and growled, "He'd better hope I don't find out he invited you for a coffee klatsch."

"Well, I'll just be getting on with the tour, seeing as I'm welcome here."

"Sit." The lieutenant pointed at a chair.

I sat, to help increase the lieutenant's feeling of effectiveness, even though I undermined it somewhat by slouching to the side of the chair.

There was a knock at the door, and Reggie poked his head around it. "Sergeant Thomas said you wanted me...." His voice died away when he saw me sitting there. "Sir."

"Attention!" Steele barked.

Training. It gets the better of the best of us. I leaped out of that chair and snapped to attention next to Reggie as fast as I ever had in the service. Lieutenant Steele's mouth twitched, and I could tell he wanted to grin. He'd got his revenge awfully fast. To spoil it for him, I flopped down in the chair again and swung one leg over the arm.

"So, Harding, in the interests of public relations, you invited your pal private *dick* Randall downtown for a little tour of the facilities, or so I hear."

"Where did you hear that, sir?"

"Where do you think, nitwit?"

"I never mentioned your name, Reg," I muttered.

"Shut up! You two know each other from the service?"

"Yes, sir," Reggie answered promptly.

Lieutenant Steele clasped both hands behind his back and started to pace in front of the window. "You're heroes, both of you. I mean that. G.I.s, the backbone of the armed forces. Enlisting in the army to protect your country."

I stared at him. Who was this man, and where did they take the lieutenant? It couldn't have been Captain Woods's little lecture about making the unanointed public welcome, I was sure of that.

"Thank you, sir."

"I suppose it's natural you want to relive old times, talk them over."

"Yes, Lieutenant, that's it—"

"But not on our time or in our house! That's not what we pay you for!" Steele roared suddenly.

I could see Reggie squint as the decibels pinned his ears back, and I wouldn't want to swear to it that my rear end didn't lift off my chair for a moment in the blast.

Steele jerked a thumb toward the open door. "Get the hell out of here! Both of you! And Harding, if I see your tame snooper nosing around here again, I'll—"

Reggie yanked me up out of the chair and pushed me into the hallway ahead of him. "Yes, sir, thank you, sir!"

I dragged my feet, but he strong-armed me to the lobby. "What'd *he* have for breakfast?"

"Probably a box of ammunition and a couple of grenades," Reggie muttered.

"That would account for his explosive personality."

"Beat it! I'm in enough trouble as it is."

"But you haven't shown me—"

"The diner. I'll meet you there after I get off duty. Around five-thirty."

With that, he opened one of the glass doors at the front and shoved me through and damn near down the stairs, except that since I mustered out I kept fit. Sit-ups and push-ups in the office every morning and a run at night.

So there I was, with no evidence to deduce anything from and no one answering any questions. It was a bit too soon to assume that Charlie would have anything for me. I could have tracked down Mr. Phil Martin, but I had a feeling it was better for my health to stay far away from that man.

And I was still walking around with a big stack of bills in my pocket. At least I couldn't be arrested for having no visible means of support, but I'd feel awfully stupid if I lost it. I headed for the bank.

I enjoyed the feeling of peeling a bunch of Cs off my bundle before I deposited it. The state of my bank balance was a whole lot healthier than my state of mind when I left, as in no longer at zero.

Reggie had asked me to lay off his boyfriend, or at least his crush, and the deal was that I got to see the photos. It wasn't his fault that he couldn't deliver, but it opened a window of opportunity for me. Time to take a look at Jazz Morgan. I headed for a phone booth to consult the book.

HE LIVED on the north side in the Negro section, of course, on Jefferson, past the open sports field, the cemetery, and the high school. It was nice enough there. The houses might be small, but you could see they cared about their neighborhood. It was well kept.

There was no Jazz or J Morgan listed in the book, but there were five Morgans of various names and initials, so I took them one at a time. Where I went, I knocked, but no one answered, despite the fact that I saw the curtains twitch at the second place. But I could understand that. A white guy standing on your doorstep in blacktown could only mean trouble.

It surprised me to find that Jazz Morgan owned a house instead of living in a rented room somewhere. Maybe tickling the ivories paid better than I suspected, or maybe it had more to do with who he worked for. It was a small house, a Spanish-style bungalow, and when I rang the bell, there was no answer. Of course, I didn't know for sure it was his yet.

"He's not at home," I heard a woman's voice say.

I turned around to take a look. The woman who was peering at me from over the porch railing next door might have been Lily McIntyre's age, but she'd lived a much harder life. Not that she was ugly. Her lined face was beautiful and kind, but her hair was grey, and her clothing was plain. She wore sensible shoes, something I couldn't imagine Lily doing no matter how much her feet hurt.

"Do you know where I could find him?" I came closer to her porch. She didn't get up. I liked that.

"That would depend on who was looking for him," she said. "You don't often see a white man in blacktown. Unless you're a cop." Her eyes narrowed suspiciously.

I grinned, thinking of Lieutenant Steele having a nice little fit of apoplexy if he heard someone mistake me for a cop. "No cop, Mrs.—?"

"Miss Rivers," she said.

"Grey Randall," I said, holding out my hand. She leaned forward to take my hand in a firm grasp and shook, very dignified.

"You're not here to collect, are you?"

She must have seen the confusion on my face.

"Collect what?"

"You're not from—no, of course you're not. My mistake. But I can tell you're no powder puff. What do you want with Barry?"

"Barry? Sorry to disturb you, I must have the wrong place. I'm looking for a fella named Jazz Morgan."

"That's Barry. Jazz is his nickname. Why do you want to see him?"

I could have come up with a cover story, but this lady was shrewd enough to see through a quick lie. I decided it might buy me more to come clean. "I'm a private investigator, ma'am, looking into the murder of Miss Marguerite Saint-Ville. I understand Jazz Morgan knew her."

She decided I was telling the truth. "Barry didn't do it, no matter what anyone told you. None of this black man assaulting an irresistible white woman nonsense. I've known him since he was a boy, and he's not like that."

I wondered if she knew just exactly how much not like that he was, depending on whether Reggie was right about him. "I just wanted to ask Mr. Morgan a couple of questions about her. So far, I've spoken with a few people who knew her, and I'm trying to find out what she was like."

"Why don't you ask him at the club where he works?"

"I don't want to interrupt his work, ma'am. Might be awkward for him."

"Awkward," she scoffed. "Since when—oh, never mind. You can most likely find him downtown on Tonopah Blvd. He plays piano in a club called Blackout there till closing. Then he goes on to another club near Fremont. A white club."

"Thank you, Miss Rivers."

"I'll tell Barry you were around asking, in case you miss him," Miss Rivers called after me.

I swear there was a malicious note in her voice, and I knew it was no use asking her not to mention that I had been there. With neighbors like her on your side, there's not much chance of taking your suspect by surprise. Which was probably a good thing for Jazz, not so much for me.

I realized when she said downtown, she meant downtown in the north side, not downtown Las Vegas. And judging from the name, I was betting that Blackout was a black club.

And speaking of which, it sounded like maybe Jazz was a betting man. Suddenly it all made sense what Miss Rivers had said about me being there to collect. I wondered whether Jazz would kill a woman for money if he got in deep enough. It was another motive, but a dicey one. I had no evidence for it beyond an inference based on an inflection from a woman I didn't know. Aside from the fact that the killer left the jewelry behind too; any experienced thief would have taken it on the off chance.

I drifted by the Blackout Club and parked the car a couple blocks down. That's another way I keep fit; never park right in front of the target. It could leave you without getaway wheels.

Walking down the street, suddenly I thought I knew how it must feel to be black in the army. Or anywhere other than blacktown. I was the only white person I could see, and every person who passed me stared rigidly ahead, not deigning to make eye contact.

I felt self-conscious. I might have to go into Blackout at some point, but there was no way I could lose myself in a crowd here. Jazz would spot me coming a mile away, and he had the advantage of home turf. If he didn't want to talk, I might find myself with a music stand wrapped around my neck.

Blacktown was practically the only place in Vegas where closing hours were actually enforced. Reggie would never admit that the cops had quotas, but if they were short a few arrests, they had a tendency to drift into the north side. Black men couldn't afford to fight back, and most of them were probably used to the occasional night in the hoosegow. Then everyone went home happy, at least if you were a cop. Maybe the colored fellas were just happy to be going home at all.

I glanced in the windows as I walked by the club. Business was slow, seeing as it was only the middle of the day, but Jazz was there, picking out a sad tune on the piano.

It's hard to judge a book by its cover, and he was a big, powerful man, almost as big as Captain Billy Woods, but he just seemed so sad. Not the usual reaction of a crazed killer, and anyone who would strangle a woman had to be a little bit crazy. Or maybe it was the guilt weighing him down.

I hoofed it back to the heap and headed for my office. I had stuff to think about. I wondered what stories Phil Martin could tell me about his piano player. I wondered what a girl like Marguerite Saint-Ville was doing singing in a secret club in a deserted warehouse district. If she wanted to be a dancer or a singer, why wasn't she hanging around stage doors or using Lily McIntyre's name to get some big-name choreographer to give her another job? Heck, she was pretty enough to go to Hollywood. And what did Miss Tina think about this white girl horning in on her turf? It seemed like a good idea to have a chat with her at some point.

I wondered if the photos Reggie had to show me were going to lead anywhere. But most of all I wondered about Miss Lily McIntyre. I had a feeling she was leading me up a rose-covered path and she knew a whole lot more than she was telling me. But until I had some lever to pry her loose with, I suspected I'd be dancing to her tune.

WHEN I had tossed my hat at the hat stand, and scored, of course, I sat down in the only chair that really helps me think and put my feet on the desk, running over the usual motives for murder: greed, fear, revenge, attempted assault that went bad, silencing a witness, etc. After ten minutes, I realized that even the chair wasn't getting me anywhere without some actual facts to think about, so I called my answering service. There was a message from Charlie.

I dialed the front desk at the library, and Mrs. Fielding answered as usual. Maybe I called there too often, because she recognized my voice and put me on hold before I could even ask for Charlie.

"Hello?"

"Hi, Charlie, I hope I'm not getting you in dutch by calling."

"In trouble with who?" Charlie actually sounded surprised that I'd be asking.

"Mrs. Fielding, your boss," I reminded her.

"She won't care. She likes me."

Well. I had never noticed any visible signs of affection between the two, but Charlie was a good worker—when she wanted to be. And Mrs. Fielding didn't look like she was equal to working the microfilm machine, anyway; I'm sure Charlie made it look hard. "So whaddya got for me?"

"I just chanced upon this item, but Miss Saint-Ville was mentioned in the list of the chorus line in a show at the Jungle Room. It's still running," Charlie said. "I'll probably have more for you later."

"Thanks, that's great!" I checked my watch. It was early yet, but dancing isn't all glamour and nightlife. Dancers have to practice, and I was hoping maybe I could catch them at rehearsal.

The Jungle Room was one of the lesser clubs in Vegas, but it ranked way above a strip club. If Miss Saint-Ville rated a slot there, maybe she really was good. But seeing as I knew nothing about her at all, at least it was a place to start on her end.

I'd been to the Jungle Room before, not on business. It was the kind of theme club that hit you over the head with a club and dragged you back to its cave and held you captive, complete with fake trees, stuffed animals that looked faintly like monkeys swinging on mechanical arms, live parrots in cages, you name it. The drinks tended to have paper umbrellas in them. And rum.

I went around to the stage door, where I slipped an old geezer a fiver to let me by. The dressing room was empty, so I wandered to the backstage area, watching girls in mismatched dance gear, but all wearing banana skirts, as they kicked and bumped and spun. I wouldn't exactly have called it a dance myself, but what do I know about it? I can't even do the foxtrot, although I'm a whiz at the tango. It was my mother's favorite; she called it the dance of seduction, and she forced me—I mean, *taught* me how to do it so she had a victim to practice on.

The choreographer was shouting insults and directions, and the girls were mostly ignoring him from what I could tell. Eventually it all came to a halt, and the girls started filing by me.

"Hey, cutie, looking for a date?"

"I might be," I said to the dark-haired girl chewing gum who'd asked.

"Will I do, sugar?"

"I'm looking for Miss Saint-Ville," I answered.

She made a face. "She's not here. Hasn't been for two weeks." She started walking away from me and unpeeling her banana skirt at the same time.

I caught up with her. "Know where I can reach her?"

She stopped and examined my face. "You seem like a sweet guy. You don't want to hook up with her, take my word for it."

"Why, was she trouble?"

"She was okay. It was her boyfriends who were trouble."

"Look, can I buy you lunch? Maybe you could tell me a little about her."

She snorted. "Sure, go to the luncheonette around the corner and grab me a cheese and pickle sandwich on white. Then I won't have to change for the break, sugar."

I went and got a sandwich for myself as well as two Cokes and some donuts. When I came back, the geezer was gone, and I just waltzed right in. Could have saved the fin by getting here later. And they say the early bird gets the worm. Well, I guess it was true—for *him.*

The dressing room was filled with half naked girls, none of whom seemed too upset when I walked in. I averted my eyes politely from their various states of disarray and went to where my dark-haired dancer was sitting with her feet propped on her dressing table in very uncomfortable-looking stilettos.

She called out, "See, girls! I told you, he's a bunny."

I scowled at her. "I'm a private dick. Hard-boiled. Grey Randall."

She giggled and stuck out her hand. "Suzy Velvour. You're going to have to work on your image, Grey. You're adorable when you're blushing."

I put the stuff down and shook. After a quick glom at me, the rest of the girls had gone back to chattering and powdering their noses. The din was deafening. "There's your lunch, Miss Velvour. Stage name?"

"Ya think? Thanks for the Coke." She slid a drawer open without moving her legs and leaned forward to take out a bottle opener. She had frightening abs. "Aren't you even going to ask?"

I opened both bottles and handed her one. "Sure, spill it."

"You're a bunny because you look at my eyes when you talk to me, not my tits." She shook her shoulders, making her breasts shimmy. Now that she pointed it out, she was only covered by a skimpy brassiere top that didn't look equal to the challenge her boobs were putting it to.

"My mother raised me polite," I growled. Somehow I didn't cotton to being described as fluffy and cute.

"She did a good job." Suzy tipped the bottle and swallowed. "Unless you're a gaycat."

I decided it was time to get the spotlight off me. "Marguerite Saint-Ville. Her boyfriends?"

"What about them?"

I rolled my eyes in exasperation. "You said they were trouble."

"Is she in trouble?"

"You don't read the newspapers much, do you?"

"Only the show-biz section. What happened to her?"

I thought if I told her all about it right away, she might clam up or start leaking tears. "She's in a jam. I'm trying to get a handle on it, but I don't have an end to pull on. Tell me a little about her."

"I don't know her very well, but she sat right next to me, so you sort of chat between numbers, you know?" Suzy started unwrapping her sandwich. "Most of the girls I've run into here and there since I've been in this business. You know, in one show or the next, but Miss High-and-Mighty just blew in here one day and started dancing like she owned the place."

"You didn't like her?"

Suzy shrugged and chewed. "She could dance, I'll give her that, but she hadn't earned the right to act like a star or anything."

"How did she act like a star?"

"Didn't really talk to the girls much. Talked hoity-toity like she went to boarding school or something. Heaven knows she was too good to socialize with the rest of us. Always had a date, always had men sending her flowers." She paused to take a bite and added thoughtfully, "Her clothes were too good, you know? And if her earrings weren't real, I don't have a close, personal relationship with rhinestones."

Maybe Suzy was smarter than I'd given her credit for after that crack about me being a bunny. "What about her boyfriends? Who were they?"

"That's just it, I never saw any of them. Maybe she was ashamed of them, or maybe she was into married men." Suzy shrugged. "Not like it's a stigma around here. Married men tend to feel guilty that they can't be seen out with you, so they're good to hit up for jewelry and flowers."

"Did she get a lot of flowers?"

"Yeah, there was this one palooka, sent a new bunch everyday. But he never signed his name, just 'Love, B.' I think she liked it at first. Then she said he was getting obsessed, like stalking her, you know?" She leaned forward and helped herself to my untouched sandwich while I thought about Barry Jazz Morgan, who couldn't risk being seen in public with a white girl.

"And you never saw this guy?"

"I saw her getting into a car one night, after work," Suzy said.

"You know the make or color? License number?"

"It was dark, but I think it was a black Ford."

Great, not too many of *those* around. I was driving one myself. "Any other guys?"

"Yeah, she liked to keep a bunch of men on tap, just in case. But the other guys came and went. This 'B' was in it for the long haul. Then one day he sent her a bunch of dead flowers." She shuddered. "Creepy."

"And she talked to you about this guy?"

"No, I snuck a peek at the cards." Suzy giggled, like she'd pulled off some complicated undercover operation instead of leaning over to glance at a posy on the next table. "Except she did seem upset the day the dead flowers came. Turned white as a sheet and said she might have to give him the slip. Find another place to work. When she didn't show up I just figured that's what she did."

"And she would have had no trouble doing that?"

Waspishly, Suzy said, "I might, but her? No way. She was the choreographer's golden girl."

"And why was that?"

"Because Miss Lily McIntyre recommended her. You know—"

"Yeah, I know who she is."

"Who doesn't? But she's *it*, you know. Everyone knows Miss McIntyre, and she knows everyone in Vegas. Everyone important, that is."

"Anything else you can remember about Miss Saint-Ville? Anything that made her different?"

"Oh, yeah, she had her own apartment. The rest of us room with other girls, and trust me, she couldn't afford a cold-water on the salary we get here. One of the boyfriends must have coughed up handsomely."

"Can I take a look at her dressing table?"

"Help yourself, but the manager came in and tossed her stuff when she didn't show up for work."

"You remember the name of the florist who delivered the flowers?"

"You think I'm some kind of librarian or something?"

Considering the librarians I knew, no, I wasn't about to mistake this doozy for Charlie or Mrs. Fielding.

"Wait a minute, it was… Frankie's, that was it," Suzy said with an air of triumph for having dredged up that fact. "I remember the two F's on the card."

"I'll have a look."

Suzy was right; they'd cleaned up. I sat down to inspect the drawers. Empty. I saw the corner of a piece of paper that had slid between the mirror and the back of the table and pulled it out. It was a florist's card, like Suzy had said, with Frankie's Flowers in a fancy script that linked the two F's.

The typed message read: *Red roses for my Rose Red. All my love, B.* Possessive. Of course, being typed, there was no handwriting for comparison, even if I had something to compare it to.

"Well, thanks, Suzy. You've been a big help." I stood up to go.

Without removing her feet from her dressing table, Suzy arched her back and put her hands behind her, laughing when she unhooked her bra-top. It popped off and hit her mirror, relieved to be out from under the strain. "I could help you more than that, lover. Maybe show you a thing or two." She gave that little shoulder shimmy again, making her naked breasts sway like ripe fruit.

Deliberately, I stared right at them and smirked. "Yeah, I can see you have a thing or two to show," I said and turned away.

"Hey, Grey! You never said what kind of trouble Margie was in."

"The worst kind," I said over my shoulder.

Suzy swung her feet down and sat up straight, her face going pale under the stage makeup. "You mean—"

"Yeah, she's dead."

THAT gave me something to think about. Margie. I wondered if Lily McIntyre ever thought of her protégé as Margie rather than Marguerite.

And with an obsessive boyfriend in tow, with the initial B. Maybe I was reading Jazz's sadness wrong. The only other B I could dredge up right now was Sgt. Bert Guthrie, and I had to hope that Marguerite had a better opinion of herself than to date a troll like him, no matter how much she got around.

Lily hadn't remembered to mention the fact that she'd gotten Marguerite the job, either, or where she worked. It would be interesting to know just who paid the rent on the apartment. I was betting either the boyfriend or Lily might be able to clue me in on that.

I checked with the choreographer, who had drunk his lunch and was too far gone to know anything, and the manager, who was too mad to remember much about Miss Saint-Ville except that she took off on him and left him in the lurch. He had thrown out whatever she left behind. An act of petty revenge in light of what happened to her, but of course he couldn't know.

After the noisy room full of perfumed girls, I needed a lungful of fresh desert air when I emerged from the club. I couldn't help thinking about how unfair life was. I mean, a straight dick would have been in heaven detecting in there, but where was the dressing room full of gorgeous naked men when you needed one? Las Vegas definitely needed more queer strip joints. Or even one.

"Fancy meeting you here."

"Are you practicing to be my shadow?" I demanded.

Artie shrugged. "I bet your shadow is having a hard time keeping up. I stopped by your office, but you're always roaming around somewhere, never sitting still in one spot."

I stared at him. "Are you trying to be philosophical?"

"Nope, just I heard your girl used to dance here and I thought you might want to know."

"Yeah, I heard that too."

"I shoulda known, two steps ahead, that's you. Plus, I got a message for you. Some broad with red hair, parked out front in a car with a driver." He nudged me in the ribs with his elbow. "Wants to see you, chop-chop. Better not keep her waiting. Those redheads got a temper, don't they, hotshot!" He gave me a leer.

"All right, all right. Thanks."

"So the redhead, she a sugar mama or something?" Artie kept it under a yell but just barely.

"If she's who I think she is, she's a client." I grabbed Artie's shirt and yanked him closer, keeping my voice quiet. "Listen, the difference between your job and mine is that I don't go around making a lot of noise, get me?"

I was always surprised when Artie let me manhandle him that way, seeing as he outweighed me by fifty pounds or so, but maybe he thought I was a bunny too. At any rate, he was tittering about it.

"Hey, gumshoe, don't forget that's my tie you're wearing! Don't get any blood on it!" he said. So much for keeping things quiet. Even though it didn't seem like anyone was taking much notice of Artie.

I went around the side of the club and spotted the midnight blue limo waiting at the curb with the engine running. I wondered if my client was planning on chasing me all over Vegas to get a report, because that would most definitely put a crimp in my style.

The back door opened, and a gloved hand curled a finger at me. I walked over and bent down to peer inside. "Miss McIntyre."

"Get in, Grey, darling," she said invitingly. "We're going for a little ride."

Those were the exact words to strike fear in a man's soul in those days, but somehow I didn't think Lily was out to dust me. At least not yet. I slid in next to her, enjoying the delicacy of her scent after the heavy, cheap perfume favored by Suzy Velvour.

"Where are we going, Miss McIntyre?"

"I told you to call me Lily. Did you find out yet that I got Miss Saint-Ville her job?"

"Yeah. Why didn't you tell me about that?"

"I figured a smart detective like you would nose it out quickly enough."

I almost wanted to tell her about Charlie, not wanting to take the credit for her work, but I didn't need to reveal my methods. "You could have saved me some time by telling me yourself."

"But then you'd have had to check up on me anyway to be sure I was telling the truth, wouldn't you?" Lily looked very pleased with herself. "I know, I read detective stories."

"Uh, those aren't always true to life, you know," I said.

"Of course not. Artistic license." She waved a hand gracefully. "But I wanted you to be able to tighten up the screws on witnesses on your own so you could give them the third degree until they squealed."

"Why are you talking like that?"

"Trying to speak your lingo, gumshoe," she said, very tough.

"Don't crack wise with me, babe," I said.

"So, tell me, Grey...." She leaned toward me, putting a familiar hand on my knee and gazing soulfully into my eyes. "Do you have a moll?"

"Uh, no, I've never really needed one," I said, wondering where we were going.

"If you need any help, keep me in mind." Lily slid her skirt up her leg to reveal a little pearl-handled revolver stuck in the top of her stocking. "I'm heeled."

"Well, thank you for the offer, but it really wouldn't be appropriate when I'm working for you," I said, trying to be tactful about it. I guess it was my day for dames to flash me. I was hoping my lack of reaction would leave them thinking I had nerves of steel. "And stop trying to distract me. It might make me think you don't want to talk about what I found out at the Jungle Club."

"Darling! I'm all ears."

Funny how some women can say darling and it sounds silly, but from someone like Lily, it was just right. I gave myself a shake back to reality. This could all be a ruse.

"I hear you got Miss Saint-Ville the job at the Jungle Room."

"So you said. And is that a crime?"

"No, of course not, but—"

"She was a good dancer. I know Jack, the choreographer. He needed a girl, and she needed a job. It all worked out." Lily shrugged. "Sometimes it's more important who you know...."

"And I heard that you know everyone it's important to know."

Lily looked pleased, as if I'd just paid her a compliment. "I *am* fortunate in having a great many friends. What else did you learn?"

I thought about giving her the lowdown on Suzy's snappy maneuver with the brassiere but decided it wasn't pertinent to the case. And besides, I was betting Lily knew all about it and could probably pull it off with more finesse anyway, not that I wanted to be there to witness it. "The girl I talked to said Miss Saint-Ville had an apartment all to herself, something she couldn't have afforded on the salary she made at the Jungle Room, and speculated that maybe she had help paying the rent from a man. She said Margie had several boyfriends at the same time."

"Margie," Lily mused in a strange voice. She caught me looking at her and said, "Miss Saint-Ville was… very young. That's the time to date several gentlemen friends, before one thinks of settling down."

The term seemed quaint coming from Lily. Settle down? I bet Lily was still sampling several men at once. "Do you know where she lived?"

"I'll check my address book when I return home. I may have jotted it down."

The car drew in to the sidewalk in front of the biggest, most expensive department store in Vegas, Ronzone's. I guess maybe I'd interrupted a shopping trip.

"Would you mind asking your driver to bring me back to my car?" I asked.

Lily nudged me, and I got out, giving her my hand to help her step out of the car. First she swung those fabulous legs out, clad in black hose. Several men passing stopped to ogle her as she emerged and smiled up at me.

"Don't be ridiculous, Grey, darling. You're coming in with me."

"Shopping?" I asked dubiously. Not my idea of a fun time. I wondered if she was going to try on dresses and ask my opinion. That could prove to be deadlier than catching a killer.

"We're getting you a new tie. You're still wearing that *hideous* one," she said, flicking the tie over my shoulder.

"No, this is the other one," I started to explain, glancing down at the one I was wearing. If Miss McIntyre thought the first one was hideous, this one didn't stand a chance. It was paisley, and even I didn't like it. I would be embarrassed to wear this tie to one of Artie's fights. Even though it was his.

On the other hand, if I had to question Phil Mar—anyone apart from the thugs I usually ended up chasing, I needed a better tie. I shut my eyes, trying to remember what kind of tie Mr. Big had been wearing when we met, but the gloss of his looks kind of blurred the details for me, and I was lost.

"I can see you in a lovely purple tie, Mr. Randall."

I opened my eyes and growled at her. "Purple!"

Miss Lily McIntyre threw back her head and laughed. You read about that in books, but she made it seem fabulous and exciting, not affected like an actress might do. "Not something bright, like an Easter egg. Something subtle, mysterious, sophisticated."

Well, no one had ever called me sophisticated before, but I was willing to learn. "I'm kind of busy—"

"Not in that tie on my behalf," Miss McIntyre said. She slipped her hand into the crook of my elbow and hung on tight. "Come along, darling. I can call you Grey, can't I? And you must call me Lily."

"Miss McIntyre—"

"We're going to know each other quite well, Grey, darling. No formality between friends. And one day you'll have to explain to me just how you came to own something so ugly." She started dragging me inexorably toward the doors. "Think of this as your moll giving you the darb steer and putting you wise, shamus."

Her fur thing made my nose itch as she swept me along into the store. I didn't want to actually *hurt* her making my escape, and maybe she did know what she was talking about with the ties, although *purple*—

Chapter 4: I Get My Man (Temporarily)

I SMOOTHED my new tie and wondered if Reggie would appreciate it. Probably not. Philistine. He had to wear a department-issue dark blue tie, and my new one was a smoky blue and pure silk. I'd never had a silk tie before. Of course, he probably wouldn't even notice how well it went with my charcoal grey suit once I started asking him questions about Barry Jazz Morgan.

My suit had passed muster with Lily, although she had muttered once or twice about how could I pick out a nice suit and be blind to the kind of tie I wore. I was glad the suit passed muster, because as it was, she'd bought me three new ties and would have forcibly thrown away the one I was wearing if I hadn't claimed it was borrowed and I had to return it. Which was true. Artie was going to be really happy to get it back.

I waited for Reggie at a table in Nancy's Diner, seeing as I didn't have to sneak up on him this time. When I first came in, Nancy commented favorably on the tie too, so maybe Lily was right.

Reggie sighed when he slid into his side of the booth. "Lieutenant Steele sent his love."

"Oh, give mine to him. And a kiss."

Reggie shivered. "Please. Only in my nightmares. Sorry about that, but you should have let Sergeant Thomas call back for me."

I shrugged. "Ask me what I did after I left?"

"You went shopping."

Guess he did notice the tie after all. I couldn't help giving it a stroke. Feely. "I went to the Jungle Room and talked to a girl who knew Miss Saint-Ville. She said that some guy was stalking her, obsessed with her."

"Yeah? Who?"

"She didn't know. Said the guy used to send her flowers and signed the card with the letter B."

Reggie looked a little wary but played it cool. "And that gets you where?"

"I also drove around in blacktown today. Found out where Jazz hangs his horn." I was watching him, but he was good. He wasn't giving an inch. "Met a neighbor lady who told me his real name is Barry."

"I should have told you that." Reggie didn't say that apologetically.

"Damn right you should have! What if he was the one sending her flowers?"

"What if he did? What difference does it make?"

"This guy sent her flowers every night, but no one ever saw him."

"So?" Reggie clenched his fists on the table and leaned forward menacingly.

"So a black guy can't afford to be seen slipping around with a white girl. She was seen getting into a car one night, and Jazz has a car, doesn't he?"

"Circumstantial."

"What kind of car does he have, Reggie?"

"A Ford."

"The witness said this was a Ford. Black."

The next thing I knew, Reggie hauled off and pasted me one with a right hook.

"Ooof!" I went down hard, flying out of the booth and landing on the floor with Reggie standing over me, clenching his fists.

"You asshole," I said, but I didn't get up because if I did, I'd have to smack him one, and I'd promised Nancy not to break the china.

"Crap, I'm sorry." Reggie held out a hand to me and hauled me to my feet. "I'm just...." His shoulders slumped, and he looked defeated.

"It's all right. Siddown." I sat down myself and wiped my nose. It was bleeding. I held a napkin to it. The last thing I needed (or wanted) was to get blood all over my brand new tie.

Nancy came over, looking amused. "I guess I should have put the fear of God into you, Reggie, instead of your friend. Here, have some ice." She gave me a dishtowel wrapped around some crushed ice.

"Thanks, Nancy." I held it to my nose. Not that I have any false vanity or anything, but I think my nose is my nicest feature, and I didn't much want to look like Artie's twin.

"Are you boys going to eat or just argue whenever you come in here?" Nancy asked.

"Eat, we're eating," Reggie said. "I'll buy."

"You'll buy the next one too. This one's on the house. But only for *you*, Mr. Randall!" Nancy said, tapping my shoulder with the eraser end of her pencil. "What'll you have? Mac and cheese is on special. Homemade."

"Have that," Reggie said with the air of a connoisseur. "Better than your mother's, I guarantee."

"Okay." I nodded and inspected the towel before holding it to my nose again. He'd never had my mother's mac and cheese, but she was a terrible cook anyway, so it was a sure bet.

"Two mac and cheese. And a couple of Cokes," Reggie said, and Nancy nodded, taking off to get our orders. "Sorry about that." His lips were twitching a bit, and I thought maybe his regrets, however sincere, were short-lived. I wondered how swollen my nose was.

"You seem pretty sure of Jazz," I said.

"You said you'd lay off," he reminded me.

"When you got me the photos. After you tossed me out of the station, I had all day to poke around. Where are they?"

He unbuttoned and reached inside his shirt, pulling out a brown envelope.

"Have to sneak them out?"

"I made copies of the crime scene photos too," he said. "They're on top."

Nancy came trotting back with our supper, and when I smelled it, I suddenly remembered I hadn't eaten lunch, Suzy having casually helped herself to my sandwich after she chowed down on hers.

I dug in. It was delicious. Nancy and her diner didn't look like much, but she sure could cook. We ate in complete silence; it was only after she'd cleared the table that I opened the envelope and took out the photos.

I was glad I'd eaten first, because the sight of that swollen, dark face would have taken away my appetite. As it was, I had a hard time keeping it down, because even for a hardened dick it wasn't pretty, and this was only a black-and-white shot.

The pictures didn't tell me much I didn't know already, but it's always good to get a feel for the scene of the crime. Miss Saint-Ville had dropped her wrap some distance away from where she ended up, like Reggie had said. Her bag was next to her limp hand, as if the killer had tried to get her to hold onto it after she was dead. She was sitting upright, propped against the wall, and her legs were crossed at the ankle, her skirt decorously pulled down just far enough that her garters were covered.

"He posed her," I said, looking up at Reggie.

Reggie looked somber. "I'm not saying Jazz could never do anything violent. He boxes some. But he was raised by his grandmother, he respects women. This is... almost mocking the victim. Pulling her skirt down, like no one but me gets to see what's under there. But leaving her face uncovered. As if he was saying she deserved it."

"So you think Jazz might kill in anger, but he'd regret it afterwards." I didn't know Jazz that well myself, but that's kind of what I thought of him. He seemed like a proud man, one who understood what the loss of dignity meant. He would have had to hate her deeply to leave the girl there like this.

"Maybe a crime of passion," Reggie said in a strangled voice. "But I don't think…." His voice petered out, and he shook his head sorrowfully.

"You don't think he was passionate about her?"

"More… confused. But what do I know?" he said roughly. "Look at the others. Publicity shots I took for Phil Martin."

"The cops, working for Mr. Big," I said. I shuffled the black and whites to the back. The first photo was of Jazz Morgan, sitting at the piano, his shirt unbuttoned to the waist so his dark skin contrasted against the white cotton, revealing a necklace gleaming on his chest. It looked like a musical clef symbol.

Reggie snatched it away from me. "Sorry, that got in there by mistake."

I wanted to chuckle, but I sensed his feelings were a little too raw. And I didn't much fancy another tap on the nose.

The next shot made me gasp. I'd seen that one black-and-white shot of Miss Saint-Ville more than once, which was enough to tell me that she was a very pretty girl, but seeing her in color turned the whole case upside-down for me.

I could have been looking at a shot of Miss Lily McIntyre, taken eighteen years ago!

The same peaches-and-cream complexion, the same coppery red hair, the same flashing green eyes, the same delicate features…. They could have been twins! Except for Lily being old enough to be her mother—

"Holy fuck," I breathed. "Thanks, Reggie. I gotta go." I stuffed the shots back into the envelope and stood up.

"You haven't even looked at all of them," he said.

"I've seen enough," I growled. Not telling me everything? That would be Lily. Fascinating, aggravating, tantalizing Lily.

"What about Jazz? Can I tell him he's off the hook for this?" Reggie called after me.

"No!" I stomped out and got in my car.

IT'S A good thing Reggie didn't follow me over to Lily's house, or he could have made his quota for the night and tagged me for speeding. I raced up the circular drive in front of a house that I could only call a mansion and screeched to a stop.

A maid answered the door after I pounded on it, dressed in one of those black maid outfits with the frilly white apron, and looked at me disapprovingly. She was smart and French, with a short gamine hairstyle and an intriguingly ugly face.

"Miss McIntyre in?"

In a pronounced French accent, she said, "I shall inquire, m'sieur. Who shall I say eez calling?"

"Grey Randall, private dick, and make it snappy, will ya?" I snarled. Looking back, I'm surprised she let me in at all, but she left me standing in the front hall while she went to inquire.

"Madame vill see you," she announced when she came back.

I followed her up a staircase that curved gracefully to the second floor, too mad to take in the surroundings. The maid tapped twice on a closed door and opened it without waiting for an answer.

"Grey Randall, private deeck," she said. And that's pretty much the last time I'm going to try to capture the way she talked. From here on out, you can imagine it for yourself.

Lily was admiring herself in a long mirror, turning this way and that to view herself from every angle. She was dressed to go out, wearing a black evening dress that plunged as far down in the front as it did in the back. One red rose was tucked into her satin belt. She was shiny with diamonds when she moved. I never would have thought one woman could shovel so much ice onto herself and carry it off, but Lily did.

"Thank you, Celestine," Lily said. She turned to greet me with a smile that faded as soon she caught the steam pouring out of my ears. "Grey, darling, whatever's happened to upset you?"

I stalked toward her, tossing my hat onto her satin-covered bed. Big enough for four, by the way.

"Which was it? Cousin? Niece? Or *daughter?*" I held out one of the photographs Reggie had taken so she could see it, one where he'd caught her in a moment of genuine laughter.

Lily went white to the lips, which were painted a luscious shade of coral red. She snatched the photograph from me and stared at it hungrily, her eyes revealing the agony, deep and profound, like someone had torn off a piece of her soul, leaving a bleeding hole that could never be filled. "Daughter."

"Why the con? Why didn't you just tell me?"

She looked up at me with dry eyes. I felt like I was caught spying on a grief too deep for tears.

"Where did you get this photograph?" Lily asked in a breathless voice. She swayed, and I was afraid she might faint, but she was made of stronger stuff than that. "I have only black-and-white photographs of her." She closed her eyes and raised her face. I could see the muscles of her neck working.

I went to her and put a hand on her elbow, leading her to a chair. "I'm sorry, Lily."

"Thank you."

I knelt beside her, afraid to let go of her as she looked at the photograph as if she were memorizing it.

"Since she died, I couldn't remember... it was as if all my memories of her had become black and white... like the photographs. I was afraid... for the first time in my life... I was afraid of the coming years. Not of growing old... but that she would fade in memory...." Lily's voice was hoarse. "Who took this?"

"A friend of mine. He's a cop, but he does photography for fun on the side," I said awkwardly.

"I'd like to meet him. He captured her spirit, that flash in her eyes, her... joie de vivre as I never could." Lily's lips trembled slightly as she looked up at me, her eyes almost emerald with the intensity of her emotion. "I'd like to thank him. I'd like to thank *you* for bringing this to me."

I felt like a heel. I'd charged in there like a mad bull, never thinking about how Lily might feel when she saw the photograph. I was just pissed that she'd lied to me. And here she was *thanking* me!

"I have a few more," I said. I remembered in time that I also had the crime scene photographs in there and glanced through the envelope, sorting out the shots before I showed them to her. I returned all the black-and-whites to the envelope, along with one shot that showed Marguerite with Jazz. I wondered if Reggie put that one in by accident as well as the other publicity still of Jazz at the piano.

Lily smiled tremulously when she took the remaining photos from me. She showed me one with Marguerite singing into a microphone, her eyes starry and focused dreamily in the distance. She looked like she was in love, but it could have been part of the act. I hadn't realized what a good photographer Reggie was; it could have passed for a Hollywood still with the way the shadows and light revealed her face.

Lily said, "He caught her love of music in that one. She loved to sing, and she could get lost in a song. She had such a bright future. I always meant to get some color shots of her, but you know how time slips away."

"Yeah, Lily, and time is passing right now. I'm sorry to press you, but I need to know the whole story if I'm going to get anywhere. Why didn't you tell me she was your daughter?"

Two taps sounded at the door, and Celestine, the maid, appeared again. She frowned at me ferociously when she saw me kneeling at Lily's side but only said, "Madame, the car is here."

Lily looked at her blankly for a moment and then said, "I can't possibly go out tonight. Tell the driver—no, I'll write a note." She put the photos down with a lingering glance and then got up, walking to a dainty little secretary tucked into the bay window. She scribbled a note and said, "Please give that to the driver to take to—my friend. He'll understand. And then make us some coffee, Celestine. Thank you."

Celestine took the note and gripped Lily's hand, searching her eyes. Then she gave a little nod and walked out of the room.

"Let's go downstairs, Grey, darling."

I felt like a murderer when she gathered up the photographs and took my arm, like I had killed all of her joie de vivre and left only a lifeless husk. But I underestimated her. Made of steel, that lady.

"Let's go to the morning room, it's smaller than the dining room. More intimate." Lily led the way and sat down at a small round table, spreading the photographs out so she could drink them in. "I'll tell you everything."

"Start at the beginning," I suggested.

"I came to Las Vegas when I was seventeen," Lily said. "I'd always wanted to be a dancer, and I had *flair*. Anyone can learn the steps, but you have to be *born* with flair, and I always had that. I attracted attention from the right people immediately."

I could see that. "Especially with that red hair."

"*And* my face and figure," Lily said, sounding somewhat more like her usual self. "I was an overnight *sensation*, if I do say so."

A swinging door opened, and I could see past Celestine into the kitchen. She put a tray onto the table and unloaded a silver coffeepot, creamer and sugar, spoons, and three mugs. Also a little plate of cookies. She poured three cups, setting one in front of Lily and handing one to me. She took the third and sat down, somewhat to my surprise, but Lily pushed the photographs over to her.

Celestine gave me a sharp look and picked them up, studying them one by one. "Elle est trés belle."

Lily nodded. "She was." She sighed and continued. "Everyone admired me, and I acquired a number of very attentive gentlemen friends. And then I found myself pregnant." She didn't look the least bit embarrassed. "An occupational hazard of mistresses in those days."

"I thought you were a dancer," I said stupidly.

"The two are not mutually exclusive," Lily said dryly. "I didn't expect him to marry me, but I did expect a sort of… understanding and support. When I told him, he refused to believe the baby was his. I kept hoping, but eventually I thought it best to leave town."

I nodded, and Celestine bowed her head, as if commiserating with Lily.

"My daughter—my *beautiful* daughter—was born in 1930. And when I got my figure back, which was very quickly, I resolved to come back here, reclaim my place on stage, and raise her with all the good things that money could buy," Lily said reminiscently. Then her voice crackled with anger. "But I was *not* going to let her suffer the stigma of illegitimacy. *No one* was going to call my darling girl a bastard!

"She was such a beautiful baby. I knew one day she would be a bigger star than I could ever be, so I gave her a name that was destined for success. Marguerite Saint-Ville." Her voice lingered over each syllable, and I guessed that it made her happy to choose a classy stage name for her daughter. I wondered if she'd ever thought that maybe her daughter might not want to follow in her footsteps. But maybe she knew her daughter as well as she thought; after all, she did say Marguerite wanted to be a singer.

"We made believe that she was the daughter of a relative." Lily looked at Celestine, who nodded.

"Did… Marguerite know she was your daughter?"

"Oh yes, but we pretended that an evil wizard had put a spell on us and if we ever mentioned it outside this house, something terrible would happen." Lily's lips quivered again. "And something did."

"Because she told someone?"

"No, I'm sure she never did. When she was sixteen, she understood, she saw through the fairytale. She rebelled and ran away." Lily shrugged. "I didn't blame her. I'd run away myself, and she had… my spirit."

She put her fingertips on the close-up of Marguerite, tracing the soft curve of the girl's cheek. "I couldn't find her myself, so I had to call upon the help of… a friend. I went to see her, begged her to come back. She refused. In the end, we compromised. I found her an apartment and a job. She didn't want it known that I was her… mentor. Wanted to make it on her own."

"Did she find out that you got her the job?"

"Yes, eventually. She was very angry, but she said nothing about running away again," Lily said. "But two days later, she was gone, and I thought it was just a repeat of the first time. I wasn't worried at first. Eventually, I'd find her again... and then—the police came—to ask if I knew her. They told me she was dead."

We sat in silence for a while. I felt drained, wondering what I would have done if Lily had told me all this the day she walked into my office. It felt like years ago, but it was only yesterday.

"Who's your friend, the one who found her?"

Lily shook her head, making her earrings flash in the light. "You don't need that. I'll tell you if it becomes pertinent, but he would never—"

"So you've ruled him out based on no evidence other than your feelings?" I asked harshly.

"He has an alibi."

"Sometimes alibis are made to be broken."

I wouldn't have thought that Lily had it in her at that point, but she fluttered her lashes coquettishly. "*I'm* his alibi." She preened a little, proud that her appeal had not diminished. "You said these shots were for publicity," she said, getting back down to business.

"That's right."

"Where was she working?"

All at once, I realized that telling Lily that her daughter was working at a queer club could lead to all sorts of ramifications for me. But I had to remember that this was just a job like any other. A private dick has to chase the clues, no matter where they lead him. "It's a small private club. Over in the train yard behind the station."

"And who hired her?"

"Phil Martin, or so I've been told."

"You haven't spoken to him, questioned him—"

"I've been following other leads," I said. I didn't want to let her know that I had been doing everything *but* talking to Phil Martin about this.

"I know him well—" she exclaimed.

"Of course you do," I interrupted rudely.

"If you need me to, I can call him, get him to come over here right now—I wonder why he never mentioned—"

"No! No thanks. I'm sure I can get in to see him. I've met him… once… but I didn't know then what I know now," I said.

"He runs several other clubs. Topaz on Fremont. That's the hottest and most popular in Vegas right now. That's where he'll be tonight, most likely. We could go over there—"

"Lily, you can't come with me," I said firmly.

"Madame," Celestine started. "You must not—"

Lily drooped in her seat, her excitement wearing away. "Of course, it was silly of me. Thank him for me, would you? For giving her a job. And she got it on her own. It must have made her feel… safe to work for him."

I wasn't sure she was aware of the irony of that statement. That was one of the reasons I didn't want her along, besides the obvious. Any man would lie to spare her pain, and who would want to say, "Yeah, I hired your daughter to work in a dangerous area where she was killed"?

"What did the police tell you about the… uh, *circumstances*."

"The murder," Lily said. She sure didn't flinch when it came to facing unpleasant truths. "She was strangled by someone taller and stronger than she was, almost certainly a man. She was not raped. She tried to defend herself."

"How did they know that? Defensive wounds on her arms?"

The smile Lily gave me was almost demonic. She scared me in that moment. Implacable, ruthless hatred glowed in her eyes, and I was glad it wasn't me that would have to face her with her daughter's death on my conscience.

"Yes. And they mentioned the heel of her right shoe had blood on it."

I remembered her performance in my office when she came to hire me. "You mean...."

"At least she hurt him before he killed her."

I didn't want to mention that pulling that maneuver might also have pushed him over the edge and made him angry enough to kill her even if he hadn't planned on it. Lily didn't need to dwell on that, especially when she was clinging to the minor comfort of thinking she'd taught her daughter to defend herself.

"What sort of nightclub is this place?" Lily said.

I took a breath. I was going to have to tell her at some point. "It's an after-hours club. Illegal. For queers."

Of course, she took it completely in stride. "Then presumably her killer didn't come from there."

I wasn't going to get into the issue of jealous T-girls right then. "I'm not ruling anyone out on that basis."

"Of course," Lily said, patting my arm soothingly. "You're a very good dick." She looked at her diamond wristwatch and said, "I'd better let you go if you're going to interview Phil Martin. Let's hope he can give you some kind of lead."

"Thank you, Lily. I guess I'd better go right over there," I said, hoping she couldn't tell how uneasy the thought made me.

She smiled at me brightly and resumed her society manner with a suddenness that took my breath away. "Thank you *so* much for coming, Grey, darling."

Like she was giving a party or something.

Lily picked up the photographs and ran a gentle hand over them. Her voice went soft with pain again when she murmured, "I can never thank you enough for these."

"You're welcome."

Celestine escorted me out and shut the door behind me. The porch light went out as soon as I reached my car, and I looked back, watching through the sidelight by the front door as her dark form moved toward the morning room, and I was glad Lily would not be alone that night.

Those were two very tough women.

As MUCH as I didn't want to, I knew I had to start at Lambda. It was only nine o'clock. That's practically daybreak in Vegas; if Mr. Martin, AKA Mr. Big, AKA Mr. Beautiful, had to make the rounds of his clubs, it stood to reason he'd make the early call at the smallest one. The secret one where he wouldn't want to be seen.

If I was in luck, maybe I could catch him there. That sentence had all kinds of wrong in it, but what I had in mind for questioning him was better done there than at a busier club.

I wondered if a man known as Mr. Big in some circles would start to think of himself as Big, like I thought of myself as Grey. If I were Mr. Big, would I send flowers to a dame and sign the card B for Big? Seemed kind of unlikely, but you never know how much a man's ego could get twisted up when he fell for a broad.

And maybe I could put the squeeze on Barry Jazz Morgan too. Yeah, I know, I thought if I could get him to talk first, maybe I wouldn't have to see Mr. Martin again. Not that I'm yellow, just that I noticed Martin's last name had the same number of letters as the word "danger."

And maybe I could see which way the wind blew with Miss Tina as well. I had to admit I was curious, I'd never really gotten up close with a T-girl who was on the stage.

The disc got me past the bruiser at the door again without any trouble. Looking over the room, I didn't see Reggie. That was good. I was going to be in enough trouble without having to fend him off as well.

Last time I was there, I'd seen Phil Martin, AKA Mr. Big, disappear behind the blue curtain on the wall, and I figured if I played it cagey, no one would notice if I slipped in back there as well. As it turned out, all my subterfuge was for nothing; that was also the way to the restroom, and some guy came along right behind me. Apparently he thought I was taking numbers, because I had to show him my fists to convince him I wasn't heading for the john to look for some action.

Once I'd shaken him off, I eased down the hallway to find Phil Martin's office. The first door I tried turned out to be Jazz Morgan's dressing room. And he was at home, so I went right in.

Without looking up, he said, "Sorry, men's room is on the other side of the hallway. First door past the curtain."

"Jazz Morgan, just the man I wanted to talk to," I said menacingly.

When he got to his feet, I had to look up at him. He topped me by about six inches. It's some trick to look *up* and scare someone, but I like to think I managed it.

"Who the hell are you, white belly?" he growled.

Kind of a strong reaction to an invitation for a friendly chat. Despite the fact that he was taller than me and bigger, and Reggie told me he boxed, I wasn't going to let him get away with trying to intimidate me with his size. Brains over brawn, right?

"Ooooh, racial slurs. I bet I can top it," I taunted him back.

"Miss Rivers told me some big-time, hotshot cop came by looking for me."

He crowded me against the wall. Looking up into those pretty amber eyes, I was surprised to see a tinge of amusement instead of anger.

"I'm just a little fish in a big pond," I said. "I'm not the law, I'm private."

"It don't scare you that I'm black, does it?"

I put my hand on his chest and shoved him away from me. "Not much." I shrugged. "I care a lot more if you're a killer."

He looked wounded. "I wouldn't kill anyone. I'm not a saint, but I'm no murderer."

"Anyone can kill, it just depends on the circumstances," I said cynically. I'd been strung plenty in my line of work.

"And who am I supposed to have killed?"

"Your girlfriend, Marguerite Saint-Ville," I bluffed.

He clenched his fists and towered over me with a threatening expression on his face. And that's when I saw it: underneath his anger, his guilt peered out steadily, even though I didn't know exactly what he felt guilty for. Yet.

"You find out who killed her, you let me know. I'll deal with him," he continued, but he backed up a step. He was turned inward now, contemplating his pain rather than me.

I stood there, not knowing quite what to do. "So why'd she dump you?"

His laugh was bitter. "She didn't dump me, man, I tried to let her down easy. As soon as I found out—"

"That she was interested in more than just the music?"

He nodded. "You do know something, don't you, little fish?"

I was getting tired of people razzing me because of my size. "I know a lot more than you think I do. She ever do the high kick with you?"

"Shit, man, check it out." He seemed impressed that I knew more than he thought I did. "She told me about that, only did that to gents that was bugging her. No need for that here or for her to ward me off, she was hot for me. I'm on the square."

I nodded, I knew he was telling the truth, but he wasn't telling me everything. "What about Miss Tina?"

Jazz snickered bitterly. "No love lost between them. Margie made fun of Tina till she was off the rails."

"So why was a classy dish like that working in a club like this?"

"Maybe you'd better have a little chat with Mr. Martin," Jazz said, grabbing my arm tighter than was comfortable.

I knew I couldn't break away without causing a ruckus. Besides, it was inevitable that I would have to talk to Mr. Big, so I said, "Lead me to him."

He snorted with bemusement.

Brains over brawn, right? I knew I could handle myself whatever came up.

He dragged me down the corridor, maybe a little faster than I would have chosen to stroll. Trying to collect my thoughts, I did my best to keep up. He opened a door, and Mr. Martin looked up from the paperwork on his desk. He was on the phone.

"All right. I understand. I'll get back to you." He put the phone down and leaned back in his chair, looking amused and untouchable. Not that I didn't want to touch him, dig? But like he would never give me the time of day. He wasn't interested in me, just waiting to hear why Jazz had dragged me in there.

Jazz dropped my arm, and I resisted the urge to rub it. The feeling started to return to my hand when Jazz said, "Caught this little fish poking around, looking for some answers."

"What makes you think you can just march in here and expect anyone to talk to you?" Mr. Martin demanded. There was a little tremor to his lips, like he was trying not to laugh.

"Talk to yourself, and I'll listen," I said.

His lips curled in a grin, and his dimples dug into his cheeks.

I don't like being regarded as the evening's entertainment. I don't know why people don't take me seriously sometimes. I mean, yeah, I may be wiry, but I'm smart. The urge rose up inside me, a dark urge. I wanted to wipe that condescending smirk off his face. I wanted to master him and force him to his knees in front of me. An unwelcome little voice inside me acknowledged that after I did that, I wanted him to master me.

I became aware that I was staring at him with my mouth open, breathing hard. I shut it with a snap and snarled, "Why did you hire Marguerite Saint-Ville—to work *here*?"

Mr. Martin and his honcho exchanged meaningful glances. "Better get back onstage and make some noise," he muttered ominously, and Jazz nodded, leaving the room and shutting the door softly behind him. I could hear his footsteps diminishing in the distance. In the tense silence I heard the piano start up in the distance and the honeyed tones of Miss Tina as she started to sing. I wondered how much noise Mr. Big thought he needed to cover up. Not that I was scared or anything.

"Something wrong with the joint?" Mr. Big asked as he stood up and started walking toward me.

I felt at a distinct disadvantage with him, but I held my ground. "She was a dame. This place is packed with men who don't have much interest in dames. And she left this behind." I opened my hand and showed him the Lambda on the silver disc.

He glanced down, and his mouth was grim as he met my eyes again, but there was a warmth in his eyes. I was beginning to wonder if he had fallen for the Saint-Ville dame too. That would have been a mood-killer for me.

"Where'd you find that?" He made a quick movement, as if to snatch it from me.

I closed my hand over it and took a step back. "Does it matter? I found it."

He prowled toward me, and suddenly I became aware that the tux was showcasing a very muscular and fit frame. He wasn't as tall as Jazz, but he was bigger than me, and unless I found a way to take control, he might snatch the evidence from me.

I stuffed it into an inside pocket and retreated while I taunted him. "It led me right to your door."

"You had to know what that symbol meant to be able to find this place," he growled. "Most *men* don't know what it means."

The faint emphasis on the word "men" was meant as an insult, but I was on the scent now. Time enough to be offended later; he had something to hide, and he'd just revealed that to me.

"Most *men* don't run clubs like this," I tossed back.

He gave a sharp bark of laughter. "You think this is my only club? It's just a business to me; I've got three others. Maybe you've heard of Topaz downtown?"

"Yeah, I heard it mentioned in passing." I hope my disappointment didn't show on my face as we continued to circle his desk, with me walking backwards and him coming after me. Maybe he was as straight as I'd feared after all.

"The other clubs are the hot spots. They pull in the major bucks.

But I'm not one to turn away an untapped business opportunity," he said. "I don't care who people fuck on their own time, their money is all green to me."

"So why did Miss Saint-Ville come here and not to one of those mainstream clubs?" I asked triumphantly.

Phil Martin was good-looking, suave, sophisticated, expensive, a lot of things I wasn't. But suddenly there it was. Confirmation. The one thing we had in common, one way he was exactly like me. He probably wasn't even aware of the look of interest warming his eyes. A straight man will look into your eyes, no problem, but there was just that little flick downward, a glance at the groin. A dead giveaway every time. So Reggie was wrong about one thing. Made me wonder what else he was wrong about.

Mr. Big, AKA Phil Martin thought he had himself well in hand. I imagine with his associates it wasn't wise to give away a secret like that.

But that downward glance meant I had an in with him, a way to force him to talk to me about just why he'd hired a girl to sing torch songs at a queer club. Didn't matter what game he was playing, pretending that he was only running this club for money; he was one of us, and I knew if I got him in the right position, he'd answer anything I had to ask.

The problem was I didn't want him to think I was putting the black on him for keeps. That could prove to be bad for my breathing, as in continuing to do so. I stopped backing away and tossed him a confident grin, now that I knew where we both stood. He realized he'd made a mistake, although he wasn't quite sure what had given him away. Mr. Martin paused in his stalking of me and looked at me with a little more respect in his dark blue eyes. "I see why Jazz brought you to see me. What did he tell you?"

"Told me he dumped Margie, not the other way around like everyone seems to think," I threw back at him.

He seemed shaken. "You don't know what you're playing with here. This goes up above me."

This time it was my turn to feel shocked. "They call you 'Mr.

Big'. Who's above you? How high does this thing go?"

"Look, for your own health, maybe you shouldn't ask so fucking many questions," he hissed.

He took a quick step toward me and grabbed my arm. Damn, that was gonna leave a mark. His fingers squeezed first, and then his thumb started to stroke me, but it was subtle, like he was trying to find out what was under my suit. Almost like he didn't know he was doing it.

"I'm Grey Randall, private dick. This is what I do," I said.

"*Grey* Randall?" He seemed even more surprised. "I see," he added slowly. I could see the respect dawning in his eyes, and that made me nervous about what he'd heard about me.

While he took a moment to think about it, I yanked my arm out of his grasp and planted my hand flat on his chest, driving him back against the wall. Even though he was probably stronger than me, I didn't have to use any fancy tricks on him.

The expression on his face told me everything he'd been trying to hide from the world—and me. There's no mistaking that hungry look a man gets when another man's touch lights a fire inside him.

He was trying to finesse a losing hand; all his talk about his other clubs was designed to throw me off. Sure, they might have been the hotspots for straight men and women, but this was where his heart was. He was right at home, and he wanted *me*. Now I could see it plain as day. I had him where I wanted him. He didn't move a muscle, just watched to see what I would do next. If I could keep my wits about me, and my dick in my pants, I was home free. I lightened the pressure of my hand, making little circles on his chest. He was built, his pecs pumped and firm. I let my hand trail down the center of his body, feeling the indent between his abdominal muscles.

He let his head fall back against the paneled wall with a little thud. He almost moaned, stopping it in time so all he let out was a little sigh.

I leaned toward him, letting my breath blow over his lips, and he parted them invitingly. I almost smiled. He wasn't going to take me in that easily; we were following my game plan now, and kissing him was not part of the scheme.

"Marguerite Saint-Ville?" I asked softly from three inches away.

"Huh?" he said thickly, his breath coming in quick pants.

"Why did she come here?"

"I can't tell you that," he said, turning his face away.

I continued to run my hand down his body. I could feel him getting harder against the back of my hand as I caressed his inner thigh.

"I don't believe you," I whispered in his ear. He shivered. Sensitive ears, huh? I don't pass up any advantage. I leaned in a little closer and sucked his ear lobe into my mouth. He groaned as I nibbled on the tiny piece of succulent flesh. I twirled my tongue around it as I held it captive between my teeth, my hot breath flowing inside the curved canal of his ear. I knew he wouldn't dare try anything now; I had him by the balls. Literally. Fondling them as I allowed my body to brush against his.

His breath was coming ragged now, whistling in and out as he pretended to resist me. Like a man gasping after a long time in the desert who suddenly stumbled on an oasis and could have all he wanted, he seemed to just give in to me. I wondered how long it had been for him. Maybe long enough that he could give even me a run for my money.

"When was the last time you saw Miss Saint-Ville?" I asked, trying a different tack.

"Fuck. You know her... know when it was," he stammered.

"I know more than you think." His body jerked as I ran my nails over his cloth-covered erection teasingly. I'd done that to myself, and I knew just how it felt and just how hard to do it. What can I say? I like to investigate. Even myself.

He was struggling to keep his composure, so I knew I had to push him over the edge. I undid one button and let my hand slide inside his shirt. I almost gasped at the heat and smoothness of his chest. Hot damn. It isn't often when business and pleasure coincide so well.

"Was she upset when she left?"

"I wasn't here—but that's what I heard.... Oh, yeah," he gasped. The first in answer to my question and the last in response to me pinching his nipple. Sensitive. I like that in a man.

"Did you know who she was when she came here?"

He tried to resist, but I twisted his nipple while grinding my leg between his. His palms were flat on the wall, as if he couldn't move. It must have been a long time for him, the way he just stood there taking what I was dishing out to him.

What he didn't know was that it had been a long time for me too. Maybe even longer than for him. I was playing with fire here, and he had me burning with lust. I was standing on the edge of a knife, and I couldn't let the blade slide in.

"Yes. I knew."

At last! Now we were getting somewhere. I pulled back slightly and undid his belt with one hand. I'm very dexterous. It comes in handy when you're picking a lock... or questioning a recalcitrant suspect.

"Why'd you hire her?"

"I had to." His voice was hoarse. "Please... please, don't...."

I unzipped his pants. They fell to his ankles. He was wearing silk boxers. Oooh. I *liked* them! Midnight blue, with a wet spot where his cock was tenting them. Very feely. "You want me to stop?"

"No! Yes, I mean, fuck! Don't stop!" He was panting, and a little drop of sweat trickled down his face from his temple.

I smiled at him, but he didn't notice. His gaze was fixed on my hand, watching as I stroked the thin fabric that was the only barrier between us. I used my nails again, and he closed his eyes, moaning with sheer pleasure.

"Who sent her?"

"No one...."

"Who was she running from?"

His eyes flew open, and at last I knew I had a clue. "I can't tell you."

"Can't? Or won't?" I asked silkily. I slid my hand inside the opening in front of his boxers, finding the hot, pulsating length of him. With one finger and a thumb, I stroked him lightly, teasing him. His hips started to flex as he sought more friction, but I pulled away whenever he got too close, keeping the pressure light.

"I can't... don't know that," he pleaded with me.

With both hands, I pulled the waistband away from his trim waist and blew downward, letting my breath cool him off a bit. In truth, I needed a little time to cool off myself. This was just a job, I kept reminding myself, but I knew I was lying. I'm a trained investigator, I can spot a lie from a mile away, even if it's mine.

He watched me, practically drooling as I pushed his boxers down to join his pants, my palms smoothing the way down his long muscular legs. Damn, he felt good.

I knelt in front of him and licked my lips. He was mesmerized, his eyes bugging out of his head as he watched me. I breathed on the head of his cock, and it jerked upward, almost slapping his belly. It was glistening with a few drops that leaked from the tip.

Fuck, I wanted to taste him. I stuck out my tongue, and he stopped breathing, holding completely still.

Less than an inch away, I stopped and said, "Give me a fact to go on. If you tell me something, I won't tease you any more. Who sent her to you?"

"Her father... I owed him a favor," he groaned, as if the information was wrenched from him against his will.

"That's a good boy," I crooned encouragingly. I hated to spoil the mood, but I had to ask. "Did you ever date her?"

"No, never. I never would," he babbled, watching my mouth.

"You never go out with women?" I asked mockingly. A guy like him pretending to be straight? It didn't add up.

"Her father—he put the word out—dangerous if he found out—a guy made her unhappy—" he puffed.

"Ever send her flowers?"

"Flowers?" he echoed vaguely, as if he'd never heard of them.

I couldn't torture him any longer. Believe me, I'd been there. It might not be fair to elicit information this way, and it sure as hell wouldn't stand up in court as a method of interrogation, but it works. He'd told me all he could, I knew that. And now it was time to give him his reward. And me. I was suffering as much as he was, but my pants were baggier, and no one had their hand on me. As far as he knew, I was completely calm and collected.

I licked over the head of his cock and closed my eyes in turn. I know some people find it bitter or salty, but to me, the first taste of a man who is hot and horny is like heaven. Just knowing he was hard for me, that I'd made him that way, it was headier than any booze could ever be. I never needed a speak to get my groove on. This was all I needed to drink.

Jazz's music wailed softly in my ears in counterpoint to the beating of my heart as I licked Mr. Big's cock, all hard and long and thick. I licked down one side and up the other. I knew the featherlight touch of my tongue was driving him crazy as his hips vibrated, tiny short thrusts as he struggled to control himself.

I moaned when I took his cock in my mouth. There's something about the heavy weight of a cock on my tongue, the shape, the soft silky skin covering the hard manly strength of it that satisfies me like nothing else can. It's pure happiness to get a man hard, get him where he'll do anything to get off, to wield that kind of power over him. His face contorted with ecstasy, his teeth clenched but his lips standing out as if waiting for a kiss as I looked up at him, softly stroking his shaft with one hand as I sucked lightly on the head. I flattened the swollen vein under the ridge and let up to feel it fill again. He was throbbing, he was so hard, the tip drooling more of his fluid as I sucked.

"Oh yeah... oh fuck yeah," he sighed in satisfaction, his eyes half-closed in a daze of lust.

I nibbled down the side of his shaft, my touch delicate but with enough of a nip to keep him on his toes. He moaned, and I could tell he liked the danger of feeling my teeth on his erection. I worked him with my hand, varying the stroke and pressure, keeping him panting and moaning with suspense. And he wasn't the only one. It was an honor to have the opportunity to worship such a fine cock with my mouth, caressing him with my lips and letting my tongue get to know him.

Just as his hips started snapping faster, I swallowed his cock, letting my throat relax as he drove into my mouth. I can only do that once or twice, but I've found if you do it suddenly the first time, the guy you're blowing will think you're keeping on with it.

I think it was the idea of it that got him so hot, because I let him pull out almost immediately. He kept thrusting, but I controlled how much I took in.

I snuck a hand lower and caressed his balls. Tight they were, tight and full. He was needy all right, tossing his head on the wall and moaning like there was no one else in the club. I worked him until I felt his balls tighten up even more and his cock swelled in my mouth. I pulled off and blew on him, the air cooling my spit.

He begged. "Please... please... let me come... make me come... please...."

I stopped his hands heading for his dick. "What's her father's name?" I gasped out. Maybe I was a little excited myself.

"Please... please," he pleaded desperately. His body was trembling so violently, he couldn't free himself from my grip. "Can't tell... you... that," he burst out.

"Who told you to hire her?"

"Mr.—Mr. X.... Now please... ah... holy... fucking... he—"

He stopped talking when I took his cock in my mouth again. It qualifies as torture when you're getting someone off and you work them up and stop right when they're about to come, and I could see I had gotten all I was going to out of him. Except for that. Yeah, I'm pretty smug about it.

I toyed with him a little more, licking him lightly and holding one hip so he couldn't strangle me by fucking my throat. Finally I had mercy and sucked him the right way, jacking him at the same time with my hand.

His movements were frenzied now, his hips quivering as he drove forward in search of his release. The first shot was so explosive I never even tasted it, but I savored the next blasts. Bitter and salty, the flavor of a man, a beautiful man. And all for me.

I would have liked to hold him as he shuddered through the

aftermath of his climax, but that could have led somewhere I wasn't willing to go. I stood up in one smooth move. For the first time, I took his lips, thrusting my tongue into his mouth so he could taste himself on me. He responded weakly, trying to hold me, but I took control of the kiss, driving deep into his mouth like he'd just done to me.

I'd conquered him completely, making him come and getting the answers I needed. Now it was time to leave. I looked back at him, beautiful and dazed as he leaned against the wall, spent, with his cock limp and his pants around his ankles.

One thing I've learned over time: a man who's just had his brain sucked out through his cock won't chase you if you leave quick enough. Especially if you leave his pants around his ankles.

I paused outside his door, straightening my clothes and wiping my mouth. I wouldn't have minded wearing his cum home, but I was working, and I had my pride. I walked quickly through the club, retrieving my hat and making it to the front door unmolested. I thought Jazz was looking after me, but I couldn't be sure, and I wanted out before Mr. Big got his pants zipped up.

The door closed behind me, and I left the smoky atmosphere for the crisp cool air outside. The moon was a shining silver disc in the midnight blue sky.

I took a deep breath to calm myself and headed for my car. It was too late tonight to chase down the clues I'd been given. And besides, I had something to take care of.

I put a few miles between me and the club, a fair distance. I kept an eye out, but I wasn't being tailed.

The scene at the club had been brutal but necessary. Sometimes people don't want to talk and they have to be cajoled. I wondered what Mr. Big thought about it now that he'd had time to calm down. One thing was sure: I'd have to watch my back for a while. Powerful men don't get to that rung of the ladder without a streak of ruthlessness in them, and he would want revenge.

I could argue that he could have shaken loose from me at any time, but it's not so easy if the thing you've been denying is suddenly on their knees in front of you.

If he could have felt the state of my aching dick though, he might have thought we were even. The urgency was off, no one was following me, and I needed some relief. I was so hard I was having trouble deciding which stick shift to grab. I pulled into a dark alley and got out, unzipping my pants. I pictured Mr. Big, no, Mr. Beautiful, as he leaned against the wall, gasping and hot for me, and relived the feel of his cock in my mouth as I stroked mine slowly. I tried to prolong it, but all I could see was that beautiful piece of meat of his, standing up for me, full and hard and bursting with seed.

I was panting as if I'd run a mile as I jacked my dick, watching the splatter of my cum hit the brick wall in front of me, glistening in the moonlight. My hips thrust wildly as I came, and I moaned his name. After taking a few minutes to calm down, I fished in the car for the hideous tie Lily had threatened to throw out. I wiped my hand on the tie and zipped up. I dropped the wet tie on the ground and got back in the car. I heaved in a deep breath and turned the motor over, checking both ways before I headed for my apartment, leaving the evidence of my evening's activities behind.

Guess I owed Artie a new tie even though I hadn't gotten blood on it. And I was still going to have to go back to interview Miss Tina.

Chapter 5: I Meet Mr. X

I GUESS I needed that. I turned in early and slept like the dead till morning. While the morning fog was lifting and the coffee was perking, I realized I had a lot to think about. Who was Mr. X? Why would Phil Martin hire Marguerite Saint-Ville to oblige him? Who killed her? Was it Jazz Morgan after all or somebody else? What did Reggie know about this that he still wasn't telling me? What else had Lily left out? And why had I allowed myself to put the moves on Mr. Big?

I could have gotten him to talk another way. No fooling myself, things would be a lot simpler if I'd just controlled myself. For one thing, I didn't want to believe it was Mr. Big who sent those cards signed with a B, but there were a lot of reasons a man could kill. Like blackmail. If Margie found out about him and threatened to go canary on him, maybe he could have been desperate enough to strangle her, but then why send flowers before she even knew he ran a queer club?

Okay, back to the case. There were things I needed to know. I called my service and found out that Charlie had called the previous day, saying she'd found something she wanted me to see, and Lily had also called that morning.

Charlie or Lily? Research or action?

A lot of private dicks prefer action, exciting car chases, sniffing out clues, shining bright lights in people's eyes and barking questions at them. Of course, most of them can't read. I'm a different kind of dick. I've always been good at research, among other things, and I could have been a scientist if the inclination took me that way. And with Charlie to do the legwork, it shaved hours off research time for me, not that I was going to tell her that.

I opted for the library first. Mrs. Fielding steered me to the crime section, where I found Charlie immersed in some book.

"Boning up?"

"If I'm going to help you track down a murderer, I might as well familiarize myself with the criminal mind," she said, pushing up her glasses.

I tried not to laugh, but if a crook could have seen her, sitting on the floor in her slacks and ugly brown cardigan, I don't think she would have struck too much fear in his heart. Tactfully, I asked, "So what have you got for me?"

She took my hand and stood up, shelving the book without looking. "I think you'll be interested in what I found out about your client."

"Okay, lay it on me."

Charlie led the way to the basement, and I was impressed when I saw how much stuff she had laid out on a long table. The library had only just started microfilming the current periodicals, so she'd gone into the archives to find magazines and newspapers. I whistled to show how impressed I was.

"You deserve the new Austen set," I said.

She grinned smugly. "Wait'll you see this." She led me to the head of the table and handed me a pair of white cotton gloves, pulling on a pair herself.

Twenty years ago, Vegas was a smaller town with fewer watering holes. But even then, good-looking dancers were hoofing it for the guys working the mines and ranches. Silver and gambling were the only news in Vegas back then, that and the dames. Men came here to forget and live it up, with gambling, booze, and broads.

And the people who lived here, well, all that mattered was what was happening here: who was killing who, who was fucking who, who lost money and most importantly, who won it.

About twenty years back, Charlie found the first piece of evidence I needed. The rise of Lily McIntyre was news, first buried in the back pages, and then she earned front-page status as she became a headliner. Her rise to stardom was marked by fewer and fewer clothes.

She was a looker, all right. She may have been correct, she might have had a bit of an edge on Marguerite; she was taller, slimmer, and her face was lovelier. More innocent, perhaps. For a while, at least.

She hit the headlines on the arms of a lot of men, high rollers, casino owners, and shady-looking fellas.

After a while, she narrowed it down to one man, Max Hamilton, who owned only one hotel and casino at the time: the Rising Star. I wondered if he'd named it for Lily. Or maybe he was honoring himself. Of course she appeared on his arm after she hit it big. He wanted the best, only the best. He was the type who saw something beautiful and had to own it. And for a while, he owned her, squiring her to openings, shows, dinners. He even gave a dinner for the mayor, and she was there as hostess.

Of course, he couldn't stop fooling around with other dames. A guy like him, why should he? He would never have thought of pledging constancy to a woman; they were there for his pleasure. And sometimes in the photos, I could see a little hurt and jealousy in Lily's expression when the novelty of owning her wore off and Mr. Hamilton began looking at the other dames again.

They were still appearing together, but less frequently, by March of that year. And then the stunner: there she was on Davie Berman's arm. Another casino owner, which meant mobster, a friend of Bugsy's. Bugsy Siegel, in case you didn't guess. After that I never found another picture with Lily and Max Hamilton in the same frame. A guy like Mr. Hamilton? He wouldn't forgive a public slam like that.

And Lily? She looked triumphant, but spiteful. Not a happy woman. Her run with Berman flared up and then burned out in two months. After her came a tall ash blonde like a cool drink of water, and Lily disappeared from the papers.

It was a whole year before her picture appeared in the papers again. The caption read, "Back from her triumphant tour through the Northeast." I pondered that. A high kicker like her, she'd have been a hit on Broadway. And usually if a star made a splash in the Northeast, that's the pool she would have dived into, opening at Ziegfeld's Follies before hitting the bright lights on Broadway. And a star like her, she would have made sure to tell the paper all that. So that was probably when she was off giving birth to Marguerite.

Why the big secret? In those days, everyone assumed a dancer was a tramp, especially if she hung out with bosses like Max Hamilton and Davie Berman. No shame in popping out a kid, it even lent a certain cachet. Lily hadn't been very forthcoming with me at all, I decided. What else was she hiding?

Moving along, I found articles on Lily: what she liked to eat for breakfast, why she preferred silk for her underwear, and how she trained her famous legs by putting her feet on two different chairs and sliding them apart as she went into a split in midair. The picture that accompanied that article really caught my attention, and I blanched, imagining the strain on the inner thigh. And what happened if you got tired and slipped?

"Grey," Charlie said. "Stop staring at that revolting picture and look here." She pointed to a magazine from two years ago.

There was Lily, on Max Hamilton's arm again, smiling at the camera at the opening of his second hotel, the Lucky Star. I'd heard Max Hamilton described as looking like a retired admiral, but he was more my idea of a modern-day pirate, tall, handsome, a charismatic but devilish smile as if daring the world to take him on, iron-grey hair, well-fed—

My eye stopped along with my heart when I saw another snap of Mr. Big, AKA Mr. Beautiful, AKA Mr. Phil Martin, the very guy I sucked off last night, frolicking with two of the finest female refreshments Vegas had to offer: a beautiful blonde dame on one arm and a lovely brunette on the other. I wondered if he ordered dessert off both sides of the cart. Given what happened the night before, I would have sworn he came down firmly on the blue team's side. Maybe he thought he'd be safer disguised with two beards. A man can hope.

It suited him. Philip was kind of silky on the tongue. I imagined calling him Phil.

Phil, could you get me some coffee? Phil, give me the paper. Phil, could you lick my cock?

Martin. Businesslike, crisp, no nonsense, powerful. There he was at the same party with Max Hamilton. Laughing with him like he knew him. Wait, hadn't he said this was bigger than him?

"Grey!"

"What!"

"Are you even listening to me?"

Always go with the safe answer, in case of snap quizzes. "No, sorry, Charlie. This photo is giving me some funny ideas about the case." She didn't have to know *how* funny.

She seemed to accept that. "From 1931 on, when Lily McIntyre made her comeback, until 1946, when this was shot at the opening of the Lucky Star, I wasn't able to find a picture with Miss McIntyre together with Mr. Hamilton. It was like they always avoided each other."

"Well, he *is* married. Isn't he?" I tried to remember. I seemed to recall hearing that he had a couple of kids with his wife.

Charlie frowned disapprovingly. "That hasn't stopped him from being photographed with *hordes* of beautiful women. Usually dancers."

"Doesn't his wife like to party?" I asked flippantly.

Charlie shoved another magazine under my nose. "She does a lot of charity events."

I expected to see a gray-haired motherly woman, innocent of her husband's licentious ways, but the photo showed a raven-haired beauty, sleek enough to have been a dancer herself. Maybe she was, once upon a time. The chorus line seemed to be Max Hamilton's preferred dating pool and he dove in the deep end. "Does she know about him running around?"

"The papers are hardly likely to print that, even if it's true. Perhaps she looks the other way," Charlie said impatiently. "But notice how he is with her and when he's with Miss McIntyre."

"You'd make a good detective," I said.

"He's happy with Miss McIntyre," Charlie said. "Not like in 1930. Something happened between them then. And now, he still dates a lot of other women, but it seems as if he's not willing to put her in the spotlight. He's protecting her. The caption there says she was escorted to the party by Vic Urban and is seen here with *host,* Max Hamilton."

"How many casinos does Max Hamilton own?"

"Two," Charlie said.

"And other business ventures? Nightclubs? Dinner clubs? Betting parlors?"

"It could take me a year to track down all of his business dealings," Charlie said in dismay. "He's got a finger in every pie as long as there's money in it."

"What about Topaz, the club on Fremont?"

"If I find out, will you take me there sometime?"

I stared at her blankly. "Why would you want to go there?"

"I've never been, and it's supposed to be the most popular club in Vegas right now."

"You'd have to wear a dress," I blurted out before stopping to strap my tact on.

"I know *how*, Grey! I *have* worn a dress before." Charlie folded her arms and glared at me. "I even *own* some."

"All right, I'll take you. If I can afford it." What could I say? I was desperate. "But if I'm buying, I get to approve the dress." I had this feeling that *if* Charlie owned a dress, as she claimed, it might not be one that would get her into the club.

"As if *you're* an expert!" she exclaimed huffily. "And I want champagne!"

"You like champagne?"

"I don't know. I've never had any, but I want to try it. And to dance!"

"Only the tango. That's the only dance I know," I said firmly.

Charlie lifted the magazine and pulled out a typed list she'd hidden inside it. She grinned at me. "I figured you'd ask. I found twenty-four clubs so far where he's part owner. Betting and racetrack interests, real estate, and he owns some racehorses. I also jotted down Marguerite Saint-Ville's address and phone number for you."

"You should go on the grift," I said bitterly.

"I played you all right," Charlie crowed.

"Enjoy your victory while it lasts." I scanned the list quickly. Topaz was on it, Zircon, another of Phil Martin's clubs, and other names I couldn't tie him to. Not surprisingly, Lambda wasn't on it. I wondered if Mr. Hamilton even knew of its existence or whether it was a sole venture for Mr. Big.

"Did you find out who did it yet?" Charlie asked.

"Not yet, but this helps," I said, tucking the list into my pocket. No wonder Mr. Big didn't want to make any waves by telling me who Mr. X was. He wouldn't want to get his financing yanked out from under him, but I was thinking that now maybe I knew who the big cheese was. Maybe Phil Martin was how Max kept his finger on the criminal pulse of Vegas. I was onto something, but what?

Not that I was going to confront Phil Martin with this information any time soon. No, I had a better idea of who to put the squeeze on next.

"Got today's paper handy?"

She heaved a big sigh but went to grab it and held it under my nose. The murder was still getting a big play in the papers, even though there was nothing new to report. So the newshounds were making it up, implying that the cops were trying to hush it up because the killer was someone too rich ever to be arrested.

Captain Woods was quoted as saying, "The Las Vegas Police Force takes pride in keeping the crime rate low. Since I've been placed in charge, the number of violent assaults has dropped precipitously. Soon criminals will realize there is no way their dastardly crimes will not receive just retribution. Las Vegas is a clean town, a safe town. There is no way that the citizens of Las Vegas will not see an arrest of the man who committed this crime. We have him in our sights, and as soon as we gather sufficient evidence, the details will become public knowledge."

Blowhard. He should run for office. I tossed the paper down.

"Thanks, Charlie. See you."

"Wait! When are we going out dancing?"

"Business before pleasure. I have a case to solve first."

BACK to Miss Lily McIntyre. The previous night I'd been too sore and it had been too dark for me to take much notice of her house. She lived in a ritzy area, Huntsridge, right on the turnaround on Maryland Parkway, AKA Showgirl Row.

Maybe it was due to the kinds of productions they danced in, but most of the showgirls owned ostentatious monstrosities that looked like frosted wedding cakes. Lily's was different. It looked kind of French to me, with a slate mansard roof, built of pale sandstone with quoins at the corners and little terraces with wrought iron railings at intervals around the second story.

I could see the tire marks I'd left on the circular drive in front of her house where I'd skidded to a stop the night before. I walked up the shallow set of stairs, flanked by low stone pillars all covered with red roses twining over the balusters.

I hadn't called ahead. Somehow I needed to surprise the truth out of her. And if that didn't work, at least pry the keys to her daughter's apartment out of her so I could search it for clues.

When the door opened in answer to my ring, I said, "Good morning, Celestine. May I see Miss McIntyre?"

Celestine gave me a gimlet eye. I had a feeling I wasn't on her good list after last night. "I shall inquire, m'sieur."

She planned on me waiting in the foyer like I had the night before, but I followed her silently. Gum shoes, you know. Dress code in the private dick manual. She led the way through the living room, where I could see a smaller alcove with shelves to the ceiling solid with books and one of those brass library ladders. I'd always wanted to try one of those.

Celestine continued on into the morning room, where we'd had coffee the night before. In the daytime, I could see why Lily liked the room. It was painted a warm yellow, which set off her coloring to perfection and caught the morning sun. The round table was cherry and sitting there, you could look out onto her garden, which was also filled with red roses.

"Grey, darling!" Lily said, as if I'd just dropped by for a social visit.

Celestine turned and gave me a dirty look for sneaking in behind her.

"Bring another cup, Celestine. You'll join me for coffee, of course?" Lily gave me a warm smile and waved her hand to another chair. She was wearing a black street dress with a red rose tucked into the belt as if even in mourning, her vibrant personality demanded some outlet.

"Thank you. The coffee smells great." I sat down prepared to nail her, but she forestalled me.

"You've come to ask me who Marguerite's father was, I expect."

"I think I know that. Mr. X. Max Hamilton."

For a second, Lily looked surprised, but then she laughed. "Well, you *are* cleverer than you look, Mr. Dick."

"So, you're not denying it?"

"You succeeded in making Phil Martin talk then?" She leaned forward. "Did you shine a light in his eyes?"

"I'm afraid some of the methods we dicks use must remain a secret, but I milked him dry," I said with what dignity I could muster. "I asked him why he hired your daughter. He said that Mr. X asked him to."

"You tricked me!" Lily seemed delighted rather than upset. "*Very* clever! I certainly fell for your subterfuge."

"Lily, you don't have to entertain me."

Her smile faded, and she stared at me. "I forgot. It's been… rather wearing."

It struck me how awful it must have been for her not to be able to claim her daughter publicly, but I didn't want to make it worse by mentioning it. "I need to see Max Hamilton."

"All right. I can set it up, I have an in. Today?"

"You said time was of the essence," I reminded her.

"So I did. And?"

"The keys to Marguerite's apartment and the address." Funny how much more real she'd become to me as I learned more about her. She wasn't just the Saint-Ville dame who died in an alley any more.

"So you can search it. And?"

I took out the florist's card I'd found stuck in Marguerite's dressing table at the Jungle Room. "Do you have any idea what that means?"

"'Red roses for my Rose Red,'" Lily murmured. "Did you notice my roses when you came in?"

It would have been hard not to; the scent was intoxicating in the hot sun. "They're very pretty."

"Marguerite loved red roses. They were her favorite flower and remind me of her. Flaming and deep and velvety. She was softer than I am, you know. She didn't have that hard edge she needed to—" Lily's voice broke. "When she was a little girl and we played pretend, her name was Rose Red and mine was Lily White."

"So she wouldn't have told just anybody her secret name?"

Lily shook her head. "I don't know. I wouldn't have thought so."

"Did Mr. Hamilton know that was her nickname?"

"He would never have killed her. He'd always wanted a daughter—he was so proud of her when he knew—" Lily raised a hand as if pushing away some horror. "He couldn't have!"

"Maybe he knows who did it?"

"Why would he protect them, when he knows—" Lily jumped up and started to pace. "No, I can't believe it."

"Get me in to see him."

"Why do you think he wouldn't see you if you called him yourself?"

"I'm just a small fish in a big pond, and he's the shark that owns it," I said.

LILY was good for it, and when I left, it was with an appointment to go see Mr. Hamilton. Of course I'd had to talk her out of coming along, because she was so keen to prove to me that he couldn't have done it.

Well, I didn't think he would have done it himself; he was too big for that. If he wanted it, he was a man who had these types of things done for him. I just couldn't think of a reason why, other than blackmail, but the relationship was complicated enough that I would have thought it was a two-way street. Besides, it didn't sound like the Marguerite I was coming to know.

I'd heard whispers and hints about Mr. X around town, but I hadn't paid too much attention because I didn't move in those lofty circles. And I never connected Mr. X with Mr. Hamilton until things started coming together on this case, but since he was a casino owner, it stood to reason that he had ties to organized crime. You didn't step off the train in Las Vegas and work your way up from bus boy to casino owner without a little backing.

As to that, I didn't want to rock the boat. The system had been going on a long time before I got there, and I had no interest in stopping it. But if he had been involved in Marguerite Saint-Ville's death, I was going to nail him for it.

Mr. Hamilton was in his office at his first hotel, the Rising Star. The girl at the front desk in the lobby recognized my name when I said I was there to see him and pointed me at the elevator to the penthouse.

The elevator jockey took me up without comment, but I could tell he was heeled. When I stepped out at the end of the ride, I found myself in a circular room with no windows. A cute dame with light brown hair and girlish freckles sat behind a desk with a phone, a blank pad, and a vase of flowers. Not roses.

"I'm Grey Randall, private dick. I have an appointment to see Mr. Hamilton," I told her.

She smiled brightly at me. "Please sit down, Mr. Randall. He's with someone right now, but he'll be right with you."

I sat. The furniture was modern and sleek, all chrome and leather. I wanted a gander at this Mr. X, to decide for myself if he was the kind of man who could kill his own daughter. But Lily didn't strike me as the kind of woman who would accept a man like that as her lover, and she seemed certain he hadn't done it.

I didn't have long to wait. A door hidden in the wood paneling opened, and there was Mr. X himself, shaking hands with another man as he escorted him out, a man I recognized.

What was Captain Billy Woods doing here, in the center of the web that Mr. X spun around the city of Las Vegas? Hard on the track of crime, as befitted the brave and handsome captain of police? Or maybe he did have political aspirations after all.

Captain Woods gave me a quick glance, and his smile grew wider in recognition. "Thank you, Mr. Hamilton. Don't worry about a thing. I'll see you soon then."

Funny thing, Big Billy Woods was taller than Mr. Hamilton, but somehow he didn't seem like the bigger man.

Sometimes when you see a picture and you meet the man in person, you're disappointed, as if he were smaller than you'd thought he'd be, but that wasn't the case with Mr. Max Hamilton. I could tell that Mr. Hamilton was definitely Mr. X. He radiated dominance and a hard ruthlessness that made you want to keep on the good side of him. Even Captain Woods seemed to be feeling the effect as he looked down at Mr. Hamilton.

I realized that Mr. X wasn't simply the owner of two casinos; he was in the business of power. Wherever Mr. Hamilton ended up, he would make certain that he was in charge.

Funny thing, when I first saw the color photograph of Marguerite, I'd thought she was an exact duplicate of Lily, but I could see the resemblance to her father when he smiled. Of course, he was all hard edges and she had softened them up some, but the likeness was there.

Captain Woods gave me his hand to shake, and I tossed him a grin as he squeezed my hand in his. I had a feeling he was this close to warning Mr. Hamilton about me, but he didn't.

"Mr. Randall, isn't it?" When I nodded, he went on. "I didn't know you knew Mr. Hamilton."

Considering that until yesterday, Captain Woods hadn't known I existed, it wasn't exactly astounding that he wouldn't have a list of who was in my address book, but I didn't point that out.

"We have an interest in common, Captain Woods," I said.

Captain Woods gave Mr. Hamilton a sidelong glance. Mr. Hamilton stood there looking suave and unthreatening, giving nothing away. "What would a private dick and an important businessman like Mr. Hamilton have in common?" From his tone, you would have thought he'd said "snake" instead of "private dick."

"We both like to garden," I said recklessly. He didn't need to know that I lived in an apartment. "He likes lilies and I prefer roses."

Mr. Hamilton surprised me by looking as if he was trying not to laugh. "I am fond of a good bloom."

"We're comparing the merits of spreading on a good, thick coat of manure or straw for the winter," I said solemnly.

"I think I can smell it now." The tightness of his lips was the only thing that gave away the fact that Captain Woods knew he was being kidded, but he had enough self control not to push the issue. He nodded at both us. "Good day, Mr. Hamilton."

I waited till he was gone and held out my hand. Hey, Mr. Hamilton might be a crook, but a guy can still be polite.

"Grey Randall, private dick." We shook. He had a firm grip. Businesslike. But he didn't try to crush my hand like Woods had.

"Ah, yes. Miss McIntyre said you'd be calling. Come in." He gestured and stood back to let me pass into his office.

"Wow, what a view!" I said, unable to suppress my reaction. The windows looked out toward Red Rock and over the other casinos on Route 91. But I wasn't so impressed that I overlooked the two gunnies holding up the wall in his office.

"I like to keep an eye on the competition," Mr. Hamilton said with a chuckle. "Have a seat. What can I do for you?"

I sat and looked over his muscle. One guy was a regular gunsel, average face, average height, average build, nothing to grab hold of if you were asked to describe him after witnessing him commit a crime, but the other one was a fireplug in that he had no neck. He was stocky and muscular, and I assumed he had to have his suits tailored. Off the rack was never going to fit him. His nose was flatter than Artie's.

"It's private," I said.

The average Joe came forward. "Stand up."

Not wanting the indignity of Mr. X watching while I was dragged up out of the chair, I stood up on my own two feet and permitted him to pat me down. "Careful. I'm ticklish," I warned him.

"He's carrying, Mr. Hamilton. Want I should take it from him?"

"You can try," I growled. One thing about being wiry, you learn how to take down guys that are bigger than you are, although the fireplug could present a challenge, especially if I had to take them on two at once.

"Don't bother, Brownie. He's not here to dust me," Mr. Hamilton said with a smirk.

"You're confident," I said. "Send them out."

Mr. Hamilton said, "I prefer to keep my men here when I meet with strangers."

"I can understand that. They make a good argument standing by your side," I said. "But Miss McIntyre sent me over to discuss something personal. Red roses."

Mr. Hamilton turned a little pale, but there was no sag to him. "Brownie, Stevens. Wait out there."

Brownie was the gunnie who could blend with a crowd; Stevens turned out to be the fireplug. He wasn't much of a conversationalist, so far he hadn't said a thing, he just nodded and went to the door.

When they were gone, I said, "Why did you ask Phil Martin to hire Marguerite Saint-Ville?"

"Right to the point. I like that." Mr. Hamilton leaned back like he was planning to dance around it. "Mr. Martin is an associate of mine—"

"You lent him your wallet to start Topaz and Zircon," I

interrupted. "But you must have other resources. Why him?"

Mr. Hamilton stared at me as if deciding how much to spill. Finally, he said, "I trust him."

"Don't you trust your other associates?"

"Mr. Martin is an honorable man."

Yeah, an honorable crook. Go figure. Not that I had any hard evidence that Martin was a crook, but if he was tied in with Mr. X, you could bet on it. I was.

"So you trusted him to what? Not to jump her? Not to sell her to whoever was after her?"

"Both of those, yes. And he has security at his clubs. As long as she stayed there…." Mr. Hamilton looked blank, completely empty.

"It's harder to protect someone than to kill them. You'd need an army to meet all eventualities."

"Yeah."

"So who was after her?"

"She never told me," Mr. Hamilton said. "I asked. She never told me."

"Did she know you were her father?"

Mr. Hamilton tried to stare me down. He didn't succeed. "Lily must trust you."

"I figured it out on my own. She just confirmed it."

"Where did I go wrong?"

"You fucked up big time letting Lily get away from you in 1930," I said. I could have kicked myself if I wasn't afraid that Mr. Hamilton might join in. I mean, getting mouthy with a man with his connections isn't usually a good way to stay healthy. Since he'd made it big, he'd left off carrying a gun on a daily basis, but I'm pretty sure he knew where to find one. Or he could just whistle for his goons.

However, my crack startled a chuckle out of him once he decided how to take it. "You're right about that. I'll rephrase it. What I meant was, how did you tumble to it?"

I shrugged. Maybe I should open a correspondence school: How to be a private dick in five easy lessons. Print the ads in the back of matchbooks. "Does it matter?"

"I suppose it's a moot point about Marguerite, but Lily—I'm married, you know. I got kids."

"Maybe we could work that out later, not that I moonlight on a lonely hearts column, but right now my priority is the man who killed your daughter, and I'm out to get him."

"I wish you luck. I haven't been able to find out a solitary thing about it. If I could help you I would."

"You didn't help her much, did you?"

He frowned and leaned forward to glare at me. I didn't let him see how it shook me. "Listen, there were reasons…. If I let it get out I had a daughter—an *illegitimate* daughter—it would have been open season on Marguerite. Blackmail, one of my rivals putting the snatch on her— I'd have had to hire that army you mentioned to keep her safe."

"Maybe you should have. It didn't work out so well the way you handled it, did it?"

A spasm of pain crossed his face, and for the first time, I saw how hard her death had hit him. "No, it didn't."

I waited till the mask slipped back into place. "Don't you have your ear to the criminal ground in Vegas? No rumors, anecdotes, bragging rights?"

He looked startled. "Now that you mention it, no."

"What was Captain Woods doing here?"

That hit a nerve. "Why shouldn't he be here?" Mr. Hamilton snapped. "As a leading citizen of Las Vegas and a major business owner—"

"I just thought he might be sharing some theory about the killer," I said mildly. "He *is* investigating the murder, isn't he?"

"Oh, I see. No, he wasn't here for that, but Woods has assured me that the police are doing all they can. He doesn't like to leave an unsolved murder on the books."

"So he does have some idea who did it," I probed.

"He seems to think she was seeing some man at the club where she was working. Mr. Martin says that she wasn't." Mr. Hamilton scowled like he wasn't sure who to believe.

I wondered if he knew exactly what kind of club Phil Martin was running. I was guessing not, seeing as he seemed pretty easygoing about his daughter working there.

"So Miss Saint-Ville strolled in here one day, not knowing you're her pop, and said, I want to walk on the wild side, can you get me a job singing in one of your henchmen's clubs?"

Mr. Hamilton reddened. "Not exactly. She was maddeningly complacent with me, thinking that I was just another older man who wanted to date her. She flirted with me after I made the mistake of giving her some diamond earrings for her birthday. I'd promised Lily I wouldn't tell her until we could talk to her together, when the time was right, but it was driving me crazy. Anyway, Marguerite called me one night from the Jungle Room; she was terrified. I couldn't go myself, so I sent a car for her."

"Why couldn't you go? Too busy?" I knew I was being offensive, but I wanted to make him talk, even if he was yelling.

Hamilton glared at me. "She's afraid some guy is out to get her. If I send two armed goons to pick her up and bring her to me, she'll panic, thinking she's out of the frying pan into the fire. I mentioned Martin to her, and she found him on her own. Brownie volunteered to make sure she got there alive and trailed after her but dropped her when she made it to Topaz. I thought she'd be safe with Phil Martin." He ended on a faintly resentful note.

"She probably would have been, if she'd stayed put," I said, hoping to put in a good word for my dream guy, even though he wasn't mine and never would be.

"She had Lily's waywardness, but not enough knowledge of the world to keep herself safe," Mr. Hamilton said. He rubbed his eyes wearily. "Marguerite had a thing for bad boys. It's always the same with sweet girls like that. Sweet but stubborn."

Seemed to me she took after her old man more than he was

willing to admit. "So she met some other bad boy and went out to meet him?"

"I don't know. She was told to stay inside the club until Phil got there to take her home, but that night she disappeared, and no one there knew to stop her. Phil regularly makes the rounds of all my clubs, you know. He would take her home last thing."

"Seems like she had Lily's talent too," I suggested. He seemed to need a chance to talk about her.

He grabbed onto it eagerly. "She had it in spades. For Lily it was dancing. For Marguerite it was the urge to sing. You couldn't stop her from grabbing the spotlight. It would have been like standing in front of a freight train and holding out your hand, shouting, 'Stop!' Headstrong."

"Like you," I murmured.

"My kids may not have gotten my brains, but they got that."

We could argue about the brains, but what was the point? I was willing to grant that he had some, given his success in business, but his brains sure seemed to turn to water where his daughter was concerned. I wouldn't be surprised if he was feeling guilty toward Lily as well, after the way he handled Marguerite's cry for help.

I took out a card and put it on his desk. "If you think of anything else, give me a call. I'm open twenty-four hours." Well, I wasn't really, I had to sleep sometime, but it sounded good, and at least my service was and they could always wake me up if it was an emergency.

My mind was spinning; why would Captain Woods even allude to a potential boyfriend at the club if he weren't prepared to back it up? Or did he mean this other joker she ran out to meet? Could it be Bert Guthrie after all? Did Captain Woods care about him enough to protect him? Maybe just because he was a cop and a cop had to be protected at all cost?

"What are you going to do next?"

"Miss McIntyre gave me the keys to Miss Saint-Ville's place," I said.

"If there's anything you need, anything at all," Mr. Hamilton said heavily, "I have resources."

"Thanks, I'll keep that in mind."

Mr. Hamilton nodded and swiveled his chair to stare out the window. The meet was over. I got up and left. And felt lucky to be able to.

ONE more errand before I went to Marguerite's apartment. Of course, if it had panned out, I might not have had to go.

I found Frankie's Florist on South 5th Street. If only Frankie had been one of us, meaning queer, I might have gotten a better description of the jasper that sent Marguerite the roses. But there was no Frankie. Instead, there was Fannie, an older lady, plump and friendly but so farsighted that her eyes looked huge behind her glasses as she peered at me across the counter. She must have needed them for her flower arranging, but I'm sure she would never have recognized me if she'd seen me on the street.

She was willing enough to flap her gums. Fannie told me that the man who ordered the nightly roses was tall and dark-haired, but as she barely cleared five feet herself, that could be considered a very relative description. It could have been me. I was just an inch short of six feet. It could have been Phil Martin or Jazz Morgan. Hell, it could have been Stevens, the fireplug.

She also told me that Frankie had been her brother, who had died five years ago. She'd always meant to change the name but never got around to it. Frankie and Fannie. You have to wonder about some parents, maybe trying to get up their own vaudeville act.

Okay, chalk one up for the killer of Rose Red. He'd chosen a blind florist with seeming care, and it appeared that was going to pay off in protecting his identity.

I thanked her and left.

Fannie did give me the names of several other men who had sent flowers from her place to Marguerite. Given what Suzy the topless dancer had said about Margie liking them married, that gave me and the cops a lot of space to move around in. Plenty of married men in Vegas who ran around on the side.

With the help of the phone book, I tracked down the few names Fannie had given me. These guys were nervous, scared of their own shadows. They didn't qualify as bad boys, and I couldn't imagine they'd held Margie's interest for long, seeing as she went for a challenge. They also didn't seem the type to strangle a dame in an alley, although I wasn't ready to strike them off the list without an alibi. The last guy got blustery with me and claimed he'd already given this information to the cops, and what was the deal? Without actually telling him I was with the cops, it amused me to leave him with the impression that I was checking up on them. But he had a good alibi with long legs and saucy eyes that he didn't want his wife to find out about. I checked her out, and he was in the clear.

Chapter 6: Hide and Seek, and Sprung

THE art of disguise can be as simple as you make it. False beards are old hat. I'd found that if you carried a clipboard or a toolbox, most people thought you were there on legitimate business, and they wouldn't stop to ask questions no matter what you did.

I found Marguerite's apartment building in a nice neighborhood, with big trees lining the streets. Quiet. Neighbors were at work and kids were in school. There weren't a lot of people visible. I parked around the corner and walked back wearing my disguise, which consisted of coveralls and a jacket with Rick's Plumbing spelled out on the back to cover my holster. I had a toolbox in my hand as I approached the downstairs door. But it wasn't just plumbing tools I had with me.

Using the key Lily had given me, I unlocked the vestibule door. The bank of mailboxes was on the left, before you reached the elevator. Margie's was stuffed. I guess Lily hadn't thought to have the mail forwarded. I opened it up, using the smaller key on the ring, and went through it. Mostly circulars and bills from department stores. I crammed it back into the box and locked it. Nothing for me.

I walked up the stairs, not wanting the elevator boy to remember me. Marguerite lived on the fourth floor at the top. The apartment had that empty feel that they get when the occupant hasn't been there for a while. If I'd wanted to take up housework, the furniture needed a good dusting, but other than that it was tidy. When she'd handed over the key, Lily told me she couldn't bear to clear up her daughter's things just yet.

Marguerite Saint-Ville had lived up to her name in decorating her apartment. It was a little overwrought for my taste. Curtains trimmed heavily with fringe, gold-framed mirrors and crystal chandeliers in the living room. The walls were painted Nile green, which probably made a nice foil for Marguerite's coloring, while all the furniture was covered in white satin, with pink velvet pillows chucked everywhere.

I could picture her languishing on the divan in a negligee with a drink in her hand, trying on her idea of sophisticated. I bet she learned it where we all did, the movies. If she'd still been alive, I could imagine sharing a laugh over it with Lily, but Marguerite was so young, it was tragically pathetic. Considering Lily's impeccable taste, maybe Marguerite would have grown out of it eventually.

But I wasn't here to scope the place out for *Better Homes and Gardens*. This was Marguerite's refuge, and I had to hope that somewhere, she'd left a clue as to who all these nameless but dangerous boyfriends were. From what Suzy Velvour and Max Hamilton had told me, I got the feeling she had the itch for older men. Maybe from growing up without a father, but maybe people would say the reason I was queer was due to the same thing. Sometimes people were just people, no rhyme or reason to it.

The living room was a wash; it looked like a movie set and was about as personal. The kitchen was small, and the only thing I learned there was Margie didn't cook. She didn't own a single pot or pan, not even a percolator for coffee. She did have a collection of takeaway menus, though. The freezer needed defrosting, but other than that, it was empty except for an empty ice cube tray stuck in the ice.

Dining room, bathroom, and linen closet all came up zero. That left the bedroom, the inner sanctum. It made sense if there were anything personal, that's where she would have kept it.

I was thorough. I even stripped the bed and lifted the mattress to check under it, which was no easy task, given the canopy draped with fussy silk curtains trimmed with velvet ball fringe. Then I had to struggle with the dust ruffle so it hung straight when I made the bed again. Her closet gave off the faint scent of roses. Her clothes hung there neatly arranged in the colors of the rainbow, with her shoes lined up below. I noticed she favored stilettos, like her mother. Her underwear was organized in silk-lined boxes inside the bureau drawers.

I don't know if the police had asked Lily to leave everything alone, or it was just that she couldn't stand to visit the apartment now that her daughter was dead, but on Marguerite's vanity amongst the bottles of perfume, next to a framed and signed photo of Lily smiling (not the same one she'd given me), stood a jewel box. I looked over the contents of the case; I'm no expert on gemstones, but Suzy was right. There weren't any rhinestones, at least as far as I could tell.

In the bottom drawer I found some letters, but they were all from Lily, written over a number of years and placed in a velvet box that had probably held chocolates at one time. I made a note to tell Lily about that. Evidently whatever trouble there was between them, Marguerite still felt some connection to her mother. Either she didn't keep any of her bills or she didn't pay them herself, because the letters were the only reading material other than a few glossy magazines in the living room.

Maybe she had no secrets or they were too dire for her to reveal them even to herself. No keepsakes, letters, cards, not even a bouquet of dead flowers. It was like she had created a setting for the woman she wanted to be. Her mother's high heels might have been too big for her to fill, and I got the picture of a young girl tottering around in them, not knowing quite how to deal. Maybe once there had been some other evidence and she tossed it. Or maybe someone else had.

I was just closing the drawer when I heard the click of a key in the lock. The closet was too easy; whoever it was would look there first thing. There was a fire escape outside the bedroom window, but I'd never manage to fight my way past the heavy drapes in time to make it out of there unnoticed. I imagined getting twisted up in them and hanging there like a helpless target for whomever walked in. I opted for hiding under the bed.

Even though I had a right to be there, it might turn out to be more profitable to see who was sneaking in and why. It could be the building manager. If it turned out to be Lily coming to keep tabs on me, I'd just look like a fool. Or I could pretend I was searching under the bed.

I grabbed my toolbox and slid under the bed on the far side from the door. Hopefully that would give the damned ruffle time to stop shaking with my movement. Marguerite had stored a vast collection of shoeboxes under the bed, and I managed to maneuver them in front of me, so if he wasn't careful about looking, he might miss me.

I was grateful that I'd formed the habit of putting everything back exactly as I found it while searching instead of tossing a joint and leaving a big mess to clue him in to the fact that someone had been there.

Peering out from under the dust ruffle, I could see a pair of black men's shoes, polished to a high shine. So it wasn't Lily coming to check up on me, unless my take on her was dead wrong. My heart was thundering in my chest, and I tried to keep my breathing slow and easy. Didn't want to give myself away by gasping like a fish out of water.

A deep sigh sent a shiver up my spine, and I curled my fingers around my gun for comfort. I thought for sure he was going to peek under the bed, but he didn't. He seemed to be sniffing the air. Maybe he was smelling the same rose scent I had. Eventually the shoes moved away out of my line of sight. I heard him open drawers and the closet doors—I was right about that, at least. Don't hide in the closet. Too obvious.

He seemed to know the place, which aroused my curiosity. If he'd been there before, he should have known where she kept it, whatever it was that he was searching for. It was a long five minutes waiting under that bed to be discovered.

Then his footsteps went out of the room, and I couldn't hear anything. I really wanted a squint at his face, but he might have been standing right in the doorway, waiting for me to come out. I couldn't see his shoes any more.

What the hell, Vegas is a gambling town, and I was willing to take a chance. Of course, not being an idiot, I squirmed out from under the bed on the side away from the door. I crawled on my elbows to the end of the bed and peered around the corner.

Wherever he was, he wasn't in the doorway. I got up and crossed the room silently, flattening myself on the wall behind the door and peering through the crack. Nothing. I caught a sound from the living room. I edged around the door and stuck my head out of the room just enough to catch a movement in the mirror at the end of the hallway. He was standing by the front door with his back to me, letting himself out. He was tall and he had dark hair, but that was all I got, because like an animal that senses danger, he started to turn but thought better of it and darted out the door, while I stood there with my gun cradled in both hands by my cheek.

I heard him shut the door and lock it. Lock it? He had a key? So he didn't pick the lock to get in here. Maybe Marguerite had given it to him, or maybe he took it when he killed her. After a few minutes, I heard faint footsteps on the walkway outside and crossed to the window in time to see him standing there, staring up at the window. I knew, with the lacy curtains under the heavy drapes and the fact that it was light outside, that he couldn't see in, but it felt like his eyes were boring holes in me. I didn't dare take a step back for fear the movement would confirm his suspicions. At last he got into a car and drove away. He wasn't driving a police car; it was an anonymous black Ford.

Of course I recognized the man. It would have been hard to mistake him for anyone else because of his height and black curly hair. It was my old friend, Big Billy Woods, captain of the police.

Why would the captain of the police need to sneak into Marguerite's apartment to search it? He had a right to be there. He had a murder to investigate, although coming here alone was a bit weird. And if he wanted it searched, he could have sent flatties to do that. And why did he have a key? That one was easy: evidence from the crime scene. All he had to do was help himself if he wanted to get in.

If it hadn't been him, if it were some other guy, would I have gone down and tackled him? Not likely. I had no evidence that he'd done anything criminal and no way to make him talk.

I scanned the bedroom, checking it against the picture I'd made in my head when I first came in. I couldn't see that anything had been taken. I have a good visual memory, and to the best of my recollection, everything was just the same as I'd left it.

I opened the drawers and checked them over. Items had been slightly rearranged, but nothing was gone. Then I opened the jewel box, and that's where I found it. Captain Woods hadn't snuck in here to take something; he'd come here to plant something. I lifted it by the chain. It was an unusual one, one bar of silver alternating with three little links, then another bar and so on. But what made the necklace special was the pendant, a circle of silver with a musical clef note in the center. Now that I had it in my hand, I could see that the symbol was formed by a tiny dragon, twisted around to form the clef. I recognized it from the photo Reggie had accidentally included in his package, the one that he'd taken back of his not-boyfriend Jazz.

I went to the window in time to see Captain Woods's car pull up to the curb across the street again. That's when I realized he was alone. Usually he had that ferret Guthrie trailing after him like they were handcuffed together.

Something must have made Woods suspicious; maybe I'd left an item out of place, or maybe he heard me breathing after all. Or maybe he just wanted to be on hand to make sure that the necklace he planted was found as fast as possible. I saw his hand reach for something on the dashboard and bring it closer to his mouth. He had a radio transmitter, even though he was driving an unmarked car. He might have decided to call for reinforcements. If he was coming back in, I needed to be somewhere else and fast.

When I saw two black and whites pull up and a bunch of officers spilled out like a Chinese fire drill, I recognized my old pal Reggie first by the camera around his neck. I didn't know the other three, and Guthrie was noticeably absent. The cops didn't even glance toward Big Billy's car, so maybe they didn't know he'd called them in from across the street.

If Big Billy had realized someone was in the apartment, it was a good play to trap me and discover the necklace at the same time. But the moment was past for intellectual appreciation of the niceties of the situation; I had to scram.

A disguise can only do so much. To someone who didn't know me, the plumbing gear would take the place of a real description, but Captain Woods knew my face too well. And he wasn't stupid; he could put two and two together. If I came strolling out the front door of the building, he'd know I wasn't there to sell tickets to the policeman's ball.

I figured with that many men, they would have both the stairs and the elevator covered. I couldn't go down, so the only way was up. I collected my toolbox and closed Margie's door behind me without checking to see if it was locked. If Captain Woods's story was that there was a break-in, that would just play into it.

I could hear footsteps starting up the stairs and cat-footed it up to the roof. I went out the door and eased it shut. Being as this was a ritzy building, there were large air conditioning units on the roof in addition to the water tank. Plenty of cover if the cops were feeling energetic enough to make the climb. I was betting that they weren't.

They were probably wondering why Captain Woods sent them in again, like he didn't trust that his men had put forth their best effort the first time. Of course, since they'd already searched the place once after the body was discovered, they would just be going through the motions. If he wanted the necklace found, he would have to make sure of it himself. Or maybe this was their regular M.O.: can't find the crook who did it, return to find evidence "overlooked" the first time and pin it on some guy who deserved to go away anyway.

I inched my head above the parapet and looked down. Big Billy's car was still there. Nothing outdoors was moving. I wondered how long it would take them and how hard they would look. My guess was they had to make it look good for the boss, because it was over an hour later before they emerged and drove away. And still Big Billy sat in his car waiting.

My stomach was beginning to think my throat had been cut, but better I should starve to death than fill up on bullets from Big Billy's gun. He was still down there. I was betting that when the report came back to him that the cops had come up empty, he would go back inside Marguerite's place and check it out for himself to see why they missed it.

If only I'd put money down on a wager with myself, I could have cleaned up big time. He waited another hour and then went back inside. I enjoyed picturing Captain Woods cursing while he searched the joint for something he was never going to find while my heart rate slowed down to normal. I have to get my simple pleasures where I can. Ten minutes later he came out and drove off. I could tell by the way he strode to his car that he was angry, but I didn't have time to gloat.

This was my chance to get off the roof and take it on the lam. So I hoofed it down all four flights and out onto the street, walking fast around the corner to my car. The meter had lapsed a long time ago, and there was a ticket on the windshield. Normally I just tore them up, but I was going to pay that one and fast. The wheels of bureaucracy may grind exceedingly slowly, but I didn't need some eager beaver sending up a report that my car had been in the vicinity on that fateful day. Someday I was gonna meet that meter maid and give her what for.

I WENT back to my office to ditch my coveralls and mull everything over.

Only three people knew about my plans to search Marguerite's place: Lily, who'd given me the key, Celestine, her maid, and Mr. Max Hamilton.

One thing I believed about Lily; she wanted her daughter's killer found, so I couldn't see her confiding in Captain Woods, not if she didn't think the cops were making an effort. If Celestine was in Big Billy's pocket because she had a secret, desperate crush on him, I should just turn in my detective's license now and look for another line of work.

That left Mr. Max Hamilton. I had evidence that he knew the Captain; I'd seen Big Billy coming out of Mr. Hamilton's office. It didn't have to mean that Mr. Hamilton was trying to stop me; maybe Big Billy called back and asked what I was doing there.

I bounced up out of my chair all of a sudden. Told you it helped me think. One the things sitting in the chair revealed to me was that I didn't have time to sit in it pondering the subtleties of how Big Billy knew I was searching Marguerite's apartment. If he planted something, confidently expecting either me or his bully-boys to find it, he wasn't just going to shrug off his disappointment and call it a day.

He had a plan for that necklace, and he had to get it back into his possession, which meant he was going to make me cough it up if he could. He might be on the way over here right now, and there I was, sitting at my desk playing with it like an idiot.

I thought of hightailing it out of there and parking the necklace with Lily, but I didn't want to set Captain Woods on her tail. She had enough trouble. There was no one else I could think of that I would wish this on either.

I heard the slam of car doors down on the street and peeked through the blinds. I was right, the cops were here, and I was sure they were on their way up to my office. I slipped the pendant off the chain, redid the clasp, and put the necklace back on over my head. I could hear them on the stairs.

I went to my file cabinet: M for Marguerite or R for Rose Red? I opted for Marguerite and slid the pendant behind the card labeled "L through O" that sat in the metal slot on the front of the cabinet, hoping it wouldn't be obvious. Hoping no one was going to look that hard. On second thought, I jammed the disc with the Lambda symbol in as well. No point taking unnecessary chances that someone might recognize it. That would just give them another reason to cook my goose.

I was sitting at my desk with my feet up when they burst in. I'd had just enough time to stuff the chain down inside the collar of my shirt before they didn't knock.

"Wow, the top fuzz calling on me. To what do I owe the honor?" I kind of belted that out, I was panting so hard, but my smirk annoyed both Captain Woods *and* Lieutenant Steele. Score one for the dick, two cops with one flip.

To my dismay, I saw they'd brought two flatties along. One was a pudgy number I didn't know, but the other was my old friend Reggie Harding. He was giving me the flat, stony-eyed cop stare, but I knew he would rather have been helping little old ladies across the street than be here rousting me. He held a truncheon in his hand that I didn't like the look of.

"A surprise party for me? It's not even my birthday," I said.

Lieutenant Steele looked angry, but Big Billy had a mean smile on his face as he leaned over and slapped my feet off the desk.

"Stand up, Randall."

"Why, is there going to be dancing?"

Big Billy's face darkened, while Reggie turned and looked out into the hallway, and I'm sure it wasn't because he was keeping a lookout. Maybe the idea of Big Billy in a clinch with a guy struck him as funny as it did me.

Lieutenant Steele was unusually quiet.

Big Billy reached across the desk and grabbed my tie, yanking me to my feet. He loomed over me menacingly.

"Hey, that's a new tie," I protested, trying to pull it out of his hand.

He shook me like a rat, and I smacked his hand away.

"Try that again and I'll run you in for assaulting an officer of the law," he threatened. "Steele, you're my witness."

Lieutenant Steele turned his back and said, "Sorry, sir, I was looking the other way."

I almost goggled at him. Lieutenant Steele sticking up for me in even that minor a fashion made this a red-letter day. I would have to note it on my calendar and send him some flowers on our anniversary.

"Garrett, Harding, you saw him."

"No sir, sorry sir," Reggie said.

I wanted to wink at him to thank him, but I was in enough trouble as it was. No need to deal him in on it.

"If you wanted my help on a case, Captain Woods, all you had to do was call. I would have come down—" I was cut off short when he shook me again. His manhandling me must have made the chain come out of my shirt, because his gaze dropped, and he snatched the chain off my neck with his other hand.

"Where did you get this?"

"I went to a store, paid down my money—" I started.

"Don't give me that. This is evidence in a murder. Where is the pendant?"

"Murder? What murder? I never had—"

"Don't play dumb with me, you lousy punk!" Big Billy raised his mitt to smack me across the face and then hesitated. "The chain broke. Is it down your shirt?"

"*You* broke it, and there was never any pendant," I lied, staring him in the eyes.

He yanked the knot out of my tie and ripped the buttons off my shirt pulling it open. When nothing fell out, he snarled at the two cops, "Find it. He didn't have time to ditch it. Take this place apart while I take him apart."

I didn't much like the sound of that. While I was confident I could have handled him if I'd met him in a dark alley with no witnesses around, he'd already tied my hands by promising to arrest me for assault if I fought back. I looked at Lieutenant Steele. Clearly he didn't approve of the direction this was going in, but he wasn't going to help me more than he had already. I didn't blame him.

Reggie and Garrett started their search on the file cabinet, carefully keeping their eyes averted from the action.

"If you tell me what you're looking for I'll help you all I can. I always like to support our local boys in blue—"

I bent over, gasping for air after Big Billy landed a punch just under my ribs on the right side.

"You broke into the apartment of a murder victim and stole evidence in an ongoing investigation. That's obstructing justice. I want it back."

I blew air in and out till I could speak again. "I didn't break in anywhere."

"So you admit you were there!" he roared triumphantly.

"Where?"

"Don't play games with me, peeper. You were at Marguerite Saint-Ville's apartment today."

"What little bird told you that?" I taunted. I had an idea that he was trying to get me to deny things he hadn't even accused me of so he could trap me. But apparently he didn't share that idea. He balled up his hand into a ham-like fist again. His idea was that if he hit me enough, eventually I'd give him what he wanted to get him to stop. It had some merit. I just hoped he'd wear out first.

He hit me again in the same spot, sending me crashing over my chair and onto the floor. I didn't make a sound other than my huffing and puffing to catch my breath; I wouldn't give him the satisfaction.

When I could talk again, I said, "Was that you parked across the street?"

Big Billy flicked a quick glance at Lieutenant Steele, but the lieutenant was too savvy to reveal any reaction to my jibe, even though I'm sure he was intrigued. He didn't miss much, but he didn't give it away, either.

"Listen, I know you were there. You took something out of that apartment, and I want it back," Big Billy said softly, his eyes narrowed.

"If it was evidence, why didn't you bag it when your boys first searched the place?" I asked. "Or maybe it wasn't there yet for them to find."

He stepped over, grabbed my shirt, hauled me to my feet, and punched me again, sending me flying into the file cabinet this time. I hoped the impact wouldn't dislodge the pendant from under the card, and my luck held. Maybe he was thinking the third time would be the charm, but I wished he'd find another spot. He was good with his hands, I'd give him that, always landing his right on the same spot, but I'd had worse.

I saw Reggie's fists clench and shook my head slightly at him before taunting Big Billy. "Was that you under the bed, then?" I gasped.

Big Billy frowned, and I thought he was going to pound me again or maybe even kick me. I think he thought so too, but Lieutenant Steele intervened.

"Someone called in a tip, Randall. Said there was a B and E at the Saint-Ville apartment. We went down to check it out."

"And you found me inside?"

Lieutenant Steele growled at me. "Of course not, you moron, you'd be in jail if we had!"

"So this same little bird also told you if you came down to my office you would find a nice surprise waiting for you here instead?"

"Maybe we should take you in and give you a going-over to help your memory!" Big Billy said.

"No, Captain. If there *was* evidence in that apartment, it's useless now that it's been removed," Lieutenant Steele said. "Let's give him some rope."

I could see the wheels turning in Captain Woods's head again, trying to find a way to turn this to his advantage. Or maybe just coming up with another angle. He glared at the lieutenant, and it was clear they had differing points of view on police procedure.

"Right, men. We're done here. Let's go." Captain Woods kicked the trashcan over as he turned to go, which was just petty, because it didn't harm me other than that I'd have to pick up all the balled up paper and put it back in. It struck me that he was pretty damn confident that I hadn't made any notes, or he'd be looking through the trash. And maybe the file cabinet too. In fact, he didn't seem to be too interested in anything else I might have had hidden on the premises in his urgency to get his hands on the pendant.

"Thanks for coming, call ahead next time and I'll have it catered," I said from my spot on the floor where I lay gasping, and I raised a limp hand to wave goodbye.

"You'd clown on your way to your own funeral!" Lieutenant Steele sounded irritated, but his lips twitched like he thought I was actually pretty funny.

Reggie and Garrett marched out behind Captain Woods, staring rigidly ahead.

But Lieutenant Steele stayed behind. "Look, peeper, we've been on the case since it happened. Did you talk to the apartment manager while you were there?"

I shook my head. "Incognito. Besides, you know how they are. Most of them won't give a private dick the time of day."

"Interesting thing. Marguerite Saint-Ville never paid her rent."

"So why didn't they kick her out?"

"I didn't say the rent wasn't paid, but so far we don't have a whiff of whoever was keeping her. Manager says she never had boyfriends up to her place."

"Maybe the meal ticket had a good reason not to show," I said. I had a feeling maybe Lily might have been paying the rent, but no point telling Lieutenant Steele that. Later on, he might get pissed at how much I was squeezing out of him while holding out on him, but he might never actually find out.

"Or maybe someone told the manager to forget what he saw."

I was about to remind him that I hadn't seen the manager when I realized he wasn't talking about me. "Papers razzing the force about covering up for someone too important to go to jail for murder?"

"Yeah, they think we're keeping the lid on."

"And are you?"

"I'm going to pretend I didn't hear that." He marched to the door and paused as he was closing it. To my surprise, he gave me a wink. "You might be half as tough as you think you are."

"Tougher," I muttered.

"Nuts," he returned, and then he was gone too.

I eased myself up to lean against the file cabinet and rubbed my ribs inside my open shirt, coughing. Through all this, they hadn't taken my gun, so when the door swung open I reached for it, relaxing when I saw it was only Artie. "No thanks, we don't want any."

"I don't got any. Why you sitting on the floor?" he asked.

"Sometimes I like a change of view," I said.

"He worked you over nice. No punching the kisser where it would show," Artie said. He went and sat in my chair, studying my torso with a knowledgeable eye. He was a pug, he knew bruises. "Gonna have a few marks."

"I'm thinking of starting a collection," I said, fondly remembering the bruise Phil Martin had left on my bicep. It had been a lot more fun collecting that one.

"Got a bottle?"

"Lower right hand drawer." Just my luck, I get belted around by the cops and then Artie comes by to suck up my booze. "This is the worst party I've ever been to."

"Be happy they didn't take you in." Artie took a swig and then, to my surprise, came around the desk and squatted beside me, offering me the bottle.

I took a drink, and the burn of the liquor made the burn of the punches fade a bit. "How did you know they were here?"

"Saw them ride up on their black and white chargers."

"Oh." Somehow Artie had a nose for trouble. He had a way of turning up in the oddest places, although normally I didn't think of my office as that odd. "Artie, you ever heard of a colored guy called Jazz Morgan?"

Artie sat next to me on the floor, leaning on the cabinet. "Yeah, he comes by the gym sometimes."

"I heard he boxes."

"Yeah, he could be good, but he's too careful of his hands."

"Well, he's a musician. Plays piano," I explained. I wrestled the bottle back from Artie and took another slug.

"Ah, that explains it. Don't want to damage the dollar-earning digits," Artie said, taking firm possession of the bottle again.

I pulled my shirt together and tucked it back into my pants. "Alliteration."

"Male or female?"

"What?"

"That literature thing, male or female?" Artie tried to look smart.

"Never mind." Weird how he could come out with them sometimes. "You ever hear of Jazz knocking a broad around? Or a fella? Ever get mad enough in the ring to start whaling on someone?"

"Nope. Like I say, he's careful of his hands."

"What about someone on the cops? Ever hear of someone rousting a hooker?"

"That would be telling," Artie said.

"Yeah, that's why I'm asking. So you'll tell me," I pointed out.

"Cops sometimes have a temper too, you know that."

I sighed. Considering I'd just been the main exhibit in a demonstration of a cop having a temper tantrum—but no use being subtle with Artie, although maybe I should try more alliteration. "You ever heard anything hinky about Big Billy? Or Bert Guthrie?"

Artie gave me a sly look. "Say I have? What's in it for me?"

"Just spit it out, Artie."

"Look, he's not a good man to cross."

"Why's that?" As I thought, given a chance to air his grievance, Artie was off.

"He likes to box too, but he likes to use a live bag. And you know where the station is?"

I rolled my eyes. Of *course* I knew where the station was. I was kind of in the same biz. But I just nodded. I was still trying to get my right and proper quotient of air after having it squeezed out of me like a tube of toothpaste.

"Right near Block 16," Artie said with a leer.

"So he goes there?"

"Stomping out crime wherever he sees it. Just has to sample it first sometimes, to make sure it really is a crime." Artie tightened his lips. "This won't stand up in court, right? And I won't swear to it."

"Come on, Artie. I just need to know."

"He doesn't approve of what they do, but he's a guy. He's got needs. He uses his size to scare them into doing what he wants. He don't like it when they got different opinions to his after he asks for their company."

"How do you know?"

"I seen the marks after he left."

I rubbed my ribs again. "Yeah, I noticed that too. Got a reach like a baboon and a forceful argument at the ends of both arms."

"You mean his fists?"

Maybe I was wrong. He really wasn't that bright. "Yeah, I mean his fists. Which one?"

"Which one what?"

"Goes to Block 16, Woods or Guthrie?"

"Maybe both. And besides, they ain't the only ones. Seen your pal Reggie there a time or two."

That shook me. Why would Reggie—but maybe it was for cover. If the whole police department trooped over there on a regular basis.... Or duh, maybe he went there to arrest someone. He was a cop, after all, and technically hooking was against the law, although not so much that you'd notice in Vegas.

"You going to sit here all day?"

"Artie, did anyone see you come in here?"

"No one ever notices me," he said.

That made me kinda sad. Maybe that's why we were still friends, sort of. I took note of him. Not too many people did. I even went to his fights if I happened to be free. "Can you get out of here without anyone noticing?"

"Of course," he said. Interesting to see he took pride in that. "I'm a pro."

"I need you to hold something for me."

"Why don't *you* just take it out?" he asked suspiciously.

"Captain Woods wants it. He's going to have someone so close behind me they'll be standing in my shadow. If he rumbles that I've got this, he'll take it from me and a killer will go free," I said earnestly.

"And you'll lose your fee."

"Yeah, and possibly I won't be breathing so good any more, either," I snapped.

I saw him work out what that meant. "So, if you're alive to earn this fee…" he said suggestively.

"There's a C-note in it for you." That was a month's dirty wages for Artie. I knew if I offered more he'd get too suspicious about how dangerous it was, and I needed him to smuggle that pendant out for me.

"Done," he said promptly, with a happy gleam in his eyes. "How heavy is it and where do I bring it to you?"

I grinned. "Bring it to that queer club, down by the train yard."

He glanced out the window. It was getting dark already. "When?"

"Say in an hour." That would give me time to go home and put on another shirt. I wasn't really keen to stumble into Lambda flashing my chest hair down to my navel, especially after that one guy tried to edge me into the restroom. Too obvious.

"Can you get me inside?"

I looked at Artie, in his worn jeans and T-shirt, covered by an ugly plaid jacket. And his ugly shoes. "Don't push your luck."

"Come on, Grey, do a guy a favor—"

"I'll try," I said. But I knew if he managed to smuggle the pendant there for me, I'd get him in somehow. Even if I had to hand him the one membership disc I had through the bathroom window after I was inside.

"Thanks. You're a pal." He rubbed his hands gleefully. "Hot flutes, ready to make sweet, sweet music. Bring on the band."

He stood up and held out a hand to me. I was grateful for it; I was already starting to stiffen up from the blows. Once on my feet, I slid the L to O card up and freed the disc and pendant from the metal holder.

I showed the pendant to him. "Don't lose this, it's important. Or the case is blown."

"Okay," he said, without urgency. He took off his watch, opened the back, dropped the pendant in, and shut it, strapping his watch on again as if he hadn't just come up with the best hiding place ever. Why hadn't I thought of that? "Okay, I'm outta here."

"How did you think of putting it there?"

Artie gave me a sly look. "Seen a guy do it a couple times."

"What guy?"

"Some guy."

Apparently Artie was no longer in a talkative mood. "Okay. See you later, Artie."

I returned to my chair to give him time to get clear. I really should have cleaned up the office, but I had stuff left to do tonight. And probably a tail to lose. The office would have to wait till tomorrow. I got up and locked the door with me on the inside so no one else could stroll in and surprise me. Damn Big Billy anyway. When this case was over, I was going to shoot him, and then I was going to send him the bill for having a tailor sew all my shirt buttons back on even though I knew how to do it myself.

Now all I had to do was hide the photos of the crime scene that Reggie had given me. I looked them over carefully. There were five photos: one of Margie propped at the end of the alley, showing her and all her belongings; two were close-ups of her face and neck, from different angles; one of her hand on her handbag; and the last one was a close shot of her shoe. It was black and white, but you could see some kind of gunk dried on the heel.

The sixth photo was the one of Jazz and Marguerite that I'd kept hidden from Lily. He was playing piano, and she was singing, looking straight at him with that dreamy look on her face. I guess a big, buffed up colored guy was about the most dangerous man she'd run across yet, at least in her mind. He never saw her. Jazz was looking right into the camera with a similar expression. It made me hope that maybe he was looking at Reggie with that sappy look. If Reggie couldn't see it, well, he was torturing himself worrying that Jazz wasn't into him when maybe that wasn't the case. They say love is blind.

I stuffed the shots back into the envelope. Considering the lack of interest Captain Woods had shown in searching my file cabinet, I could just as well have put them in the L through O drawer in a folder labeled *Marguerite Saint-Ville, crime scene photos*, but instead I took my weights out of the bottom drawer where they were filed under "W" and moved the entire cabinet.

I took the envelope that Reggie had given me and taped it to the floor. Then I moved the cabinet back and returned the weights to the bottom drawer. I tried to rock it, but it was heavy enough to be discouraging to a casual searcher. Besides, usually people don't think of moving the heavy furniture. It seems permanent.

WHEN I made it out of the building, it was still just light enough outside to make it easy to spot Sgt. Bert Guthrie, Captain Woods's loyal and ferrety sidekick. I'd wondered why he hadn't attended the party upstairs; it wasn't often you saw Big Billy tooling around without him. It made me glad I'd hidden the envelope upstairs instead of taking it out to mail to myself, which had been my other idea. If he'd seen me with it in my hand, I'm sure he would have taken it from me even if he had to shoot me to get it.

Guthrie was casually propped in a doorway, stiffly holding a newspaper in front of his face, as if he actually knew how to read. I'd never noticed how outsized his hands were for his body before. I went over and batted the paper down.

"You taking the first shift?"

"You owe me a nickel, you dick!" He seemed upset that I'd ripped his paper, shaking the pages at me.

"I'll go slow, just in case. First I'm going home to change into something decent." I flipped the edge of my shirt, but he wasn't interested in the fact that I'd lost all my buttons. "Then I'm off to the

Flamingo for a night on the town. Going to meet Bugsy Siegel for a drink."

"He's dead, peeper," Sergeant Guthrie said.

"Damn! So that's why he hasn't been returning my calls." I shook my head.

"I heard you thought you were a comedian."

"I try to live up to my reputation," I said modestly.

"Try harder. Maybe I should run you in and you can be tonight's entertainment for the boys down at the station."

"You know, you would have been right at home in Hitler's Germany," I said. I watched his face as the meaning sunk in. "You'd have to work on your moustache a little, but—"

"I *should* take you in!" He dropped the paper and pulled out his gun, aiming it at me with no attempt to hide it.

"Did Big Billy tell you to shoot me in the middle of the street with people watching?" I smirked at him. Annoyingly. And it worked. He *was* annoyed, but he did glance around enough to notice the people staring over at us.

"And if you do, you still wouldn't know where it was. And I couldn't tell you, because I'd be dead."

He went all cagey at that, remembering his assignment. He put the gun away and even attempted a condescending smile. He was going to have to work on that too. "I could throw you up against the wall and frisk you."

"You think Woods didn't already try that? Or maybe you think I just like giving peep shows?" I flapped my shirt at him again.

He poked his finger into my chest to emphasize each word. "You shouldn't mess with the police if you want to stay healthy."

"And you should trim your nails."

He couldn't resist: he darted a glance at his fingers and then growled softly. "Watch your step, shamus. Wouldn't want to see you get hurt."

"So that's why you didn't come up with the captain. I never knew you cared so much," I said. I took out a nickel and flipped it to him.

He dove after it as if after swallowing a thumping from Big Billy, I was just going to toss him the pendant on the street because he scared the bejeebus out of me.

"For the paper," I said.

Guthrie was shaking with rage when he realized what it was. "You'll get yours, *dick!*" he hissed at me.

I shook my head at him. "Empty threats? Big Billy didn't buy himself any bargains when he bought you. So how's the wife?"

"I'm a bachelor, just like my dad. Runs in the family," he said.

I wondered if he realized what he was saying but decided to hold my laughter in until I could enjoy it without breaking a rib. "Your girlfriend then."

"Women. Got no use for 'em." He spat on the sidewalk to make sure his feelings were clear. "Or you either."

"The feeling is mutual, Bertie."

I turned and shuffled away to my car. He made an effort not to be obvious about following me, while I waited courteously for him to remember that tailing a man in a car on foot was doomed for failure. He was doomed anyway, he just didn't know it yet.

While he was getting into his car and starting the engine, I pondered the implications of his statement. He might not have any use for women, but he wasn't queer, I'd bet on it. Maybe Guthrie preferred to rent his girlfriends by the hour. Less wear and tear on everyone, and in Vegas, he could have a new one every time he felt the urge.

Just to show him how it was done, I lost him before I got home. Of course, he knew where I lived, so I had to shake him all over again as soon as I went out, decently clothed for public consumption. For fun I went over to the Flamingo, hoping he'd think I really was meeting someone. I drove into the parking lot, backing into a spot near the front so I would be ready to leave when the time came.

He parked at the other end of the lot, front end in. I led the way inside and lost him amongst the roulette tables and slots. He got a little distracted, getting so fancy with his tailing me from behind machines and trying to eyeball me in the mirrors, I was already ducking outside while he was still maneuvering. I watched him through the window, figuring I had a ten-minute lead while he made sure I wasn't still inside.

I lucked out when a truck came by just as I left, giving me some cover. It would have been fun to stay there and watch him, maybe even instructive, but I had a busy night ahead of me.

I watched my back, taking the long way around. It wouldn't have surprised me if Guthrie had double-teamed me, but if there was another shadow, he must have been doing air reconnaissance. If the cops weren't onto Lambda, I was damned if I was going to lead them there, even though Big Billy seemed like he might be wise to it, as he had a nose for sin. I especially didn't want him there tonight, as I had a feeling I would be seeing Reggie. No way did I want to blow his cover. Although if he were smarter, he'd stay out of there until this caper was over. But who was ever smart when they were thinking with their dick?

Chapter 7: T-Girls and B-Boys

WHEN I parked the car down in the train yard, I had on a clean shirt, dusted off and looking as good as new. At least where people could see it. The bruise on my right side was coming along nicely and promised to be a lovely shade of purple by tomorrow. I wondered if Lily would call it subtle and sophisticated. Not that she was ever going to see it.

I made a strong effort not to scuttle toward the club bent over like a caveman. I wouldn't want anyone to think my primal instincts had gotten the better of me, although the chance of looking at Mr. Martin, AKA Mr. Beautiful, did have certain... *effects* on parts of the anatomy. On the other hand, the spot on my lower right side where Captain Woods had pounded me was starting to hurt, but a limping dick wouldn't strike much terror into the hearts of evildoers.

I didn't bother looking for Artie. Ten to one he was around somewhere. And sure enough, when I got closer to the door, he fell into step beside me.

"You're gonna get me inside, right, Grey?"

"I'll do my best, Artie. Listen, do the cops know about this place?"

"Hell, yeah. Why shouldn't they?" Artie said easily.

"Just a little matter of five years in the slam for being queer," I retorted.

"That's only if you get caught in person doing the dastardly deed," Artie said. "And even then, you pretty much have to be the one taking it up the ass. If you're just standing there getting blown, it's not such a big deal. If you know how to deal."

I laughed. I'd have thought Artie only went in for the big deals, if you get my drift.

"So how does this place survive without its customers getting rousted?"

"Are you for real, Grey? You call yourself a hard-bitten dick, and here I bet you believe in fairies too." Artie went off in a fit of laughter that ended with a hoarse cough. Sometimes he liked his own crappy jokes too much.

Okay, maybe I got a chuckle out of the crack about fairies too. "You're saying the cops are on the take?"

"Give me a break. Everybody in Vegas sucks on the casino tit," Artie said. "This kind of club is nickel and dime stuff."

"Where do you learn all this stuff?"

"I probably spend more time in men's rooms than you do."

No doubt about that. "So how is it done? Some cop walks in and threatens to break heads and the owner forks over a bribe? They negotiate?" Speaking of which, I dug out a century and gave it to Artie. No sense in me having to buy him a drink because he was flat. Plus I owed him for convoying the goods.

Artie gave another guffaw. "You're kidding, right? If you don't know—tell you what, ask your boyfriend."

"What boyfriend?"

"The owner, Mr. Big."

"Phil Martin? He's not my—" I shut my mouth quick.

"Don't you know how big he is yet?" Artie hooted at his own wit.

I could feel my face getting red. Artie couldn't possibly know— "So he's in bed with the big players *and* the cops?"

"Why don't you ask him?"

"Maybe I will."

Damn and blast. I'd hoped that maybe I'd seen the last of Phil Martin, but things kept coming back around to him. I guess maybe I was going have to look at him again. See if he was the kind of guy who could put his hands around a dame's throat and squeeze. With my luck, I'd find out his middle name started with a B.

I knocked and held up the disc to the peephole. When the muscle opened the door, he merely nodded at me, but he almost keeled over in a swoon when he saw Artie. I was thinking I'd have to argue to get Artie inside, but instead the gate guardian said, "Hey, rough trade. Long time no see."

"How long?" Artie asked with a chortle.

Artie. Flirting. In a raunchy way, but flirting nonetheless. I'd never seen that before. I stopped to watch. It's never too late to learn something new, although I doubt I'll ever be using any of his pick-up lines.

"Long enough. I got a break coming up in fifteen," the door goon said with a grin. "I'll meet you there."

Artie gave him a bright smile and a nod. In an undertone he said to me, "If I'm lucky, I can squeeze one in before then. Get it? Squeeze one—"

I dislodged his elbow from my bruised ribs. "Yeah, I got it, very clever. Gimme your watch."

"Oh, yeah, right. I forgot."

I guess Artie was in such a hurry to squeeze in another appointment, he just handed me his watch and took off behind the curtain. Suited me. The fewer people who saw me flaunting the pendant around, the better.

When I walked into Lambda, there was nothing that said Mr. Big had to be there. After all, he had other clubs to run as well, where he didn't have to hide behind the curtain. Topaz was the most popular nightclub in town in a prime location on Fremont. But this was Wednesday, and I'd heard he would be here.

I spotted Reggie. He gave me a nod when I went to his table and sat down uninvited and unwelcomed, and then he ignored me. I watched him watch Jazz while turning it over in my mind.

The color that matters most in Vegas is green, so the blue uniform didn't usually get in the way when a man is out to get some of what he thinks he's got coming to him. It was no big surprise to find out the cops were on the take too. It's easy to say the cops are dirty, but I wondered how the negotiations were conducted to the satisfaction of both parties?

I pried open the back of Artie's watch and took out the pendant.

"Where did you get that?"

I looked up at Reggie in surprise. He sounded angry, and he looked like he was about to snatch it out of my hand. "I found it. In Marguerite Saint-Ville's apartment."

His face changed, showing a flash of anguish, and then it was gone. He looked a little green around the gills and stood up as if he was about to leave. "That's it, then."

I grabbed his wrist and held on, and he went down in his seat to get me to turn him loose. "Hold on, Reg, I need to ask you some—"

"Let go of me!"

"Where have you seen this before?"

He didn't want to tell me, but it was his telltale glance at Jazz that explained his big reaction. "You gave this to your boyfriend?"

"He's not my boyfriend, but I did give it to him," Reggie said dully, all the fire going out of him. "He wore it—for a while. Then he said he lost it."

"Well, maybe he did."

"Where did you say you found it?"

"Marguerite's—you think he gave it to her?"

"He stopped wearing it soon after she started working here."

"Maybe she nicked it from him."

Reggie laughed. "Yeah, right. A dame wearing diamonds and she couldn't afford to buy a necklace of her own, so she snuck into his dressing room when he was onstage and copped it."

"It could have happened that way. Did you ask him about it?"

"Would you?"

"Yeah, I would have. I would have wanted to know."

"But *you* don't give a damn. *You* don't care who you run over when you're after the truth, do you?"

It made me feel bad to realize that I hadn't thought about how he might take it when I'd asked, and that made me angry. "You want me to believe you boys in blue handle witnesses like a delicate flower?"

"Maybe a witness who's supposed to be a friend!"

I bit my lip. "Sorry."

"Okay."

"Can we talk now?"

Awkwardly, Reggie said, "Sorry about earlier, at your office."

"I notice you didn't flinch when Woods took a poke at me."

"That would have made it worse."

"Yeah, I know." I watched his eyes stray from me over to Jazz again. "Listen, Reggie. It wasn't in her apartment when I first got there. Maybe he didn't give it to her."

"What're you talking about?"

The hope in his eyes just about slayed me, he wanted to believe in Jazz so bad. "When I got there, I tossed the joint, nice and careful, put everything back just like I found it. Well, while I was in there, I heard someone at the door—"

"And you tiptoed out the fire escape?"

"No, I went under the bed. I didn't have time to monkey with the window. Anyway, when he left, I checked the jewelry box and this was in it." I waved the necklace at him.

"You probably just missed it before."

I shook my head stubbornly. "I knew something was different, so I closed my eyes and visualized what it looked like earlier...." I shrugged. "When I opened it up, this is what jumped out at me. So I took it along. Figured it had to mean something. And then *you* showed up, along with the other boys in blue."

Reggie laughed without mirth. "It would have meant something if it had been there when we were sent to search the place. I wondered why he seemed so certain that something had been overlooked."

"Who are you talking about?"

"Who planted it?"

"I couldn't see anything from under the bed. Just a pair of shoes."

"Yeah, and I bet you cowered under there until tomorrow. Don't string me, Grey."

"I didn't see him do it, you understand, but when I checked out the window…."

"Yeah?"

"Captain Woods."

"Big Billy. Double B. The boss," Reggie said. "Why am I not surprised?"

"Why *aren't* you surprised?"

"Big Billy really enjoys closing a case, especially a hot one."

"So I've heard. And he's not above helping the evidence along a little bit, is he?"

"I don't know anything for sure. It's not good for him if a case goes cold." Reggie seemed like he wasn't going to budge from that. I decided to send up a flare and see if I could light him up.

"And this is how he urges it along? Puts the frame on someone if he can't find the real deal?" I was surprised to hear the outrage in my voice. I thought I was a little more jaded than that.

"Maybe he wants to make a run at the Sheriff's job. You know how it works, the more cases you close, the better it looks. He likes to keep his percentages low," Reggie said.

"You think Captain Woods put it there to set Jazz up?"

"Got you wondering when I told you I gave it to Jazz, didn't it?"

"Maybe you put it there for revenge."

Reggie glared at me, and I wondered if I'd taken things too far. "Don't push your luck, Randall. Friendship only stretches so far."

I breathed a sigh of relief. Maybe someday I'd learn how to handle an interrogation with a little more tact, but when I got on the trail, sometimes I forgot to look to the right and left. "So why would Big Billy have it in for Jazz?"

"He doesn't care about Negroes. Maybe he heard Marguerite had a thing for Jazz." Reggie shrugged and settled back to watch Jazz some more.

"Where would he hear that?"

"I don't sit in his pocket, Grey."

"White girl, black boy. That would sell in most places." I swung the pendant absently, watching the glitter as it caught the light. "So Big Billy is dirty."

"Didn't say that."

"Come on, a law-and-order type who goes to plant evidence in the girl's apartment? It's a little late to backpedal, Reggie. I have it on good authority that he's in bed with Mr. X—"

Reggie's hand clamped over my mouth to shut me up. "Not here, you idiot!"

I pulled his hand away. "What? Why not?"

"Because Mr. Martin works for Mr. X, and his walls have ears." Reggie nodded at the sarcastic number, who glared at us but kept his distance, even though Reggie's glass was empty and mine nonexistent.

"Who searched the place after she was first found?" I asked.

"Captain Woods took a few men over. Guthrie was there, I think."

"You think Guthrie knew the girl before?"

"Guthrie?" Reggie laughed. "You think he was a crossing guard on her first day of school and she kicked him in the shin, so he waited till she was an adult and killed her? It's not like you to be whimsical."

"All right, what was so important to send you guys tearing over there to rip the place apart today?"

"You'll have to get that someplace else. Try Lieutenant Steele." Reggie sniggered at the thought. "I've already told you too much."

"And if I ask if you'd swear that Captain Woods sent you to search Saint-Ville's apartment?"

"Just doing my job," Reggie said. There was an unpleasant hint of triumph in his eyes. "Like any good cop. Just following orders."

"Where have I heard that song before?" I snarled.

He went white with rage. "Look, you've done enough damage for one night. Scram!"

"Sure," I said. "Thanks for nothing. I'll tell your boyfriend you sent me when I go to ask him about this." I flipped the pendant like tossing a coin, and Reggie made a snatch for it, but I was too quick for him. "Tails. You lose."

IT WAS simple enough to slip behind the curtain unnoticed and find my way to Miss Tina's dressing room. Jazz was still onstage with the rest of the band, but she was busy touching up her makeup when I found her room.

Her hair was down and hanging in waves around her face. I noticed three wig stands. Two of them had wigs styled in an updo, one black, one blonde. Quick way of making a costume change.

She caught my entrance in the mirror and gave me an automatic, seductive smile, fluttering her false eyelashes. "The men's room is back towards the bar." She spun on her stool and looked me over coolly. "Unless you came to see me, honey."

Her voice was like honey too, slow and dripping with sweetness. Of course, she was speaking slowly for a reason; it helped her keep the tone in a higher range. She was good; if you weren't in the know, you might have thought she was a woman for real. She had a very pretty face, and her makeup was artfully applied, making the most of lush lips and big eyes. But the tell was her brow bone was too pronounced, and her shoulders were angular, rather than soft and rounded.

She was wearing an evening suit, with a long tight skirt that had a lot of ruffles at the bottom. The jacket had little puffed sleeves and a peplum, which helped add curves to her lean hips. It was made of satin and very shiny. Too shiny, if you ask me. And she'd made sure of overkill by also loading on a rhinestone belt.

"I've heard you sing," I murmured. "You're good."

She lost interest in me after a once-over. "Thanks, hon. Be a dear and run along, I have to get ready for my next set."

"But not as good as Miss Saint-Ville."

That lit a fire under her. She turned and glared at me. "That one-note no-talent doxy? She had nothing on me!"

"She had a beautiful voice."

"Listen, buster, all she did was sing! I'm putting on a full act!" Her voice had dropped some, but either she was in good practice or she had a naturally high voice.

"She was some dancer too. But you couldn't compare with her, a real woman," I managed to slip in and stop the tirade. "So you got rid of her."

Miss Tina laughed, but I didn't see a lot of humor in it. "I didn't have to. Mr. Martin saw through her airs and graces quick enough. He was going to fire her." She reached for a jar of some unguent on her table and twisted the lid without success. She absently handed it to me to open for her despite being ready to claw my eyes out, as if it were just natural to get some man to do it for her.

I unscrewed the lid and gave it back to her. Her hands were slender and smooth, with nails filed to perfect ovals. "Where'd you hear that? Jazz tell you?"

She shot me a suspicious look. "Jazz wasn't interested in her. They liked talking about music. That's *it*! He *never* bought her line."

"So Mr. Martin told you that you had nothing to worry about, he was going to toss her out on her ear—"

"Not exactly."

"What's that mean?"

"Well, it never came to anything. She was killed, not far from here. Or hadn't you heard?" Miss Tina shrugged and went back to her reflection in the mirror, smoothing the cream on her neck in an upward motion. I could see her Adam's apple bob as she did it.

"You know how she died?"

"Somebody choked her. Probably couldn't stand listening to her sing any more," Miss Tina said crudely. "I'd have stuck a shiv in her."

"Someone who wanted to shut her up?" I asked.

She tilted her head back and looked at me from under her heavy fake lashes. "Who the hell are you anyway? Why are you so nosy?"

"It's my job to be nosy. I heard she teased you, made fun of you."

Miss Tina stood up and ran her hands up her body, cupping her bosom. "You think she made fun of this? I've got it good, I can show a man a good time both ways."

"Good for you, but it doesn't answer my question."

"Scram, buster. I don't have time for small fry." She lost interest in me again.

And I was out of interest for her. She seemed capable of wishing a murder on someone, but her idea of femininity would have limited her methods. I couldn't see her tackling a healthy girl who could fight back and actually managing to strangle her without help. Actually, I pictured Miss Tina screaming and flapping her hands if she broke a nail. If someone had held Marguerite still, Miss Tina might have been able to fall on her with a knife, but that would have been it.

I backtracked to Jazz Morgan's dressing room. I was sitting there flipping the pendant in the air when he walked in after his set. The canned music had started up soon after, which was good for me if things got too loud.

Not that I thought it would come to trading punches, or I'd have brought more muscle than my own. It's just after slipping around after him and seeing him so sad, I had a feeling he needed to talk to someone. Might as well be me; I needed answers.

"What are you doing here, little fish?" He dropped wearily onto a chair and shuffled some sheet music on the table into a neat pile.

"I heard this belongs to you." I held out the pendant on the palm of my hand.

He sat up, and his face became animated for the first time since I'd known him, but he stayed cautious. "Looks like one I used to have. Where did you get it?"

"I found it. In a dame's place."

"No fucking way."

"Yeah, I heard you weren't much for the broads."

"People will say anything." He shrugged, but it was too late to play it cool. I'd seen how his eyes lit up, and his fingers were twitching with the need to snatch it out of my hand.

"People are saying you gave it to her."

"I didn't! I told you, I lost it."

He hadn't actually told me that, but Reggie had. I guess both of them wanted to believe that real bad. I shook my head and gave him a nasty smile. "Next you'll be telling me that bad men broke into your house while you were asleep and stole it."

"Look, the person who gave me that—let's just say I never would have given it to *her*—no matter what happened between us," he stammered.

I laughed. "You need a vacation. I didn't even give you the name of the chippy."

"She wasn't a chippy. She was a nice girl! Maybe a little—" He shut up when he realized I'd tricked him.

"I didn't even mention who we're talking about, so how do you know she was pure as the driven snow?"

"Look, man." He ran his hands through his curls. "I'm no stoolie."

"Who're you trying to protect?"

"It's not that." He bent forward, resting his elbows on his knees, and covered his face with his hands.

I waited. I had a feeling he needed to tell someone what was going on.

"It was the day after she was killed."

"Marguerite Saint-Ville?"

"Yeah. Cops pulled me in, said I was speeding. One mile over the limit." He gave me a bitter smile. "What that really means is keep off the white streets, nigger. They cuff me and take me downtown. So far, business as usual. That's when it went off the rails.

"Captain Woods, he comes into the interrogation room, lets his boys get in a little workout on me. Then he lifts the necklace and pockets it. Says it's more suited to a woman."

"And you thought he was sweating you because you're queer?"

Jazz gave me a hard look, but he didn't deny the accusation. "A— former friend of mine had recently given it to me. That—friend is a cop. I thought Woods was onto us. What else could I do?"

I nodded, feeling a little bitter myself. I'd seen enough of it in the service. Queer is bad enough. Queer *and* black? Might as well just sign your own death warrant and save them the trouble. "Then what?"

"He let me go."

I could hear how surprised he still was. "What did you think he was going to do?"

"Take me for a long walk in the desert, maybe not alone," Jazz said. "Big Billy doesn't like niggers much, he comes over to the north side for 'sport' now and again. Plays the music to watch us dance."

I'd seen that done before, shoot at a fella's feet to keep him tapping. "So, you didn't check with your 'friend' about all this?"

Jazz stood up and turned around, tugging his shirt out of his pants and holding it up so I could see. His back was a mess of fading bruises and welts. "Think I want to advertise this?"

"My God," I breathed, forgetting all about being hard-boiled. I wanted to punch someone bad, and it wasn't Jazz. "Big Billy?"

"Not personally." He tucked himself in and sat down again. I noticed for the first time how he kept from leaning against the back of the chair. "He just sat in to enjoy the floor show."

I was in danger of getting lost in the side issues. Not that what happened to Jazz wasn't important, but I couldn't quite see how this tied in with the case. And even worse, I had no idea how to fix it. "So this Saint-Ville frail, did you have a thing for her?"

"You ever meet her?"

"Not alive."

Jazz shook his head. "You nailed it, I admit it. I'm queer, but I never met a woman like her before. She was... so alive. Fascinating. Sometimes there was a flash in her eyes.... It was like she had me in a spell or something. And best of all, we both loved music. That's what we'd talk about. I didn't even realize she wanted me until that last night. She followed me in here and put her arms around my neck—I tried to get her off me gently. If I left a bruise on a white woman—" He shuddered, and I guess his back was light compared to what the punishment for that might be. "She ran out of here crying. And then the next day I heard she was dead. I didn't find out until later just *how* she died."

Sounded like her daughter *did* take after Lily. That joie de vivre she'd mentioned... Lily had that too, even with the death of her daughter hanging over her. "When the cops pulled you in, did they ask you anything about her?"

"Just did I have a taste for white meat, but I thought they were talking about—"

In my line of work, you listen to a lot of lies, so you get to know the ring of truth when you hear it. Jazz was spilling his guts, and there was only one thing he kept dancing around. In a way, I had to admire him. He had to think that Reggie was in on what happened to him at the police station in some way, but he still wasn't going to go canary on him being queer.

It made me feel a little sad that I might never have someone that felt that way about me. And considering how I'd ridden roughshod over Reggie's feelings earlier, I felt a little urge to play cupid for them.

"Reggie thinks you fell in love with her. He didn't know about what Big Billy was doing to you. He's not in on the frame."

Jazz looked up at me quickly. The expression of hope on his face almost made me want to go and slip on a pair of wings. I hated to spike his uplift, but I still had questions.

"What time did you have this conversation with Marguerite that night?"

"On my last break, about one a.m."

"So she tore out of here, crying, and you went after her—"

"I didn't go after her. What would I have said?"

"That she made you want to be a real man?" I had to chuckle, but I did it on the inside where he couldn't see. What dame didn't want to hear that, and what worse thing could you say if you were a queer man?

"I thought it was better to just let it drop," Jazz said, a little defensive. "I knew she'd get over it."

I didn't blame him. No man wants to face a dame's tears, and that goes double if you're not even taking them to bed. Clearly he didn't know much about broads, though, if he thought letting it drop would make anything blow over.

"So you went for a walk—"

"I went back onstage and played until two-thirty a.m.!" Jazz exploded. "You can ask anyone, the bartender, any of the customers—"

"Who are all going to put their hand on the Bible in court and say, 'Yeah, I swear I saw the colored guy playing at this queer club where I usually hang out'," I jibed.

"Fuck!" Jazz turned and made a fist, and for a minute I thought he was going to punch the wall. But he thought better of it, reminding me of Artie saying he was careful of his hands, and just twisted them together instead. "I'm screwed."

"Let's hope this doesn't ever get to court," I said.

"Who the hell *are* you?"

"Didn't I introduce myself earlier? Sorry. Grey Randall, private dick." I stuck out my hand, and he stared at it like no white man had ever offered to shake before.

His hand was bigger than mine, and when he stood up, I could see he had at least six inches on me. In *height*, dammit! Not a man I really wanted to tangle with if I got on his bad side.

"Reggie and I were in the service together." At his questioning look, I was tempted to shake my head to reassure him, but he was a suspect that I had cornered, not a friend.

"I was in the service too." He released my hand, and I could see the anger flooding back into his face, taking the place of the sadness. "So, Mr. Private Dick, you come barging in here, asking all these questions. Why?"

"I'm investigating Miss Marguerite Saint-Ville's murder. When I found out the necklace was yours—"

"Instant suspect." He stared at me suspiciously.

"Yeah, go figure," I said. "Maybe you'd better find a place to hole up for a few days. Stay away from your usual haunts. I spoiled the first frame by snatching this when it was planted, but Captain Woods is probably going to try again. For some reason you're his pigeon, and cops don't like open cases lingering on the books too long."

"Why me?"

"I was hoping you knew."

Jazz pursed his lips. "Captain Woods just naturally doesn't like spades, but he never noticed me to pick me out of a crowd before."

"You think he heard about Miss Saint-Ville having a yen for you?"

"Who knows? He has ears."

"Even here? In a queer underground club?"

"You'd have to ask Mr. Martin about that. I'm sure he's got a payroll." He caught my look and laughed. "Cost of doing business in Vegas. Support your local crooked cop."

I was beginning to think all the cops were on the take. "Well, thanks for your time. By the way, I dig how you play."

"Thanks, little fish."

I left his dressing room, realizing he hadn't had much of a break. But from the gleam in his eye when I talked about Reggie, I had a hunch that things might be looking up for both of them. I was looking forward to hearing Jazz play when he was in a better mood.

And now that that was cleared up, things were pointing Phil Martin's way again. He knew where Marguerite Saint-Ville was the whole time she was hiding out. Someone could have called him when she tore out of here in a state, and he could have gone after her, found her walking and cornered her, although I didn't know what reason he'd have. Unless he had a yen for her too. And there remained the matter of Mr. Big's payroll activities. Who was he paying to stay in business, and who was paying him? Because however big the fish, there's always a bigger one higher up on the food chain. I wasn't quite sure how I was gonna sweat that information out of Mr. Big. I mean, I already pulled out the stops the first time I questioned him. Where was I gonna go from there? Shoot him? I didn't want to do that for purely selfish reasons.

And the other problem was where was I going to stash this pendant so it would be there when I needed it? Big Billy wanted it, and he had the resources to look everywhere I went. I'm sure he wouldn't lose any sleep if his boys tossed my apartment and office every day without a warrant, and he might even think he could sweat it out of me if he put more effort into it. I wasn't willing to put Artie or Jazz on the spot by giving it to them to hold.

I started to chuckle when I thought of the perfect hiding place. Lieutenant Steele knew, but I was betting my life that Woods wasn't aware that I knew Reggie, or he wouldn't have brought him along to my office. Reggie was a cop; he could hold it for me. In fact, while he was at it, he could answer a few more questions.

I WAS so concentrated on going over to demand answers from Reggie I never even noticed Phil Martin, even though he was standing there big as life flashing his dimples like he owned the joint. Which he did, so I guess he had a right.

When I walked by him, he grabbed my left arm, I guess just to even up the mark he'd already left on the right, and said in a tone of seductive menace, "Can I buy you a drink?"

I wanted to say, "Oh yes, please," but I was working. I pulled my arm out of his grasp and snapped, "Not now, I don't have time for this!"

He looked startled and a little angry, but then he chuckled and let me keep going. I was glad to see he had a sense of humor, because life with a man—what was I saying? There was no future in this. Besides, I'm sure he just wanted to get his revenge.

I stalked over to Reggie's table and shoved him back into his seat when he stood up.

"Fuck off, Grey! Whaddya think you're doing?"

I grabbed Reggie's wrist and twisted until he gave. "You're not going anywhere until you tell me about everything you saw that night."

To his credit, he didn't pretend not to know what I was talking about. And to my shock, Mr. Phil Martin sat down at the table with us to watch. He even flagged down a waiter and ordered scotch all around. On the house.

"Hey, *I* didn't hire you, remember?"

"But you want to make sure Jazz stays clear just the same, don't you?" I hissed.

Mr. Martin's smile faded, and he leaned forward, looking back and forth between us like a tennis match.

"I want him cleared, yeah," Reggie admitted with a quick glance toward Mr. Martin, who was frowning now.

"So who called the cops when they found the girl?"

"Anonymous." Reggie shrugged like it was no big deal, which it probably wasn't; they probably scored two or three anonymous calls a day. After meeting Big Billy and Lieutenant Steele, I'm sure I'd rather not deal if I'd found a dead body, so I'd call from a pay phone too.

"And who was first on the scene? Captain Woods?"

"No, Sergeant Guthrie, his shadow. The Captain didn't show till after the meat wagon took her away. Couple hours later."

That turned all my ideas upside down, but you have to make the theory fit the facts, not the other way around.

"What time?"

"Shouldn't you have asked all these questions when you first got the case?" Reggie asked nastily.

"Would you have told me?"

"No."

"Why are you telling him now?"

We both turned our heads and stared at Phil Martin. I think we'd forgotten he was there, which is quite a feat when you consider he was the most gorgeous man in the room. I shook my head at him and growled softly, "Shut up and stay out of this."

Phil Martin couldn't have realized the only reason Reggie was answering my questions now was that I'd lit the fire of hope for him, but he would never be able to admit that out loud, especially to me.

Mr. Martin stared at me for a second and then trotted out those disarming dimples. I swear, I could have hidden a dime in each one of them, and I wondered if he had a matching set down lower, on his ass—but this wasn't the time for monkey business.

"Time of death?"

"She was still warm when we got there at two a.m."

"Did she have any marks on her body? Something the paper didn't mention?"

Reggie stared at me, his dark eyes almost black. "How did you tumble to that?"

"A scratch on the back of her neck?"

"Like someone yanked a chain off," Reggie said as if he hated to admit it.

"Keys?"

"In her handbag, with a hanky, makeup, and her coin purse."

I let go of his wrist and dug out the pendant, tossing it to him like a coin. "Here's a hot potato for you to hang onto. Don't let Jazz have this back till I say."

"Burning your fingers?"

"All day, ever since I pulled it out of the broad's apartment from under your noses." I rubbed my side until I realized I was doing it and stopped. "And whatever you do, don't let Woods cop that you have it." I stood up to go.

"Don't you even want to hear about the blood?" Reggie asked, as if he wanted to get one back on me.

"It was on the heel of her shoe," I said.

"So you're grilling me to see if what I tell you matches up with what you already know?"

"You're a tough nut to crack. I just wanted to see if I could."

"Listen, Grey! Those photos I gave you—the ones from the crime scene, you still have them?"

"Yeah, why?"

"Because the file got lost—somehow." Reggie looked furious and fearful at the same time. "Including all the negatives."

"And I have the only copies?"

"Be careful, Grey."

I nodded. I could see the wheels spinning behind Mr. Martin's beautiful blue eyes and Reggie's dark ones. I probably wasn't alone in drawing certain conclusions.

I had to make a conscious effort to straighten up without groaning. If there was a time not to be seen waddling in pain, in front of Phil Martin was it. I didn't realize he was following me until I was almost to the door, when he grabbed me. I grunted and coughed.

"You all right?" he asked.

"Fine. Thanks for a swell evening. I'm busy."

He laughed at my less than gracious exit line and said, "Aren't you even going to corroborate Jazz's alibi before you go?"

"Is there any point? You think anybody in this club is willing to stand up in public and say they were here and they swear Jazz never left his piano?" I looked around the room and grinned. "They probably wouldn't even give me their real names."

"You've got a point, but what about me?"

"Who says you wouldn't lie for him? It would be easier than finding a new piano player."

His brows knit together, and I felt the palpable force of Mr. Big's personality. "It's not about the club, he's my friend."

Somehow I got the feeling he'd be a good friend too, the kind you could depend on—but that line of thought wasn't going to get me anywhere.

"All the more reason to lie, then," I pointed out, even though I was kind of impressed that he, a white guy at the top of the heap even if he was a crook, would claim friendship with a black piano player. "I wasn't hired to prove him innocent anyway. I'm after the guy who did it."

Phil Martin's face got shuttered then, and I had the feeling that he might have an inkling of who I was after. "I wish you luck with that."

"While I've got your attention—"

He moved in closer to me and put his hand on the wall by my head to fence me in. I could feel the warmth of his breath on my face. "You've definitely got my attention," he muttered with a glinting smile.

I didn't move away, although I wanted to run like hell. But he didn't know that, and I had work to do. "*While* I've got your attention, how do you bribe the cops?" From his expression, I realized maybe I'd been a little too blunt.

He seemed to be trying to decide whether to sock me one or laugh. Luckily he opted for disbelieving laughter. *And* he looked around self-consciously after taking his hand off the wall, which made it a little easier for both of us to breathe. I got the feeling he'd forgotten that he was standing where anyone could see us. And for me—just having him so close again that I could smell him—

"You're a firecracker when you're hot on the trail of something, sunshine, you know that?"

"It's a touchy subject, isn't it? I can't imagine if Lieutenant Steele walked in here that you'd say, 'Here's five large, please look the other way while I knock off a few guys'," I said.

"I don't rub out my customers too much, it's bad for repeat business," Mr. Martin said sarcastically. "And Steele isn't a likely touch anyway."

"So how do you tell? Take out an ad in the police gazette?"

Mr. Martin sighed. "I'm giving away the company secrets here, but first of all, word gets around about cops who are looking to build up their pension on the side. Secondly, there's an etiquette to it, like anything else. He finds some petty violation and suggests that I have it taken care of by a certain date, while implying that he'll look away for a suitable sum."

"How do you know when it's enough?"

"If I get a thank-you card, okay?" he growled. Exasperated looked good on him. If I were going to pursue anything, which I wasn't, I'd have to make a point to ride him just to watch the splash.

"Anyone dressed in blue come around to collect that night?"

For a moment I thought he wasn't going to tell me, but he was smart. Maybe even as smart as me, which made—but never mind about that. "It *was* payday, now that you mention it."

"And who picked up the bag?"

"Guthrie. Sgt. Bert Guthrie."

"He's the one who put the finger on you?"

Mr. Martin sighed. "It's more complicated than that. Word comes down from above, this day every week and this much. Guthrie's a runner, that's all. I don't know for sure who he takes the package to."

"Yeah, don't try to sell me the Brooklyn Bridge. I taught your granny how to suck eggs."

Far from pissing him off, Mr. Martin seemed to find that funny. "You're so smart, don't you figure it's healthier for me not to know the details if I'm asked?"

"You've got a point. I'll take it under advisement. One more thing. Humor me: say you're some dame's bank account and you don't want it known that you're paying the rent, how do you go about it? Hypothetically speaking, of course."

At first he looked surprised, and then angry, but he decided to play ball. "Of course. The easiest way would be to slip an envelope of cash under the door."

"Is that what you do?"

"Do I look like I need to pay a woman to stick around?"

"Seems more likely you have to thin the crowd by beating them off with a stick," I said honestly.

He laughed. "I try not to leave any bruises."

"Where it shows, at least." I found myself rubbing mine and quit. "What if you don't want the manager to open the door real quick and catch you ditching the envelope?"

His eyes got suspicious then, like he knew where I was going, and I realized I'd gotten the last useful hint out of him. "Maybe I set up a post-office box for the guy."

"Or maybe you own the building?" I suggested.

His face closed down. "Seems like an expensive way to bankroll a cheap date."

"You could always up the rent for the other tenants to even it out."

"If they were old and ugly enough," he agreed.

"What's your middle name?"

He looked surprised at the sudden change of subject, but he answered. "Andrew. Why?"

I let out a grateful sigh. "No reason. Okay, that'll do for now," I said, checking my watch. "Right now I gotta go see a dame."

"So I'm dismissed? Thanks, Mr. Private Dick. In return, I'll let you off the hook for now," he said with a feral smile. "But don't go too far."

"Or you got ways to find me, I know," I said in a bored tone, even though he was making me a little nervous.

"I don't usually let a man shake me off, Mr. Randall. It's not good for business—or my image. But it was kind of hot watching you work."

With that, he turned and walked away. I guess he knew the truth of that old adage "always leave them wanting more."

I wondered what I'd said or done that made him just let me walk out of there, but whatever it was, I was glad for it.

Chapter 8: Setting a Trap

IT WAS getting harder to stand up straight as the night wore on, but I was hot on the scent now. I hoped Lily would be at home, and alone. Somehow I didn't think I'd be real popular with Mr. X if I interrupted them in the middle of the horizontal tango.

I was in luck. It was late, but Lily was used to night hours from her old job, so she was just getting in herself when I turned onto her street. I recognized the taillights of her Lincoln as it turned into her circular drive.

I gave her a few minutes and then followed, parking behind her limo. It sure was a nice ride. I stroked the glossy enamel and then put a hand to my side, hoping I'd make it up the shallow steps and inside without keeling over.

When I knocked on the door, Celestine answered and glared at me disapprovingly. "It is too late. Madame is not receiving—"

"She'll see me," I said, pushing past her rudely. I walked into the living room and was treated to a sight of Lily spinning in the middle of the floor, her arms held out gracefully and the chiffon of her skirt swirling around her like a dark cloud.

"Mr. Dick! What are you doing here?" she exclaimed, and she stopped on a dime.

I admired her ability to do that, both the way she put me at a disadvantage and the spin. She didn't even look dizzy as the fabric of her dress swayed around her and fell into place. "Lily, we need to talk."

Her colored driver had a piece out and had it aimed at me. "I'll take him out, Miss Lily."

I really hoped he wouldn't try. I had no doubt I could handle him; after all, he had at least twenty-five years on me, but at this point in the day, I was sure it would have hurt me more than it would hurt him.

"No thank you, George. This is the private dick I hired. He must be here to report on his progress," Lily said, holding a hand out toward him. I nearly had to squint to keep from being blinded by the sparkles shooting out from the huge rock on her hand. Not to mention the choker clasped around her slim throat and the diamond bracelet on her wrist.

"Put it away, Georgie," I growled, "if you don't want to eat it for breakfast."

"I recognize him, Miss Lily." To my surprise, he chuckled and lowered the gun. "Skinny boy like you gonna try to feed me? I was putting fellas like you down when you were in diapers."

"Wiry!" I burst out, surprising even me. Sometimes even I wonder about what comes out of my mouth. I'm sure he didn't give a damn that I hated it when people called me skinny, and he wouldn't if we ever had to tangle, because I would win, but I still had to set him straight. "And I've been out of diapers for quite some time."

"Had a chance to learn some tricks, eh, boy? Want to show off your muscles for the lady?" he taunted.

Lily came to me and laid her hand on my arm. "Although ordinarily I *adore* it when men fight over me, I would very much like to hear your report before the first round, Mr. Dick."

"Mr. Randall," I corrected her automatically, keeping one eye peeled on George.

Celestine came in to back him up, and at the sight of her ugly kisser I almost gave up right then. Two against one, they could have had me. Especially if they thumped me in the wrong spot.

But Lily was by my side, facing them down for me with a smile. "He's finding out about Marguerite for us. Make some coffee, Celestine. And George, put away the gat. Come along."

When she said "come along," I thought she meant me, but evidently it was going to be a conference. Lily led me into the morning room, and George was right on my heels.

"Please, sit down."

I don't know if the society dames in town looked down on Lily because of her start in show business, but it grabbed me how she was always such a lady. I sat, a little heavily, and let out a grunt when I hit bottom.

"Are you all right, Mr. Randall?" Lily asked, proving that she could remember my name after all.

"Fine, thanks. It's just been a long day."

George held a chair for Lily, which I should have known to do myself, and then sat down next to her, as if he were her equal instead of her driver. I didn't mean that like it sounds, just that there seemed to be a deeper relationship than just between a society woman and some employee.

Celestine came back in with the tray, and that made me sit up. The coffee smelled good. Coffee smells good any time of day to me, but there was something about Lily's coffee that was extra good. Or maybe it was just Lily. Lord knows I wasn't going to give Celestine the credit.

Celestine poured out four cups, and I was interested to see that she remembered how I took it. She also fixed up a cup for Lily and George before sitting down with us.

"The three musketeers?" I muttered.

Lily snickered. "I told you he was cleverer than he looks," she said to George. He nodded, but Celestine remained unconvinced. "So tell us what you've learned, Grey darling."

I guess we were back on a first-name basis. "The police have been running in circles trying to find out who paid Marguerite's rent."

She stiffened for a moment, quite a feat sitting down, but that dame had a spine of steel. "And you found out before they did?"

"I think I'm looking at her meal ticket."

"Very good." She gave me a stately nod, acknowledging the hit. "Except it was really Max. He owns that building. The manager was told that the rent was paid for a year in advance, so he didn't bother her."

"Lieutenant Steele said she never brought any of her boyfriends up there."

Lily had her hands folded, like a little girl being quizzed at school. "At least she retained that much sense of self-protection," she said tartly.

"So what did she do for money?"

"She had her job. I assume they paid by check."

I waited. "Can I see her bank statements? And why weren't they sent to her apartment? Or did she toss them out?"

Lily rolled her eyes. "They were sent here. She never looked at them. Marguerite had over ten thousand dollars in her account when she died."

"Dancing must pay better than I thought," I said.

"When we set her up in that apartment, I opened a checking account for her with five thousand dollars. Unbeknownst to me, Max put in the same amount." Lily smiled reminiscently before adding, "And of course, Marguerite charged her clothing to me. All she had to do was pay for her meals."

Nice life, if you can live long enough to enjoy it. "Do you know the papers are implying that a man whose name is too important to whisper was keeping her and that's why the case will never be solved?"

"A temporary public relations problem. Max will survive it, he always has." Lily waved it away. "Besides, *we* know he didn't kill her. Once you unmask the real killer, that sort of innuendo is always quickly forgotten."

"*If* I unmask the real killer. How long have you suspected who killed your daughter, Lily?"

"I still don't know for sure, but the moment I heard she was dead—I suspected."

"So why have you had me running all over town trying to dig it up?"

She gave a bitter little laugh and tapped her hand on her forehead. "Of course, silly me, I could have just called the police, couldn't I?"

"Maybe not, but you could have told your boyfriend, Mr. X."

George made a sudden movement, but a quick glance told me he was just surprised, not preparing an assault. Celestine's hot black eyes gave away nothing.

"I did. He won't believe it," Lily said, and I got the sense of how bitter that had been for her.

"Because the cops are in his pocket, so they wouldn't do anything to piss him off?"

"Yes." Lily's lip curled sarcastically. "And they say *men* are the logical sex."

Okay, no argument from me there. Whatever intuitive leap had caused Lily to arrive at the same hypothetical solution as I had, if we were talking about the same person, I wasn't going to dislodge her from her perch, and besides, that wasn't what I was being paid for.

"I have no evidence that would stand up in a court of law."

George spoke up. "It doesn't have to go to court."

I nodded. It surprised me a little that he was so deep in Lily's confidence, but I was guessing it was a lonely life. For all of them. "There's something missing, though."

Lily tilted her head questioningly.

"You like a lot of glitter," I pointed out.

She glanced down at her jewelry with an endearingly embarrassed look. Maybe she was a little overloaded, but she could carry it. "You must think I'm just a magpie," she murmured. "But I do like a little sparkle."

Celestine's black eyes were on fire as she snapped at me. "Madame has *earned* the right to wear these jewels!"

"I'm sure she has," I said courteously, as Lily giggled silently in the background at the indelicate implications of Celestine's remark. I pointed at the fine platinum chain with the diamonds that disappeared down into her décolletage. "But for a woman with a predilection for the big rocks, you always wear that one modest chain, no matter what other necklace you have on. Why?"

Lily stuck her hand into her cleavage, clutching something before slowly pulling it out. Compared to her other jewelry, the locket could be described as sweet and simple, not something I would expect to see an eye-stopper like Lily wearing. It was shaped like a four-leaf clover, with a field of red enamel sporting a graceful spray of white lily of the valley on it. She opened the locket to show me a photo of her daughter on one side and a lock of red-gold hair on the other.

"Marguerite had a matching one," I guessed.

She nodded. "Hers was white with a red rose, and she had a photo of me inside. At least she did when I last saw it."

"He took it after he killed her," I said, thinking aloud.

"But why? Why would he take it?" Lily's voice was as close to a wail as I guessed she would ever get, with her iron control.

"Trophy. Some killers like to keep score," I said. "You saw the marks on her neck where he yanked it off?"

Her face went expressionless and hard as she nodded. "Find the locket and you find the killer."

Glancing from Celestine to George, I got the sense that this was Lily and Marguerite's family. They had always been together, and now with this shared tragedy, they would do whatever it took to support Lily. I wondered just how long they'd been with her. Maybe they'd been around to watch Marguerite grow up from a baby into a young woman.

"Who are your suspects? And why?" Lily asked.

I sighed. "It's a long story."

"We've got all night, Mr. Randall," George said. I think he was over wanting to give me the bounce.

I started to talk, telling them about the anonymous stalker boyfriend who sent dead flowers and signed himself "B." For Jazz, I glossed over the queer part but didn't spare Lily the news that her daughter thought she had the hots for a black man. That didn't seem to make any difference to her, although I thought she understood at least one possible motivation for killing Marguerite.

"Marguerite dated a fair number of men," I started tactfully, "but the way I see it, I've got four suspects. Unless there's someone I don't know about yet. They all had opportunity and at least two of them were on the spot, but the motives are a little foggy. One is Barry Jazz Morgan, piano player—"

"He didn't do it." George shook his head vehemently.

"You know him?" Lily turned to him.

"Since he was a kid. Just can't believe Barry would kill a woman," George said.

"And you, Grey?"

"I don't think he did it, either."

"But you've been fooled before."

"Yeah, but something doesn't gel for me there." I waited, but Lily didn't want to flog it to death. "Captain Billy Woods of the police. So far I have no evidence that he even knew Marguerite, I've got nothing on him other than he tried to frame Mr. Morgan. I was in Marguerite's place under the bed when he came in to plant a pendant that belongs to Mr. Morgan. I've heard Woods can't stand to leave a case unsolved. Maybe it's gotten to be an obsession with him, a score he has to win, and that's all there is to it."

"But if you saw him actually plant the necklace—" Celestine said.

Lily was quick. "He didn't. He was under the bed. Grey could identify the shoes, but they aren't nailed onto Woods's feet permanently. Damn!" She got up and started to pace. "Max would never believe you based on that evidence, it would have to be something you witnessed. Who else?"

"Sgt. Bert Guthrie." The name didn't seem to ring a bell with any of them. "You wouldn't know the name of the crossing guard at Marguerite's first school, would you?"

"I drove Marguerite to school everyday," George said.

"It seems Guthrie is something of a woman hater, unless he's lying about that."

"Unless he's a nut with a campaign to wipe out all the women in Vegas who sing or dance, you'd have to prove to me that he had a grudge against her before I'd buy him," Lily said.

"He'd have his work cut out. And there's Phil Martin." They looked at me blankly. "Ahem, also known as Mr. Big."

"He would *never* do it! He knows me! He knows Max! He knows what Max would do to him if he—"

"Easy, Lily. We can strike him off the list later, but we have to include him for now." No need to tell her that listing the pros and cons for him had been driving me crazy since I met him. Whatever his motivation might have been, it kept running up against my desire to believe he couldn't have done it, if only because his blood didn't run hot for women. But I could see that my feelings might be affecting my slant on Mr. Big, so for that reason alone I had to leave him on the list.

"If you don't need the satisfaction of seeing the killer go to trial—" I started.

"I don't care about that," Lily waved it away. Her face was like some ruthless goddess of retribution, hard as stone and carved into a beautiful icon. "It doesn't have to be a public humiliation."

George patted his side pocket. "I could take care of him, Miss Lily."

"No, George, I couldn't let you take that kind of risk. If you were caught—I couldn't bear it." Lily stopped pacing to pat his shoulder. "Besides, I want Max to *know*, to accept who did it. Neither of us will ever be able to—"

I wondered if the death of their daughter had brought them together after so many years apart and now it was threatening to drive them apart. If they didn't both believe the same thing, I could see how Lily would push Max away again. And maybe his pride would get the better of his sense again and they would part acrimoniously.

If I'd had wings, I'd have been groping for them for the second time that night. "I can think of a way. If all we have to do is convince Mr. Hamilton who did it—"

George chuckled without humor. "And then let justice be done in the way of the west."

I shivered at that. I knew what he meant.

"But what do we do?" Celestine asked.

"We set a trap," I answered. "And we find the proof."

Okay, we were all on the same bloodthirsty page. From the intent look on all their faces, I was glad I wasn't going to be the one walking into that trap.

We talked till the sky was light, and I never did make it home. Celestine showed me to a guest room upstairs, and I slept in my shorts.

"NOT black," I said.

Lily pouted charmingly. "I look good in black. Besides, this is more of a steel grey."

"You do. But it would be better if you wore another color. More eye-catching. Red, maybe."

Lily swirled in front of the bank of mirrors in her dressing room, carefully watching her own reflection and the graceful movement of her gown before handing out a fashion tip to the wise. "Don't ever let anyone tell you that a redhead can't wear pink. But *red*! That color *is* a problem." She patted her coppery curls complacently. "It tends to clash."

"I stand corrected. How about a color other than red or black?"

"Why are you so anxious to get me out of my clothes, Mr. Dick?"

"I'm not! I mean, not in front of me, anyway!"

She giggled with glee when she saw my blush. "Don't worry, darling, I'll preserve your modesty."

"Marguerite didn't have any black in her closet," I said. I closed my eyes, remembering how she had her dresses arranged by color.

"She had youth on her side," Lily said with a sigh. "A fresh young thing can wear anything and look beautiful."

I thought she could do with a lump of sugar. "You don't look old enough to even have a daughter," I said. "You're the most beautiful woman I've ever met."

As I'd hoped, the compliment cheered her up. Probably because it was true.

"Merci beaucoup." Lily tossed me a smile in the mirror and opened a closet door, pulling out a frothy pink concoction. "I haven't worn this since…." Her voice trailed off, and she drooped a little before holding the dress up in front of herself.

"You're right about redheads in pink, but no strapless getup, either."

"This is a gown, not a getup," Lily scolded me. "You're being very critical."

"Listen, I'm no fashion editor, and I'd love to see you peacock it some other time. But part of being a successful moll is dressing for the job. You don't want that top to fall down around your waist if you have to swing into action, do you?"

Lily cast the dress aside dramatically, but I noticed that she aimed it for the chair, where it floated in for a successful landing. She wasn't going to mess up her gown, despite her dramatic gesture. "So, you *do* need a moll!"

"Yes, Lily, I admit it. Would you please be my moll tonight?" I asked.

"You should be down on one knee," she said, crossing her arms.

"Hey, I'm not proposing! And only if you help me up after," I said. She'd seen the bruise after all when she'd come into the guestroom to wake me and won my heart forever by not making a fuss over it. Also, she brought me coffee. What a dame. And after several cups of her coffee and some judicious stretching, I was good as new.

The door to the dressing room opened to admit Celestine, who was carrying a boatload of gowns in pretty colors over her arm. She glared at me. "You should not be here, m'sieur."

"I'll go out when Miss McIntyre is ready to change," I said defensively.

"It is not that." Celestine was obviously not concerned with the proprieties. "It spoils the effect to see Madame in the moment of transformation."

"I'll leave that to you," I said tactfully. I had my reward. Celestine actually smiled at me for the first time and made a motion that might possibly have been a curtsy.

"I have brought this for you to try on, Madame. Your private deeck is right, the pink is too daring for this operation. It should be unveiled upon a more auspicious occasion."

Okay, I wasn't going to go on with her accent, but I kind of dug it when she said "dick" that way. Also, I wouldn't have put it quite the way she did, but I still thought going strapless would be tempting fate. Especially where we were going.

There was a folding screen in the dressing room, and Lily retired behind it to try on some of the dresses Celestine brought in. They looked brand new to me, so I wondered if maybe they'd been retired out of Lily's closet at the death of her daughter. But none of us mentioned that, we just danced around the subject.

"Tell me, Grey darling, do you have a girlfriend?"

"Well, I have a friend and she's a girl," I said with a snicker, thinking of Charlie.

"I'd love to meet her one day," Lily said, coming out to peacock a daffodil yellow gown in the mirror.

I would never have thought that shade of yellow—with that hair—but she looked wonderful. "You probably would, but she's not at all like you, Lily."

"They never are, my dear," Lily said. She threw me a roguish glace over her shoulder before returning to her study of her reflection. "I'd forgotten how good I look in yellow."

It sounds arrogant, but it really wasn't. In fact, it was almost somber hearing her assess her appearance. She'd been in grey and black for a very short time, but—

"No, this doesn't give off the right ambiance," Lily decided.

"I have it, Madame," Celestine said.

Lily disappeared behind the screen while I went over the plan again, listening to the silky rustlings of fabric and undertone conversation between them. I realized that Lily was speaking French, and she sounded as fluent as Celestine, who came out first to announce, "Voila!"

When Lily appeared, she took my breath away. The dress poured over her body like a river of silk, with sequins furnishing glints of light as she moved. It fit her like a glove, leaving nothing to the imagination and yet tantalizing with hints of what lay underneath. Long sleeves made the dramatic plunge of the neckline even more exciting. Bronze sequins were artfully placed to follow the curves of her perfect figure and clung to her body down to the knee, where the skirt fanned out in ruffles that flowed like water around her feet when she took a step.

"Magnifique, Madame," Celestine murmured, her eyes shining with pride and her hands clasped in satisfaction as one who has excelled in her chosen vocation.

I would have thought the bronze might have washed Lily out, but instead it was the perfect shade to set off her creamy skin, and the sheen brought out the gold tones in her red hair. She looked like a tall flute of champagne, effervescent, bubbly, and expensive.

Lily smiled at me. "You may close your mouth, Grey. I'll take your silence as a compliment."

"You—you sure can," I stammered.

Celestine pulled the pins out of Lily's hair, ruffling the curls and quickly putting it up again in a totally different style, with curls artlessly cascading from a topknot. I was beginning to see that she had her uses. "What jewels, Madame?"

I was glad Lily was being given a say in her own appearance, but I spoke up. "Only that chain and locket for the necklace."

"And my diamond drop earrings," Lily said. She poked a foot out under the skirt, and I could see a gold, strappy high heel. "Perhaps a bracelet or two."

"Or three," I said.

Lily smiled to acknowledge the hit.

Or it may have been how I looked in my new tux. There are advantages to having money. She'd had someone bring over a selection from the store, and I tried them on in the comfort of her guest room, where no one had to listen to my occasional grunt of pain. Lily seemed pretty used to sizing up a man, in many different ways. Or maybe she snuck a peek at the label in my suit when I was asleep, but I looked almost as good as her in my penguin suit. She even tied my bow tie for me. With *flair*.

WHEN it was time to leave for the party, Lily gave my heap the evil eye and called for George. For the first time, I was embarrassed by my car. I also didn't want her buying me a new one of those; first the tie, then the tux; who knew where it would end? She'd already paid me for the job; these were extras. I didn't like owing.

She didn't offer, though. While we waited for George to bring her limo around, she gave me a quick lesson in fur wrangling, so I wouldn't drop her stole when we got to the party.

I wasn't sure if the butterflies jumping in my stomach were for the fact that I was going to a private party at the richest casino in Vegas or because we were going to confront a killer. Despite Lily's flirtatious demeanor, I had a feeling I had the best moll in Vegas on my arm that night.

Take that, Mr. X.

Not that I'd say that to his face, seeing as he was the one throwing the party, or soirée as Lily called it.

George let us out at a private entrance at the Rising Star, around the side, where we walked in on a red carpet that had been rolled out, but it just added to the exclusive atmosphere.

I had to wonder if Lily had researched the room and dressed accordingly, so that she was perfectly attired to play out her big scene. Or maybe she was already familiar with it, seeing as this was Mr. X's turf. The circular room was gorgeous, all done up in rich tones of cream and caramel and gold. Heavy silk drapes hung from floor to ceiling. The round tables gleamed with silver and crystal under chandeliers casting prismatic rainbows everywhere. Perfect for a sparkly redhead.

I asked her, "Was this room designed as a setting for you?"

She laughed with delight at my observation. "Very acute of you, darling."

I was suspicious. "Did you have a hand in it?"

"Perhaps," she said, airily waving her hand at a dark-haired couple.

My heart skipped a couple beats when I glanced over and saw him. It was my first sight of Mr. Phil Martin, AKA Mr. Beautiful, looking right at home in a classy tux, arriving at the party with a tall and beautiful brunette on his arm.

The way they gazed into each other's eyes as he took her wrap made me wonder if the conclusions I'd drawn about him were correct despite the copious evidence I'd collected that his inclinations lay elsewhere. Maybe he swung both ways. They looked so right together, so at ease, as if they'd known each other a long time. Which made me wonder even more about Marguerite. If he could put on an act so good it fooled me knowing what I knew, maybe he could also strangle a woman in cold blood and never think about it afterward.

I looked at Lily reproachfully and then realized she had no reason to know that I needed to be warned in advance whenever Mr. Big was going to pop up at some event. She wouldn't have a clue how he made my mouth go dry and my dick grow hard. I put a stop to that right away, though; I wasn't going to be held hostage by an unruly body part.

Mr. Martin led his date further into the room, and then I saw his head come up and his nostrils flare when he spotted me.

I wasn't up on my Emily Post of what to do at a straight party when you unexpectedly run into a closeted man whose cock you recently sucked, especially if it was completely your idea and he didn't get a lot of say in the matter.

I mean, I'd seen him once at his club since then, but this was a very different setting, and we both had women on our arms now. At least there I had him beat; however much younger his date was, Lily out-glammed every woman in the room.

He sucked in a breath through clenched teeth, his lips tightening with lust for a moment. The look in his eyes almost made me start moving his way, but then he controlled it. The yearning disappeared behind the civilized smile as he turned to the beautiful woman at his side, escorting her to a table where he sat down with his back to me.

That got me off the hook; I was able to take a normal breath again, and just in time, because Lily turned to see what had me mesmerized.

"Did you see him?"

"What? Oh—no, he's not here yet." I guess everyone wasn't as enthralled with Mr. Big as I was. But of course, Lily knew him quite well, and maybe she was used to how beautiful he was. Maybe the stunning effect wore off as you accustomed yourself.

The room was on the intimate side, and it was nearly full when we got there. With Mr. Martin safely ensconced on the far side of the room, I pulled out a chair that put Lily sitting with her back to the door, a spot I'd wager she'd never settled for before. I helped her with her stole, grateful for the lesson earlier when she beamed at me.

There was a live band in an alcove: piano, violins, sax section, traps, and even a clarinet. The dance floor was crowded with couples dressed to the nines, and the sparkle coming off the dames was almost blinding in the dim light. But there was a sense of anticipation, and the party wasn't really going to get off the ground until the host arrived. There was a buzz in the room when Mr. Hamilton made his entrance with a beautiful girl no older than his daughter on his arm, pausing at the door to take in the crowd.

"What color is her hair?" Lily leaned over and spoke out of the side of her mouth without moving her lips in the most approved moll style.

"Uh, blonde," I said, when I caught up.

"Good," she said with satisfaction. She sniggered at my confused look and explained, "Max doesn't care for blondes that much."

Well, however she chose to look at it. I realized that she must be used to seeing him with other women. Unlike earlier in their relationship, Mr. Hamilton seemed to be trying to protect Lily from public scrutiny lately. And maybe his wife's. Although tonight was a different deal. The blonde was just for window dressing, because Lily was with me.

"Let's dance." Lily stood up and kept her shoulders still, moving her hips seductively to the rhythm, holding out her arms to me invitingly.

I swear, she must have had eyes in the back of her head. Precise to the moment that she stood up, Captain Woods entered the room. He had a redhead with him too, but the pale, freckly kind that couldn't hold a candle to the flame of Lily's hair, figure, and personality. Not that he could see any of her personality with her back turned, although her figure and hair drew his attention like a moth.

Sgt. Bert Guthrie came in behind him, alone and in uniform. He really didn't seem to have much use for women, as he sneered at the couples whirling by. But his eyes were drawn to Lily as well as she swayed in front of me. I guess Lily was right when she said redheads were very noticeable.

Even if it weren't in the script, I couldn't have resisted her.

"Remember, I can't dance," I growled as she rested her hand on my shoulder.

"Just keep in time to the music," she encouraged me. "Try to remember, slow, slow, quick, quick."

We did little more than undulate to the music, handicapped as we were by my inability to foxtrot and the pressing need to keep her face turned away from our quarry or quarries.

Mr. Hamilton had paused to speak with Woods, but now he led his young date to a table. Big Billy tagged along behind, escorting his date. He was good; after that first quick glance, he only glanced at Lily once on the way. I don't think he even noticed me. Guthrie, on the other hand, blatantly stared at Lily once he spotted her.

"Did we get a nibble?"

"More like a chomp, I'd say." I yanked her around so he only got her back as he tracked her.

"Grey, darling, release the death grip you have on the back of my gown instantly or face dire consequences," Lily ordered.

I let go immediately, afraid that she meant to sic Celestine on me as revenge for any creases I might have inflicted. "How am I supposed to steer, then?"

She gave me a Reproving Look. "You're not. I'm leading. But don't worry. I won't challenge your masculine pride by suddenly taking off with another gentleman. However skilled."

Her purring voice reminded me of how she delighted in a dirty innuendo. She might get on with Artie like a house on fire.

It proved to be quite a challenge to keep Lily turned away from Mr. Hamilton's table and on the other side of the room from our suspects. I resorted to simply telling her where they were, and she did the rest. Despite the gravity of the situation, I could tell that Lily loved to dance. There was something in the expression on her face that told me she could hear something in the music that I never would, like she knew the composer's intentions and translated them through her movement.

Phil Martin waltzed by and paused, tapping my shoulder to indicate he wanted to cut in. To dance with Lily, of course! The room would have spontaneously combusted if two men started dancing cheek to cheek. Clearly, despite my insistence that he be kept on the list of suspects, I suspected that Lily and Mr. Hamilton did not agree, because here she was, letting him see her face.

Mr. Martin unloaded his unfortunate date onto me and took off with Lily, whirling her through the crowd expertly while still managing to keep her turned away from Mr. Hamilton's table. She smiled impishly at me and wiggled her fingers. I realized that she lied about taking off on me with a better dancer. Phil Martin never crashed her into another couple even though they were moving at a good clip. Her flowerlike face was aglow with pleasure. For her, I could see dance was the way she knew best to express her true self: a passionate, intense, woman. It was her art.

"I have to learn how to do that," I muttered.

"I wish you would," Mr. Martin's date answered. "And soon."

She clearly lacked the personable nature of her date for the evening. Looking at her bored face, I was about to apologize when the band segued into a familiar rhythm. I pulled her tight against me and took control, leading her through a masterful tango. She was breathless and thrilled when the music stopped and I returned her to her table. She handed me her fan, and I set up a tornado of air while she caught her breath.

"What did you say your name was?" she inquired with an arch look.

"I didn't, but it's Randall, Grey Randall." I thought it was probably better to leave off the dick part; she seemed a bit overheated as it was. "And you are?"

"Celia Fraser," she said.

"Pleased to meet you," I said, trying not to sound *too* pleased.

Mr. Martin brought Lily back at that moment, and from his expression, he had guessed that he was performing a life-saving service right then; I had no idea how to escape Miss Fraser's clutches. Luckily for me, he was a much better prospect, and the mere sight of his handsome face apparently dimmed Miss Fraser's memory of our tango.

"Phil darling, your friend is a marvelous dancer," Miss Fraser simpered up at him.

I was right; she sounded like an idiot calling him "darling." Or maybe I was just grinding my teeth because she was stomping on my turf, even though I hastily reminded myself that I had no interest in him whatsoever. None!

"Is he?" Mr. Martin gave me a speculative look.

"Miss M—Miller!" I improvised hastily. "Let me get you a glass of champagne."

"Thank you, Grey darling," Lily said. "And thank you, Phil, that was a lovely turn around the floor you gave me."

Mr. Martin had his hand on Lily's back to guide her over to me, and I shivered at the thought of his hand on my skin—but this was no time for idle speculation.

Miss Fraser seemed to resent the fact that both Mr. Martin and I were paying attention to an older woman, and she said spitefully, "You must be exhausted, Miss Miller, to dance for so long at your age."

"Oh no, that was nothing! I could go on all night," Lily said blithely. She turned to me. "Grey darling, I'm parched. Get me something to drink at once, or I shall expire on the spot!"

"Immediately, Miss Miller." I led her away, listening to her stifled giggle.

"What a rude, boring girl," Lily said. "Phil could do so much better."

"Maybe he didn't want to waste tonight on a real date," I suggested. "Time for your disappearing act."

Lily nodded, and I led her to the bar, procuring a glass of champagne for her. "Stay right here for five minutes unless one of them approaches you."

"Should we synchronize our watches?" Lily teased. Note: Lily wasn't wearing a watch.

"Just meet me in the ladies' room in a few minutes," I said.

She nodded and contemplated the bubbles in her glass, carefully keeping turned away from Mr. Hamilton's table.

I WENT to scope out the ladies' room before I let Lily loose in there. Yeah, I know, that sounds weird. The maid sitting in there guarding the hand towels thought so, too, when I opened the door and walked in without a sign that I knew I was in the wrong place.

I held out a sawbuck to the girl and told her, "Fade if you don't want trouble."

She looked at the bill and then at my face and decided she wanted a quieter life. She scooped the money and vanished.

Glancing around the ladies' room, I could tell men were definitely getting the short end of the stick. For some reason, dames rated a couch! And the stalls were marble, no urinals, which when you think of it makes perfect sense, but they also had baskets of cute little soaps and linen towels and big fancy mirrors. No wonder they trooped in there in herds. Or maybe it was gaggles. I could just imagine Charlie seeking sanctuary from some party in here, curling up on the couch with her feet tucked under her (to the detriment of her dress) and with her new Jane Austen in her hand.

There was a starburst inlaid in the center of the circular marble floor in colors of cream, beige, and pink. Each sink had its own marble counter sculpted into a curved shape that mimicked the circular theme from the nightclub, with gold-shaded lamps glinting in the mirrors. There were upholstered chairs for the ladies to sit on while they touched up their war paint.

The mirrors had curtains swagged at the top and cascading down each side for a touch of elegance, and there were vases of white orchids, for crissakes! Real ones! Pretty containers of womanly things like lotion and powder were scattered around.

No one was in there except me, so I beat it down the hall and found the service passage just where George told me it would be. I pushed open the door to the rear of the hotel and found George and Celestine waiting there. Silently, Celestine entered, and we returned to the ladies' room together. This time she went in ahead of me and waved me in once she'd inspected for visitors.

She took the maid's place at the counter with the towels.

"I don't know what'll happen when he walks in, but if he tells you to scram, don't go too far," I instructed her.

"Of course. I know what to do, Mr. Deeck," Celestine said.

"Randall," I muttered. At least Celestine looked the part, having worn her maid outfit to the shindig.

The door opened behind me, and I whirled around with my hand on my gun, drawing a sigh of relief when I saw it was only Lily.

"I hope you weren't planning on squirting metal if any random lady came in to powder her nose," she said.

I could tell she was strung up and tense by the starriness of her eyes. For the first time, it occurred to me that as beautiful as she seemed to me, she must be a real stunner when she wasn't in mourning.

I drew out my hand to show her it was empty. "I have better reflexes than that."

"I'm counting on it," Lily replied.

"Don't let him corner you over there," I said, pointing to the dead end at the apex of the circular counter. "Stay right here. When he comes in, the angle will be wrong for him to see your face in the mirror. Play him as long as you can."

"I know," she said. "Time for you to take a hike, shamus."

"We got the bulge on him, babe."

She gave me a wink, and I winked back. Then Celestine winked at me with a completely solemn face. I gave her a wink too before I went and hid in one of the stalls. Luckily, in a swell joint like this, the doors went down to the floor and I didn't have to teeter on the john to hide my feet. I left the door ajar so I could watch through the crack. I'd never forgive myself if I gave him a chance to hurt Lily.

Now the waiting, the hardest part of the private dick biz. Waiting to see if my hunch was going to grow wings and fly. If George had done his part, Barry Jazz Morgan knew where we were, and the other three suspects were lined up out in the party room somewhere. I'd proved to myself that any one of them could have done it, which meant I was wrong on three of them, or possibly two if one of them had an accomplice, but I knew who I was putting my money on.

He was hidden from my view behind the door, but I saw Celestine stiffen a tiny bit when the door opened. Lily was sitting in front of a mirror, apparently absorbed in taking an inventory of her face.

"You. Out."

His voice wasn't loud, but Celestine's head swiveled to face him. She was staring right at the killer of her darling, but her face gave away nothing. I saw a bill wave at the door. She arose decorously and took it from him, slipping past the man hidden by the door.

He came into the room and let the door close behind him, standing against it to prevent anyone from entering. "Rose," he said. His voice was completely different when he pleaded with her.

Lily didn't move. From where he stood, he couldn't see her face in the mirror, but that meant she couldn't see him, either. She sat completely still, her powder puff in her hand, leaning forward slightly, waiting.

"My Rose, you've come back to me." He took a step forward into my view, and I would have congratulated myself on winning my bet if I didn't need to keep on my toes. Time for that later.

Captain Billy Woods came up behind Lily and put his hands gently around her throat as if that were a familiar and comfortable hold for him.

Lily didn't let him get set. She slipped out of his grasp and up onto her feet in one fluid movement, turning to face him. She glared at him as he fell back, beginning to stalk him, almost like a slow dance step moving to a beat that only she could hear, dragging the toe of her shoe on the floor behind her with every step. She looked as menacing as it was possible for a beautiful woman to look while driving back a man taller and bigger than her.

"You're not Rose, but you look... just like...." Woods's voice petered out as he gave ground.

"But I couldn't be Rose, could I?" Lily's voice was throaty, almost seductive as she accused him. "Because you killed her. Did you think I was her ghost?"

Woods seemed mesmerized, staring at her as if he couldn't believe his eyes. "I didn't... I never could... I thought she was... she was... I wanted her to be okay...."

"You thought she was okay even though you felt the life slip out of her body when she went limp in your hands?" From her voice, you would have thought she was a nun urging him to confess. She sounded almost compassionate.

His face was tortured as he studied her. "You don't know...." He reached for her.

"Don't touch me!" she spat at him. "No!"

The word seemed to do something to him. I saw his face change; something ugly and inhuman moved behind his eyes and told me it was time to stop the play. He must have been beyond all rational thought if he figured he could get away with murdering another woman with hundreds of people dancing right outside the door.

He reached for her, intent only upon his plan, wrapping his big hands around her vulnerable throat, and started to squeeze.

Lily was a good student; she remembered what I'd taught her. She clasped her hands together and thrust them upward between his, her shoulders breaking his hold and pushing his hands away.

By then I was there, ready to take over.

I guess I had something to prove both to myself and to Big Billy. His gun was safely stowed inside his buttoned-up jacket, so I didn't pull mine, either. I'd take him with my hands, and damn the six inches he had on me.

I grabbed the back of his jacket and yanked him away from Lily. He was quick for a big man, and he turned to find out who was behind him. I knew he had the advantage of reach on me, so I braced my hand on the marble counter and leveraged a foot up to kick him in the balls. He twisted away, and I caught his hip. He grunted and bent over, bringing himself closer to my height.

Before he could straighten up, I grabbed his wrist with my left and hung onto him so he couldn't dodge the full force of my blow as I punched up under his jaw, following it up with a quick chop to his throat.

He gagged and put both hands up to his neck, leaving his torso unprotected. I planted my hand on his chest and drove him back against the wall. He gave a gurgling scream that caught my attention, because I hadn't pushed him *that* hard. He brought his fists down, and I could see I wasn't the only one willing to fight through the pain. I had to make this quick, or he would have me.

I feinted a right hook at his jaw, and when he covered up, I nailed him in the middle of his chest with a short jab, right over his heart.

He screamed loud that time and slid down the wall, gasping in pain.

"Lily, your gun."

"I've got him covered," she said in a raspy voice I hadn't heard from her before.

I glanced over my shoulder to see her aiming the gun at his head with both hands outstretched in front of her. "Hold that thought," I instructed her.

I pulled Billy's tie off, much like he'd done to me at my office. In fact, I liked the parallel so much, I ripped his shirt open, scattering the buttons everywhere, just to drive it home that our positions had been reversed. Now *I* was in the driver's seat. He tried to kick me, and he had long legs. He might have tried again until he heard the click as Lily cocked her gun.

"I wouldn't try that again, Captain," she said grimly. "You present a tempting target, and I've never been one to resist temptation too vigorously."

We were both staring at the bandage on his chest when the door opened and Max Hamilton walked in, except he wasn't Max Hamilton. He was clearly attending our private party as Mr. X, his face cold and implacable. His two goons, Brownie and Stevens, followed him inside. Hard behind them was Phil Martin. I'd never seen him look so grim. He shot one quick glance at me, but then he went back to helping Mr. X glare at Captain Woods.

Clearly, despite my insistence that Phil Martin be considered as one of the suspects, someone had told him what was going on. The look on his face told me that to Max and Lily, there was no doubt he'd earned the right to be there as one of them, to look Marguerite's killer in the face. To tell the truth, I was so glad it turned out not to be him I couldn't be too pissed.

If it hadn't been for the situation, it might have given me a laugh to see Mr. X and his muscle standing around in the dainty ladies' room, especially with such menacing faces.

Celestine and George came back in and took their places behind Brownie and Stevens. No one gave them a second glance, like they had a perfect right to be there. And Celestine had accessorized her ensemble with a gun, holding it steady on Captain Woods.

I put out my hand to rip off the bandage, and Big Billy made a grab to block me.

"Hold it, Woods," Mr. X commanded in a voice that sent shivers up my spine.

Apparently it didn't do much for Big Billy's temperature, either, because he froze in place.

At that moment the door opened again, and a society dame stood there staring at us all stuck in place. The look of shock on her face was priceless. It didn't take her long to scope the scene before she backed out and fast. Brownie moved to deposit his weight in front of the door to prevent any other surprise entrances.

I proceeded with the unveiling. It was an ugly wound, small and perfectly round but oozing unhealthy looking gunk from the reddened hole. "Guess you have a little infection, Captain. Too bad you didn't get this taken care of earlier."

"I can explain," Big Billy started.

I didn't kid myself. I may have put him down on the floor, but he wasn't scared of me or Lily. It was Mr. X and his goons that kept him behaving like a gentleman. If he'd been a bit smarter, he might have noticed Lily's finger turning white on the trigger, but he wasn't looking her way.

I tossed the used bandage into the trash receptacle and went to wash my hands. It wasn't the infection; it was touching Big Billy himself. It made me feel dirty. I couldn't resist sneaking a peek at Phil Martin, but he was fixed on Billy.

Then I went and took the gun out of Lily's hand, even though she held it steady. No shakes. I clicked the safety and handed it back to her, patting her hand gently.

"Why don't you explain the situation to me, then." Mr. X's voice was quiet, like cat feet but with claws, but I didn't kid myself that he was safe to have around the house.

"It's—it's a bullet wound, suffered in the line of duty," Big Billy stammered. He pulled his shirt closed and covered himself.

"It's where she stabbed you with the heel of her shoe," I said. "She knew how to do a high kick and she used it to defend herself. But that wasn't enough to keep you off her, was it?"

Mr. X just waited.

"I'm not talking to you, punk," Big Billy growled, but his voice had lost a little of its oomph. I think he was beginning to realize the odds of talking himself out of this one were low and zero.

"Talk to *me*, Woods. I'm listening, and I'd like to know just how you killed my daughter." He never raised his voice, but he stopped Woods cold. I could see what made Mr. X so dangerous. You never knew when he might explode into action, but the possibility was there even though he was keeping it on a tight leash. I wasn't sure I wanted to see the tiger out of the cage.

"Your—*your* daughter?" Suddenly Big Billy looked terrified, like he'd realized there was no way out of here for him except feet first.

"And mine." Lily stepped forward, claiming her daughter in public for the first time, although it was a small public, and from the lack of reaction, I suspected Brownie and Stevens already knew it.

Phil Martin darted her a glance before returning to watching Big Billy, and I liked him for it. Like he was sort of looking out for her.

"Look, I didn't know—I thought your daughter's name was Marguerite—" Billy started.

"Marguerite Rose Saint-Ville." Lily's voice tolled out the syllables like a bell ringing his doom.

"You can't prove a thing! I got this wound in the line of duty! You can ask Guthrie! He'll back me up."

"I'm sure he'll say anything you tell him to," I interjected smoothly. "It doesn't matter, though. I bet I can prove you killed her. There was blood on the heel of her shoe. If we get a phenolthaleine test done, I'm willing to bet it'll turn out to be blood."

Big Billy's lips twisted into a triumphant smirk. "Go ahead and test all you want. You won't find a thing."

"Yeah, I know. You know all about forensics, don't you? You probably washed it off, but if I were to pry the rubber tip off her heel, how much do you want to lay down that I'll find some dried blood and the lab will be able to match it to your blood type?"

Billy seemed uneasy, and that made him angry. "How did you hear about the blood? There are no photos—" He stopped short, probably realizing he'd made a mistake.

"Yeah, you made those negatives disappear, didn't you? Or was it Guthrie, acting on your orders? Well, doesn't matter, because there's still a print in existence, and I have it." I snapped my fingers at him. "Maybe you should have gone looking for that instead of planting that pendant in her apartment."

That gave me an idea, but I didn't want to get between Billy and Brownie's gun. "Stevens, gimme his watch, would you?"

Silently, Stevens padded over and planted his foot on Big Billy's thigh, grinding his heel into the muscle to discourage him from taking a chance. Good move, I was going to have to remember that one. He bent and unbuckled the watch, tossing it over to me. Of course I caught it, snatching it out of the air one-handed. I could have been a ball player.

I had to get out my jackknife, but I pried the back off, and Marguerite's missing locket fell out onto my palm. I held it where Lily could see it, white enamel with a red rose in the center. "He had to have a trophy. How many, Billy? She wasn't the first, was she?"

Lily gasped and sent Billy a look of pure hatred. If looks could kill, Celestine would have been second on board the hate train, and George would have been punching the tickets.

Lily took it from me and opened the locket, turning it to show first me, and then Mr. X, that her own photograph was inside. I was hoping it made her happy to see that Marguerite had indeed left the photo there, even though under the circumstances…. She fingered the lock of red-gold hair tenderly.

Billy hung his head and mumbled, "I really loved her."

"You're sick!" Lily hissed at him. "You killed her because you loved her?"

Mr. X interrupted. "I don't care why he did it. Take him out to the car."

"Wait!"

We all turned to look at Lily. Except for George and Celestine—they kept Woods nailed in place with the daggers of hatred in their eyes.

"Do you believe me now, Max?"

"Yes, Lily." Max held out his hand and gave a thumbs-down.

"Stevens, Brownie?"

Both men nodded.

Lily turned to each of us one at a time, as if commanding a verdict.

"Grey?"

"If we're taking a vote, I say yes. He did it."

"And you, Phil?"

"I have no doubt." He nodded as he said it.

George clenched his fists, and Celestine glared at Big Billy. That seemed good enough for Lily.

Big Billy had one last gasp left in him. "She let a colored boy put his hands on her—I couldn't—"

"Take him away, boys."

Brownie and Stevens bent to lift Billy off the floor. He towered over them too, but he looked kind of pale. Maybe he didn't like it so much when the tables were turned. The ugly thing was still peering out from behind his eyes, and I pitied Marguerite, trapped in that alley with him, but I admired her for fighting for her life like she had.

"*My* car," Lily spat.

I was interested to see they both just nodded at her order, like it was the same as coming from Mr. X.

George opened the door. I was amazed that he'd been allowed inside the hotel at all, but maybe he slid by the rules because they knew that he was Lily's driver. I was glad to see that he was going to be a witness of this as well. He held the door for the two goons to shuffle Big Billy out.

Mr. X disappeared and became Max Hamilton again, going to Lily and putting his arms around her.

"I was right," she said.

He chuckled, which sounds weird right then, but it wasn't. I got the sense that these two had laughed a lot together, maybe between screaming fights, but they had something good. "You were right as usual, Lily. I should have listened to you."

When Lily whispered something and Max bent his head to hear her, caressing her back with his palm, I turned away, not wanting to intrude on such an intimate moment. Then they broke apart, simply holding hands.

I went to open the door for them.

Lily stopped and stroked my cheek with her hand. "Thank you, Grey. You were magnificent."

"You weren't so bad yourself, Lily," I said.

"Was it true, what you said about the blood under the heel?"

"There's always a chance, but—" I shrugged. "Who knows what he did to all the evidence, if it's still there or if he tampered with it. A good lawyer could raise a reasonable doubt."

"Not if he never gets the chance," Mr. Hamilton said softly. "Let's go."

Mr. Hamilton looked at Phil Martin and jerked his head slightly. Mr. Martin nodded and slipped away, returning to the nightclub with one last glance at me. I knew I'd never see him again. He couldn't take the chance after what happened between us, now that I'd gotten to Mr. X. It was just too damn risky for him. I'm a private dick, I know these things.

"You're not coming, Grey," Lily said. She held my face between both hands, kissing first my right cheek, then my left, and finally her lips on mine. She had an incredibly seductive allure, but with Mr. X standing right there, ready to stake his claim, it wasn't something I wanted to wonder about long. Aside from the whole equipment dilemma. But as long as he wasn't wondering about me.

"Where are you going?" I asked stupidly.

"It's a beautiful night for a drive in the desert," Mr. Hamilton said.

"How are you going to keep the press and police from getting onto this?"

Mr. Hamilton gave me a smile, and it wasn't a nice one. "Come on, Lily, let's get going."

She touched her finger to her lips and planted it on mine. "I'll call you tomorrow, Grey darling."

"You're a great moll," I said. "Proud to have you on the job."

She smiled. "Don't you forget it, Mr. Dick."

I trailed along behind them in the hallway to the service entrance and watched as they walked out together, hand in hand, into the desert night. I bet Max Hamilton might never have seen the service area behind the hotel before, aside from when it was being built, but it was the right way to take out the garbage.

I caught some movement over by the trash barrels and realized that Barry Jazz Morgan was standing there watching, his skin blending in with the darkness. After George had shut the car door for Lily and Max Hamilton, he looked over at Jazz and gave a little nod. It made it complete somehow, that Jazz was there too, to witness Big Billy on his way to meet justice.

George got into the driver's seat, and I watched the car pull away. I looked back at Jazz, and his hand came up. He gave me a crisp army salute before he turned and walked out of the empty courtyard.

That was it.

My job was done. I'd caught the man, and now I felt tired. Even worse, I felt I'd crossed the line somehow. I didn't just figure out who did it; I set up a showdown knowing that it was going to lead to his death. It's one thing to bring your man in and allow twelve good men and true decide his fate, quite another to bait a trap, knowing the tiger is waiting right there for the mouse and is armed with a gun. Even though this mouse was more devil than rodent.

In the excitement of setting up the sting, I hadn't quite looked at the implications of what I was doing, and that bothered me. I might not have put a gun to Big Billy's head myself, but I knew he'd never be seen alive again in Vegas.

Yeah, he deserved it, and yeah, Lily had taken a vote from all of us, an impromptu jury, but still….

I walked around to the front of the casino, skirting the club where all the merriment was still taking place, and realized that my ride had gone as well.

There wasn't a taxi in sight, so I was going to have to hoof it.

That would give me plenty of time to chew things over with my conscience. I pulled my bow tie loose and opened my collar before setting out for my office. It was closer than my apartment, and this wouldn't be the first time I crashed there.

I looked up at the stars, shining clear and bright in the desert sky, able to compete even with the neon lights. A star arced across the sky and flamed out. I made a wish on it, even though I knew it wasn't going to come true.

At least Big Billy had a nice night for dying.

Chapter 9: Never Say Never

WHEN these dark moods hit, I don't turn on the lights. I liked the way the neon lit up the office at night. I sat down and pulled out the bottle, taking a long swallow. I was surprised that Artie had left me anything to drink. I pulled on my tie some more and unbuttoned my collar, hoisting my feet up onto the desk and leaning back in the chair.

I'd seen enough killing and death in the war. When they left the hotel, I felt as if Lily had put me on the outside by not letting me come along, but I didn't need to see another man die. I closed my eyes, wondering if I should bother going home or just sleep there.

The smell of cologne told me if I was going to sack out, I should have locked the door first.

"Hey, Grey," a familiar voice said in the dark.

I cracked one eye open. Reggie looked pink in the red glow of the neon; Jazz was darker, more of a purple.

"You two look like you found the rainbow," I said sourly.

Jazz in particular was smiling. I'd never seen him smile before. He was very handsome when he did. And Reggie was pretty chipper too. Guess he was feeling lucky.

"We had a chat," Reggie said. His eyes slid to Jazz and away when he caught me watching him. "Thanks for clearing Jazz."

"All in a day's work." I took another slug from the bottle.

"You look gloomy," Reggie observed. "I thought it was a red letter day, catching the killer and all."

He wasn't supposed to know anything about that. He was a cop, for crissakes! Who the hell—Jazz. Of course.

"I don't know what you're talking about," I said distinctly.

"Parades, confetti, the roar of the crowd, you solved the case. You're a hero."

"Yeah, I'm sure Lieutenant Steele will want to shake my hand, right after he books me as an accessory before the fact."

"He won't hear about it from me."

"It's not like he's going to fail to notice when Woods never shows up for work again," I pointed out.

"Maybe he won't be too upset over it," Reggie said. "Woods took the brakes off some cops who don't know when to say when. All in the name of public safety."

For Reggie, that was like saying Woods corrupted the entire force and let them edge into being more crooked than the crooks, justifying his actions in the name of the law.

"And you came over here to tell me that?" It wasn't making my conscience feel any better.

"No, this is a snatch," Jazz said cheerfully.

"Come along quietly and we won't put the cuffs on," Reggie affirmed.

What the hell was going on? He couldn't really be arresting me for what happened—? My brain ticking over, I held out my wrists. "I'll come quietly, Officer."

Reggie looked surprised, but Jazz didn't know any better.

When he came closer, I broke for the door. Reggie snapped the light on, and Jazz tackled me, swinging me up over his shoulder. I grunted as his shoulder got me in the ribs, but I started to kick, aiming for where it hurt.

He slapped my butt, and I let out a sound somewhere between a shriek of outrage and a shout. It barely stung, but he startled me. And maybe I was a little drunk.

I gasped, "Who put you up to this?"

"Phil Martin," Reggie said. "Careful, Jazz. Mr. Big only likes the bruises he puts there. Don't mark him up too much."

"What the hell?"

"Phil's a friend." Reggie's smile was smug.

"You told me he was straight!"

Jazz couldn't suppress a snort of laughter, which made an earthquake rumble in my gut as I was hanging ass up over his shoulder at the time and getting pretty lightheaded.

"Yeah, and if you asked him, he'd tell you I was straight too. Friends lie for their friends sometimes."

"Oh yeah? What about me?"

"If he asked, I'd tell him you were straight." Reggie gave me the eye. "If you wanted me to."

Well, that answered the question about why a cop felt so safe sitting in a queer club. Phil Martin might be a crook, but there was a higher brotherhood that superseded other loyalties. Not that I thought he'd put them up to this out of a desire to deepen his friendship with me.

Queer he might be, but Phil Martin wasn't the type of guy who was going to let my innovative questioning techniques slide without getting his back.

"Put me down," I ordered. To my surprise, Jazz did so and steadied me as I staggered from the head rush. I was still a little lightheaded, but I ducked under his arm and lurched for the door again.

Jazz caught me in two steps and grabbed both my arms. "Will you quit that?"

"No," I panted. Hey, at least I was honest about it.

He wasn't even breathing hard as he held me motionless despite my effort to squirm out of his grip. "Get his belt, Reggie."

I froze for a moment in terror. What were they going to do? A belt swung hard could hurt, and I didn't even want to think about what the buckle end might feel like. Reggie fumbled at my waist, freeing my belt and feeling a good bit of me in the process. I'd never suspected him of that, but he looked kind of gleeful while he was doing it. I guess he was enjoying having the upper hand after me shaking him down for information.

Jazz circled the belt around my arms and buckled it, pinning my arms to my sides. Huh. That was going to make it difficult to run for it. It threw my balance off, as I found out when I backed up a step and almost cracked my head on the doorjamb.

"Got your cuffs?" Jazz asked Reggie.

Reggie pulled them out and cuffed my hands in front of me. Jazz pushed me out the door.

"Where are your keys?"

"My keys? Why?"

"So I can lock up your office," Reggie explained patiently. "It cuts down on crime like breaking and entering if you lock the door when you leave."

"What does it matter if I'm not coming back?" I asked.

He lost patience and searched me thoroughly, including spots where I would not have considered stashing my keys, but eventually he found them and locked the door, pocketing the keys himself.

Jazz's hands on my shoulders kept me from stumbling on the stairs, and when we emerged from the building, Reggie stepped up to a very swanky car. One that couldn't have been his. Jazz let go of me to unlock the door, and I took off, running clumsily up the street. He was faster than I'd thought he'd be and had me up and over his shoulder again before I'd gotten more than half a block.

"Try that again and you can ride in the trunk," he growled.

"Fine by me," I retorted. Maybe I could kick out a taillight and flag someone for help. Where's a cop when you need one? Oh right, unlocking the car door while sniggering at my predicament.

Jazz got in the back while Reggie kept a hold on me and shoved me in after. Jazz wrapped his arms around me and put one of his legs over mine. I struggled continuously while Reggie drove, and Jazz responded by giving me a grope. I let out a ridiculous squeak of alarm, and Reggie laughed some more.

"Hold still and he'll quit," he suggested.

I held still. Very still. Jazz had pulled me closer, and I tried not to wiggle, because he seemed to enjoy it.

I hadn't even noticed which way we were going until we pulled up in the alley behind the Lambda club in the train yard. We had another brief skirmish while getting out of the car when I thought I saw another opening for escape, which led to me being delivered to Mr. Big butt first, slung over Jazz's shoulder again.

Where was Artie when I needed help? I thought he was supposed to have a nose for trouble, although I suspected that being Artie, he either already knew about this and didn't think I needed help or was too busy laughing his ass off somewhere to lend a hand.

Phil Martin laughed at the presentation. "Don't tell me he refused my gracious invitation."

I couldn't see Mr. Big, being upside down with a view of Jazz's broad back again.

"He wasn't very receptive, but we tried not to mark him up," Jazz said.

"Put him down."

Another head rush for me. Jazz hung onto me until my vision cleared, and I had to swallow his embrace till I recovered.

"What the fuck?" I snarled.

"He's not too friendly, is he?" Phil Martin asked with a satisfied grin.

I tried to harden my heart against him, but he was just so impossibly sexy standing there by his desk, his skin glowing like burnished gold in the pool of light from the lamp.

"Let me go," I demanded, as surly as I could manage. It didn't seem to intimidate them, especially as I was still trussed in handcuffs and my belt.

"I think I said we have a little unfinished business last time we spoke," Phil said suavely. Damn, he was gorgeous. My knees wobbled. I was beginning to think he might have something on me in the business of interrogation.

"I have nothing to say to you," I said.

"Did you search him?" Phil asked.

"No." Jazz grinned. "We thought maybe you'd like to do that yourself."

Reggie and Jazz held me still when Mr. Big approached. He slipped his hands into all my pockets, finding the Lambda disc. He held it between his slender strong fingers and put it on his desk. He also got my wallet, my gun, and my goat with his groping.

I thought I understood. I was about to pay dearly for the firm grip I had on his balls that one time. Like any alpha male, he was going to get his revenge. I just hoped that Reggie and Jazz weren't going to stick around to watch.

As if he'd read my mind, Phil nodded toward the door. "I'll take it from here. Thanks, boys. Time for me to have a little chat with Mr. Dick here."

Reggie winked at me and followed what I assumed was now his official boyfriend out of the room.

Phil walked toward me, and I held my ground as long as I could, but finally I broke and took a step backward. He smiled and continued to drive me back until I felt the hardness of the wall on my shoulders. I was cornered then, and I wondered why I hadn't tried to make a run for it like I had with Jazz, the belt around my arms notwithstanding.

Phil reached for me, and I controlled myself, not wanting to let him see me flinch. He wore a little smile, like he knew just what I was thinking and was enjoying it. He unbuckled the belt and let it fall to the ground at his feet.

"In case I need it," he said.

I didn't believe for a minute that he was just going to let me go. He had something on his mind. He leaned over, and I thought he intended to kiss me, but instead he sniffed me. Delicately.

I shivered, and he hadn't even touched me yet. It was beginning to look like I might get my wish to have him master me. I just hoped it wasn't going to be painful.

"Look, if this is about my questioning you, it was all part of the case. I'm a private dick," I said nervously.

He curled his index finger around the chain of the handcuffs and lifted my hands. "Was it? I was kind of hoping you only used that 'technique' on me."

I glanced up to watch as he kept raising my hands above my head in time to see him drop the chain of my cuffs over a hook driven into the paneling. I could swear that hook hadn't been there last time I visited his office.

"I had it installed just for you," Phil said with a pleased smirk. "I hoped that maybe *I* would get the chance to question *you*."

"What do you want to know?" I asked. My voice didn't quaver. Much.

"I think you know."

He ran a gentle finger over my cheekbone. "Why is that cheekbone a little higher than the other?"

"It had a little run in. With a fist," I said.

"Tough guy."

My tie was hanging open, and he slid it out from under my collar without touching me. He started to unbutton my shirt, and I twisted my hands, but the hook was just high enough that I couldn't get loose.

"From the first time I saw you, I wanted to see those lips wrapped around my cock." He lifted a hand to stroke his thumb over my mouth, and I had to resist the impulse to suck it in.

"Well, glad to oblige. Just think of me as your fairy godfather making your dreams come true and let me go," I said.

He went back to my shirt, pulling it out of my pants. "Oh, I have a lot more dreams, and I dream big."

I swallowed hard. This was one hell of a fucking time to find out I was turned on by being held captive. Of course, my captor being a gorgeous man was a leg up. I might have been trying a little harder to shake loose if it were a woman toying with me.

I felt the tickle of my shirt against my skin as he pulled it aside.

He chuckled and ran his fingers over my chest. "I never thought you'd have hair on your chest. Not too much. Just right. Nice."

I had nothing to say at that point. My stomach muscles quivered under his touch as he slid a finger inside my waistband. He was looking at the bruise on my side.

"Big Billy?"

"He was good with his hands."

"He hit you." Phil frowned.

I rolled my eyes at the ceiling. "I ran onto his fist. By accident."

"I'm sorry," he said gently.

I let my head fall back onto the wall with a little thud and started to laugh.

"What?"

"You've got me chained to a wall and you're worried that I got a bruise?"

"Seems like you're enjoying the being chained up part," he said with a wicked grin, scraping his nails over my fly. "And yes, I *am* worried."

I was glad of the wall at my back. It had been so long since someone had touched me that way, my dick was stiff and aching. It was only a matter of time till I broke. "You're not giving me much say in the matter."

Phil frowned and stepped back, which gave me a little reprieve. "Like you gave me any."

"You could have gotten away." My words fell like a stone into still water, and I was afraid maybe I'd gone too far.

Then he smiled. "I know." He leaned forward, and the sensation of his lips against my throat had me arching in a vain attempt to feel his body against mine. He mumbled against my neck, "I'll stop if you ask me to."

They say that curiosity killed the cat, and I guess that's going to be my downfall too. He gave me an out, but I wanted to know what he was going to do. And if I was going to like it.

When his fingers found my nipples, tracing circles around the aureoles, I couldn't have spoken, even if I had wanted to get away. I pushed forward into his touch in spite of myself, asking for more. He obliged, pinching the nubs softly between his fingers and thumbs, pulling on them just a little. I groaned with pleasure.

"You like that, don't you?"

I turned my head away, ashamed to let him see how much. There was a storm raging inside me; I wanted it and I didn't. I felt one of his hands move up to my neck, and he rubbed his thumb over the little dip between my collarbones. I knew if he pressed hard enough just there, he could cut off my supply of air, but his intentions seemed to be benign. He grabbed my chin and turned me to face him.

"You're nice and s—"

"Wiry! I'm not skinny!"

Phil Martin chuckled. "I was going to say slim. Any problem with that?"

I shook my head, my cheeks burning.

"You're the sexiest dick, private or public, that I've ever seen, you know that?" He released my chin and bent to take one of my nipples in his mouth.

"I know. I've seen my competition," I gasped.

I wanted to grab his head and press it against me, but of course I couldn't. All I could do was hang there and let him explore me, which he did very thoroughly. He nibbled at my throat, tested an ear lobe, yes, definitely sensitive there, blew in my ear. He nipped and sucked at my nipples until they were as hard as my dick. He licked a line down the center of my torso and blew on it.

When he stood up his face was a little red, even though he was still dressed to the nines in his tux. I couldn't resist looking down to check the bulge in his trousers. The evidence was there, he was enjoying this as much as I was. What can I say? I'm a dick, and observation is my game.

He started on my pants, unbuttoning and unzipping me. Too late, I realized my pants had nowhere to go but down, and I widened my legs. It was a vain attempt.

My boxers weren't in his league, but Phil didn't seem to care as he watched me lose the battle with gravity.

When my pants were in a puddle around my ankles, his smile turned into a leer. "Nice legs. All three of them."

I looked down and was confronted with the sight of my boxers tenting in front of me, with my dick acting as the pole. "Thanks."

He put his hands on my hips, and one of us let out a breath. I'm not even sure who, or if we did it in unison. I bit my lips as he slid a hand around to press my shorts between my cheeks and stroked over my hole. I could feel myself clenching frantically as he touched me through the fabric.

I could feel the shape of his cock pressed against my thigh. He was right up against me, staring into my eyes, rubbing my ass and squeezing....

I let out a shuddering breath. At first I'd been afraid of what he was going to do, but now I was afraid he wasn't going to do what I yearned for. What if he just planned to unwrap me and take inventory? What if—

He turned me to face the wall, and I waited. I could feel him tangle with my clothes.

"What're you doing?"

"Struggling with your damn shirt and jacket," Phil growled.

I had to snicker. "Want me to help with that?"

"Is that a clever ruse to get me to let you go?"

"Might make it easier."

"I've got you right where I want you," he answered. "I'll manage."

He yanked my shorts down and lifted my shirt. His hands were so warm when he cupped my cheeks, and I felt his breath on my neck.

"What an ass," he murmured.

He sounded awed. I've done a lot of running to stay fit and it was nice to know that it paid off. His hands were rhythmically squeezing my buttocks almost hard enough to bruise, and I pushed back into his grip.

I wanted him to take me right there, ravish me against the wall, but I didn't know if I could admit it to him. I could hear his breath coming ragged, and his grip shifted to my hips. I knew I'd have marks there tomorrow to remember him by in case I was in danger of forgetting.

"I'm not going to fuck you unless you ask me to." His voice was low and shaky. "Although now that I've got that delectable backside on display, it'll be hard to resist."

It was nice to know that same lust that was burning through my body was getting to him too.

He stepped away from me, and I gasped at the loss of contact. I couldn't decide which was worse torture, him touching me or when he stopped. I could hear noises but couldn't make out what he was doing. Then I made some inarticulate little sound when his fingers, slick with Vaseline, slid in the valley between my cheeks.

The gentle caress made me arch and twist in my chains whenever he brushed over my hole, pulsating with desire.

"This doesn't have to go any further," he said.

Giving me another out. "What if I want it to?"

His hands left me again. For some reason I couldn't bring myself to twist around to look at what he was doing. This strange seduction was all about sensation, his hands on my body, my skin.... I heard the unmistakable snap of a condom. He was playing it safe, and I was glad of it. Being in the service had taught a lot of greenhorns about all the diseases you could catch.

Then his warmth was against my back again, one of his arms wrapped around my waist, his lips at my ear and the solid hardness of his cock drifting over my hole but never pushing at it.

The heat became a full-on forest fire, crawling slowly under my skin, and I wanted him to touch me. My dick was aching with the need to be touched. "Please," I whispered.

He bent his head a little closer. "What did you say?"

I wanted to feel his skin against mine, naked, unencumbered by clothing. I wanted to turn around and leap into his arms, wrap my legs around him and beg him to take me.

He sucked on the skin of my neck just under my ear. I don't know if he knew how close that pushed me to orgasm. Maybe he could tell by the moan I let out.

"Ask me," he said insistently in a low, throaty voice.

My hips bucked, and my blood roared in my ears. He held me tight against him, so tight I could barely catch my breath. He cupped my balls gently in his hand, and I would have collapsed if not for being chained to the wall.

"Please...."

"Say my name." His voice was raspy, as if it was taking everything to control himself. "I want you to ask me...."

"Phil." It was the first time outside my thoughts I'd called him by his first name, and oddly it made the moment more intimate, almost too much so. "Phil, please...."

He slid a finger smoothly into me. My inner muscles flexed around him, my toes curled, and I started to tremble.

"Oh fuck, I'm going to—"

"Don't come yet," he ordered. "Ask me."

"Phil, dammit, would you just fuck me!" I burst out.

He chuckled at my vehemence, and after a moment I joined him.

"Are you sure?"

"Would you just fucking get on with it?" I demanded.

"How can I resist an invitation like that?" He sounded a little breathless, which made me glad I wasn't the only one.

I missed his finger when he took it out, but then I felt the head of his cock bump against my hole. I ground back against him, and he pushed inside.

It hurt and it burned and I wanted it so badly, to feel a man inside me again. It had been such a long time. "Fuck me." That time it was more of a soft plea. The fire inside me flared up and shot to my groin.

He pushed harder, and then he was inside me all the way. The sensation from where his cock touched me inside radiated outward, taking the pain and turning it into a pleasure so rare it filled me up.

"Grey Randall," he groaned, sounding almost like he was in pain.

His hands skimmed over my chest and belly, fingering my nipples and sliding through my chest hair as though he couldn't get enough of the feel of it. Every place his fingers touched, my nerves sang out, yearning to feel that caress again. I leaned my head back against his shoulder, pleading wordlessly for more as a low moan worked its way from my throat.

He pressed me against the wall almost harshly as he started to piston in and out of me, his cock brushing over my prostate with each thrust.

When I felt his hand wrap around my shaft, stroking me in time to his thrusts, stealing my breath, a force built in my chest, channeling right to my dick, propelling me into the inevitable slide to ecstasy.

I wanted him to fuck me faster and harder. I wanted him to kiss me. The thought shocked me into momentary coherence, but then I was lost in feeling again. His hand grabbed my hip, holding me still as he propelled his cock into me, harder and deeper than ever, and it still felt like it wasn't enough. I pushed my ass back to meet him, reveling in the feeling of his muscular body covering me, dominating me.

Sometimes I can stop it, but this time I didn't want to. The sensation vibrated right through my body as I chased for the release I needed. I had no conscious control; I had totally given myself into his hands. He was almost slamming my hips into the wall.

My orgasm was so strong I almost passed out. No coherent thought, no energy for vocal cords, I was almost paralyzed as I spurted over his hand.

I felt his cock swell inside me, and he pressed me harder into the wall, his fingers where they were still wrapped around my dick pressed into my belly with the weight of him against my back. It felt better than anything I'd ever experienced before, like I could never get enough of Phil inside me, holding me, owning me... and that scared the hell out of me.

"Oh God," he breathed. His hips jerked against my ass, and he froze. We stayed like that, him throbbing inside me, until he slipped out and his grip slackened around me.

"You okay?" he asked.

"I think I'll live," I muttered, and then I let myself get pulled under.

DIMLY, I felt tingles in my arms as the blood started to circulate. My knees sagged, and then I felt myself being lifted.

"You weigh a ton," Phil complained.

"'S'cause 'm all muscle," I slurred.

His chuckle sounded affectionate as he staggered toward the couch in his office. He sat down rather suddenly with me on his lap. "Yeah, that must be it. Wiry."

I couldn't move or open my eyes. I let him maneuver me as he pulled my pants up and buttoned my shirt. I must have passed out briefly again, because the feel of a glass against my lips made me start. I prefer to think it was just a matter of all the sleep I hadn't been having finally catching up with me.

"Water," Phil said. "Do you remember who I am?"

"Mr. Big," I managed.

He laughed. "That's the first time I've ever felt I really earned the title."

"You did," I assured him. I clenched my cheeks. I had a little more to remember him by now. "Holy fuck."

"Was that 'holy fuck, I liked it' or 'holy fuck I'm never doing this again'?" He sounded sort of anxious.

"I didn't stop you." I suddenly realized I was resting my head on his shoulder and decided it might give him the wrong impression. I pulled myself away from him and up. Somewhere along the line, he'd freed me from the cuffs. "I've got to get going."

"Clients beating down your door?"

"Dying to get in to see me."

He didn't think it was funny. "I'll take you home. You can't get a cab around here this time of night."

He turned to the desk to get his keys, looking remote and unapproachable. Also hot, magnetic, and eminently desirable. I waited for him to warn me not to say anything about him to anyone. Then I wondered if his *modus operandi* to keep the news about him being queer under wraps was to kill off whoever he fucked. He looked like he could do it. Maybe he had.

"Let's go."

I waited as he locked the doors, feeling a little unsteady on my feet. I couldn't figure out what he was expecting from me. Flowers? That I'd ask to spend the night with him? Waking up in each other's arms? That sounded way too appealing, and it just wasn't in the cards for queers in this town.

He led the way to his car, unlocked the door, and got in, leaning over to open the passenger door for me. I got in and sat staring straight ahead.

"Where do you live?"

I told him and we rolled. When he pulled up in front of my building, he didn't kill the engine, just sat there with his hands clenching the wheel. His hands that had been roaming all over me....

"Thanks for the lift."

He turned to me, and his eyes glittered in the dark from the one light on my street. "Maybe next time I'll even kiss you."

"Maybe there won't be a next time."

He looked grim.

I leaned forward and kissed him. It made me feel a little better to take back some of the control I'd let him have all evening. It heartened me when I felt him respond eagerly, opening his mouth to my tongue. I put everything into that kiss, everything I couldn't say.

It was madness, one man kissing another man in a car right on the street. Granted, the street was empty and it was getting on toward morning, but it was a brilliant madness that stabbed right through me. I might never get another chance to kiss Phil Martin, and I wanted everything I could get.

Finally I pulled away and touched his cheek. He put his hand over mine. Then I got out of the car.

There was nothing left to say.

I MANAGED to stagger up the two flights to my apartment. I didn't turn on the light because I didn't want him to see me watch him leave. I had to wonder if I'd ever see him again. We were kind of in the same business, just on different sides of the fence. It stood to reason that our paths might cross again.

I had a feeling it would be wiser if I made sure they didn't. He'd shown me just what I was missing in playing the lone wolf, and that also highlighted the danger I'd be in if I changed the game plan now. Mr. Big, AKA Mr. Beautiful, AKA Mr. Martin was a hell of a good-looking guy and a good lay, but too rich for my blood. He was intrigued by me now, but neither of us could afford a long stretch inside. We were playing with fire if we thought this could go any further.

It was a one-time thing. It happened. Now it was over.

One of my private dick rules was to never get caught with my zipper down. I realized it was down now, though it wasn't really my fault, as Phil Martin was the one who dressed me afterwards. I pulled it up, even though the cat was long gone out of that bag.

His car was still down below, idling at the curb. Maybe he was waiting to see my lights go on. He'd be waiting a long time for that.

Finally he put it in gear and drove off. I watched the distinctive taillights of his Lincoln as they went down the street. They flashed once as he touched the brakes and then turned the corner.

I tried to remember the last thing he'd said before he let me out of his car.

"You haven't seen the last of me."

I hoped not. I really hoped not.

CATT FORD lives in front of the computer monitor, in another world where her imaginary gay friends obey her every command.

She likes cats, chocolate, swing dancing, sleeping, Monty Python, Aussie friends, being silly, spinning other realities with words, and sea glass. She dislikes caterpillars, cigarette smoke, and rude people who think the F-word (as in faggot, or bundle of sticks) is acceptable.

A frustrated perfectionist, she comforts herself with the legend about the weavers of Persian rugs always including one mistake so as not to anger the gods, although she has no need to include a mistake on purpose. One always slips through. Writing fiction has filled a need for clever conversations, only possible when one is in control of both sides, and erotic romances, where everything for the most part turns out happily ever after.

Visit Catt's blog at http://catt-ford.livejournal.com/.

Also by CATT FORD

http://www.dreamspinnerpress.com

Mystery & Romance from DREAMSPINNER PRESS

The Bones of Summer
Anne Brooke

CUT & RUN
MADELEINE URBAN
ABIGAIL ROUX

Murder Most Gay
John Simpson

ZERO at the BONE
Jane Seville

http://www.dreamspinnerpress.com

www.ingramcontent.com/pod-product-compliance
Lightning Source LLC
Chambersburg PA
CBHW071333250626
47159CB00004B/1586